JUST THIS ONCE

THE KING FAMILY

LENA HENDRIX

Developmental editing: Paula Dawn, Lilypad Lit

Copy editing: James Gallagher, Evident Ink

Proofreading: Julia Griffis, The Romance Bibliophile

Model cover design: Echo Grayce, WildHeart Graphics

Model cover photography: Wander Aguilar

Cover model: Valerio Logrieco

Discreet cover design: Sarah Hansen, OkayCreations

To the good girls, the nerdy girls, the girls who were more into books than boys–Whip King would like a word with you . . .

LET'S CONNECT!

When you sign up for my newsletter, you'll stay up to date with new releases, book news, giveaways, and new book recommendations! I promise not to spam you and only email when I have something fun & exciting to share!

Also, When you sign up, you'll also get a FREE copy of Choosing You (a very steamy Chikalu Falls novella)!

Sign up at my website at www.lenahendrix.com

AUTHOR'S NOTE

Just This Once references the death of a parent (off page/not detailed, but referenced), a mother leaving her children, and suspected child neglect/abuse (off page).

This book also contains explicit sex scenes with a main character sporting a Jacob's ladder piercing. (Big shout out to Tabitha for calling it a "glitter dick" and forever changing my life for the better). I did all of the necessary research so you don't have to—I seriously had to bleach my eyeballs after that. Google at your own risk. For those unfamiliar, Whip's piercing is a set of three barbells on the underside of his glorious *ahem*.

So what do you say . . . should we see what the fuss is all about?

ABOUT THIS BOOK

Whip King cannot be the man for me.

Cocky, pierced firefighters are perfect for late-night rom-coms, but in real life they're nothing but trouble. Especially when you find out they work for your dad—***after you've already slept with them.***

Moving to my parents' small town was supposed to be the fresh start I was looking for. When a disastrous Valentine's Day leads to an unexpected encounter with a sexy stranger, and ends with the hottest night of my life, I didn't think I would ever see Whip again.

Imagine my surprise when one of my sixth-grade students has a medical emergency and it's Whip who shows up, looking hot as hell, to save the day. I should be embarrassed at how we left things, but instead I'm furious he doesn't seem to remember me.

So I scrape my pride off the floor, lift my chin, and pretend there's nothing between us. But that can last only so long. ***Stolen glances melt into forbidden***

touches, and once we give in to temptation, we can't keep our hands off each other.

Nothing has ever felt so right, but my guarded heart won't let me believe in happily ever after with a man like him. Opening up to Whip may be the hardest thing I've ever done, and every time we agree to one last time, we both know it's a lie.

How many times can we keep telling ourselves ***just this once*** before we realize that, when it comes to love, once is never enough?

ONE

EMILY

*W*HY AM *I settling for a medium-ugly man who won't stop staring at my tits?*

I questioned all my life's choices. *Safe and predictable* held less appeal as I watched my date dribble spaghetti sauce on his chin. I blame my mother. She had insisted that a blind date on Valentine's Day was exactly what I needed to move on with my life after everything that happened last fall.

More like a spiraling descent into absolute nothingness.

Insert Dickie Johnson.

Dickie's mother worked with mine as an administrative assistant at the local police station, and both had hatched the plan to pair us up.

Dickie. Freaking. Johnson.

After my parents had moved to the coastal Western Michigan town of Outtatowner, I learned quickly that almost everyone who lived there had some kind of quirky nickname. Unable to hide my horrified expression, Mom had assured me that nicknames seemed to be reserved for those who'd grown up in Outtatowner and not for a substitute teacher who had barely made it through week one of her new residency.

My parents claimed the nicknames were one of the many things to love about their charming small town. Dickie could have been Richard or Rick or, hell, even Bob, but around town, he was known solely as Dickie. The people here wore their nicknames like a badge of honor.

After being twenty-five minutes late, he'd copped a feel not once, but twice, on the short walk from the restaurant entrance to our secluded table. If that wasn't a bad enough start to our date, Dickie droned on and on about his real estate licensure without asking a *single* question about me. Honestly, that was fine, because the less he knew about me, the better. All I needed to figure out was how to make a graceful exit without having to hear about cutting the date short from my mother.

"I closed the sale on this very storefront." Dickie waved a hand in the air. "So, if you're thinking about dessert"—he winked at me—"I get a discount that I can stack with my coupon."

I nodded and hummed a response, but his words didn't register, since I couldn't stop staring at the orange splatters of sauce clinging to the square patch of hair beneath his lower lip.

"Are you even listening to me? I was highlighting my financial prowess, but I see you're distracted." Dickie laughed and sucked in his lower lip, his tongue darting across the hairs. "It's a flavor saver."

My eyes lifted to his. He waggled his eyebrows at me, and my stomach curled in on itself.

I blinked and shook my head. Surely I hadn't heard that right. "I'm sorry . . . a *what*?"

His forefinger and thumb smoothed down the coarse

hairs beneath his lip. "You've never seen a soul patch?" His eyes flicked down my front and back up, his words sinking in.

A flavor saver.

"Okay." I forced a tight smile, then gently removed my napkin from my lap and placed it beside my plate. "I think it's time to go." I scooted backward, the scraping of stiff chair legs against the wooden floor filling the restaurant as I stood.

Dickie rose, reaching into his sports coat to remove his wallet. "Yeah, okay." His chuckle bounced off my back. "Yeah, let's do this."

My eyebrows cinched down, and I shook my head as I gathered my purse and stuffed my arms into my coat. "Um . . . no. Let's not. Thank you for tonight. It's been . . . interesting. Good night, Dickie."

Without waiting for him, I headed toward the door as fast as my slingback kitten heels could carry me.

"Hey. Wait up!" Dickie called behind me, but I was determined to escape the restaurant as quickly as possible. The February wind sliced through me as the attendant pulled open the ornate door with a flourish. My plan to run away from my problems was already starting to bite me in the ass when I realized it included *actual running* in the harsh Michigan winter. I lowered my head, wrapping my arms around my middle to ward off the chill.

"Wait, please. I have one more thing I need to ask you."

My patience was thin, but the absolutely pathetic look in his eyes wore me down. "What is it?" I bristled against the cold.

He sucked in a breath and held up his palms. "Let me ask you this—are you tired of the nine-to-five grind? Are you looking for a way to gain financial independence and live a life of freedom?"

"What? Are you serious right now?"

Dickie rocked on his heels expectantly, completely oblivious to the fact I was actively freezing to death in my dress.

I held out my palms. "Um, I think I'm good."

He leaned in. "Plain good is *not* good enough, Emily. You deserve the best! And that's why I want to introduce you to an amazing health supplement line. These products are game changers. They'll improve your energy, your immune system, your mental clarity . . . basically every aspect of your life!"

Cue internal groaning . . .

I shook my head. "Oh, wow . . . that sure is . . . something." I nodded. "So . . . I'm leaving."

Dickie followed me step for step as I hurried down the sidewalk. "Oh, Emily, you don't get it. This isn't about money—it's about investing in your health! Think about it. What's more important than your well-being?"

I shivered and cut across the roadway where I knew he'd parked his car. "Well . . . my bank account, for one thing."

When a car honked at us, he simply waved a hand. "Ha! You're too funny. But seriously, our products are an absolute bargain for the value they provide. And the best part is, if you join my team, you can earn commission by selling these products to your friends and family!"

I clenched my jaw, trying to keep my eyes from rolling to the back of my head and getting permanently stuck. I hummed through gritted teeth. "Sounds like a dream. Your car is that way."

I gestured down the roadway, and his smile melted from his face. "Oh. Well . . ."

I threw one hand up in a salute. "Night!"

I knew full well my car was parked two blocks in the *same* direction as his, but extending this date from hell was the last thing I needed, so I scurried away in the opposite direction.

Dickie called to my back: "You didn't even hear the best part! Your first ten customers get a free starter kit!"

I ignored him, and my heels pounded on the sidewalk like every building on Copper Street was on fire. I could feel his gaze behind me, but I didn't dare look back. Seeking refuge, I darted around the corner onto Main Street and hid behind one of the large concrete flower planters that lined the main thoroughfare.

Still shivering, I waited a few minutes before peeking around the corner.

Thankfully, he was nowhere to be seen. I breathed a sigh of relief as my body sagged against the rough concrete planter. Soft yellow light spilled out of the large bay windows in front of me. *King Tattoo* glowed from the sign, and I paused. My gaze skated over the shiny black chairs and black-and-white-checkered tile.

I could do it. I could break free and get something dainty and unexpected tattooed, just because. Something just for me . . .

Indecision locked me in place as I shivered against the cold. My eyes adjusted to the light as I stared through the storefront window. Two men stood inside, one behind the counter and the other leaning over it.

Both were so impressively built that I couldn't help but stare. The one leaning over the counter and pointing caught my attention. My eyes moved upward, from his boots to the musculature of his thick legs before pausing at the curve of his butt.

No man should have an ass that fantastic.

As if he could feel my eyes locked onto him, the man straightened and started to turn. I shook myself out of a stupor and hurried down the sidewalk. During my attempted escape from the date from hell, I realized the only other place open on Valentine's Day evening was a general store.

I needed refuge. Warmth. *Chocolate.*

The bell clanked against the glass as I pulled open the door, and a whoosh of hot air coasted over my brittle skin. My heels danced on the linoleum as icy shivers racked my body.

The man working behind the register only nodded before turning back to his magazine. "Evening."

I gave him an apologetic smile before digging my phone out of my purse. Of course my cell battery was nearly dead from mindlessly scrolling videos while I'd waited for Dickie to show up. My car was only a few blocks away, but I was chilled to the bone, and I couldn't risk him waiting around for me. My finger hovered over my stepdad's contact. He would rescue me in a heartbeat, and I could worry about picking my car up tomorrow.

I closed my eyes, fully aware of the man shooting concerned glances at me from behind the register.

You don't need saving. You don't need anyone.

I took a deep breath and remembered the grin on my stepdad's face when he told me about his plans to cook for Mom and share their own romantic Valentine's Day at home. After nearly twenty years together, my mother and stepfather were still very much in love, and I had always thought of my stepfather as "Dad." It was something that gave my bitter twenty-five-year-old heart a tiny bit of hope. My mother had found her second chance at love as a single mother, so there was no good reason why there couldn't be *someone* out there for me.

Right?

You have to let someone in if you want them to know the real you. To love the woman you try to hide.

My mother's words rattled through my head. Letting someone in meant being exposed.

Vulnerable.

That's a big no fucking way.

I'd done that once and was in absolutely no hurry to do it again. Besides, I had a successful and fulfilling career as a middle school teacher. In my previous district, I had joined every committee and was a force to be reckoned with in the teachers' union. I was going to be principal one day. I had big plans. Dreams. None of which hinged on a man. Especially one with a *flavor saver*.

I needed only a minute to collect myself, defrost for a moment while I waited for Dickie to leave, and then I could head back toward the restaurant and find my car. As I stepped deeper into the store, the sticky-sweet smell of creamy milk chocolate hit me like a wall. Pink-and-red stuffed animals were strewn across the metal shelves, clinging to each other with hopeful eyes. As I passed a pair of monkeys, I flicked one in its plastic eyeball.

Down the aisle, I spotted the half-off Valentine's Day candy and decided that drowning my sorrows in sugar was the only logical choice. My stomach rumbled as I stepped up to the barren shelves. Most of the good stuff had been picked over, leaving conversation hearts and a smattering of chocolate oranges. I scanned the shelves, crouching down to see if there was any hint of dark chocolate hiding somewhere. Frustrated, I shoved aside the boxes, sending a few tumbling to the floor.

My eyes caught on a small, hidden bag of individually wrapped chocolate squares.

Dark chocolate caramel with sea salt? Yahtzee!

I clutched the package to my chest before lifting on my tiptoes to peer over the metal rack. Thankfully the employee behind the register had lost all interest in me as he flipped through the pages of a magazine. I just needed a minute.

Sinking to my butt, I smoothed my skirt over my tights and kicked off my heels. I opened the package as discreetly as I could and slipped one decadent square out of the bag. After unwrapping it, I closed my eyes and let a bite of chocolate melt on my tongue. The bitterness and salt warred with the creamy caramel.

I moaned.

Looking at the morsel of salted dark chocolate, I sighed. "Looks like you're going to be the only pleasure I'll be getting tonight so . . . damn it, I'm going to enjoy you."

I rolled my tongue around the salted caramel coating my mouth. "Oh my god, you're good."

Throat clearing jolted my attention away from devouring the chocolate. A steady rhythm of heavy boots walked up the aisle, and my eyes landed on a pair of scuffed-up work boots as they stopped at my side. My gaze followed the long trail, up well-worn denim, over trim hips, and across a broad, masculine chest before landing on the face of the man from the tattoo shop.

His eyes were piercing, so blue they looked almost gray. It was a stark contrast to the thick mop of hair that hung across his forehead. His features were strong, but not severe. The lift at the corner of his mouth confirmed he'd definitely overheard me nearly coming to orgasm from a piece of dime-store chocolate.

My heart caught in my throat as the handsome stranger looked at me with a devastating smirk. “Theft is a punishable offense, you know.”

TWO

WHIP

The last thing I expected to see was a heart-stoppingly gorgeous woman on Valentine's Day tearing apart the candy aisle like a feral raccoon digging through trash.

I recognized her as the stunner who'd stopped in front of my brother's tattoo shop before scurrying away. After she dipped into the general store, I used the opportunity to make a little detour on my way home.

From the end of the aisle, I had watched her aggressively push candy aside until she clutched a bag of chocolates on the shelf with a triumphant smile across her face. When she sank down and tore into the package right there on the floor of the general store, I was more than intrigued. The moan as the chocolate slid across her tongue shot straight to my cock.

She definitely wasn't a townie. I had lived in Outtatowner my whole life, and I would have recognized someone as achingly pretty as her.

I crossed my arms to keep from laughing as her wide eyes stared up at me at being caught. Her eye color pulled me in. Not quite blue, but not quite green either—more of a smoky hue. *Very interesting.*

"Um . . . ," she mumbled around the chocolate before wiping at the corners of her mouth with a shy laugh.

I lifted a hand, and she moved to get up. "Oh, don't mind me," I said. "But I plan to pay for my discount chocolate." I stepped closer, scanning the near-empty shelves before frowning down at her.

I harrumphed and crossed my arms.

"What?" she asked around a mouthful of chocolate.

My scowl deepened. "You stole the last one."

The woman swallowed, the muscles working in her delicate neck as her throat bobbed. "Not stolen, impending purchase."

"Ah." I nodded, dismissing the sad variety of half-off candy. I reached for a plastic container full of red-, pink-, and white-striped candy corns and held it up. "What do you think Valentine Corn is?"

The woman glanced up, her shy smile simmering with humor. "I was too afraid to find out."

I flipped the container back onto the shelf next to a box of conversation hearts and sighed. "Probably a safe bet," I said.

She shook the bag in front of me. "Want one?"

My mouth hooked into a grin.

Fuck it.

I gestured to the space next to her. "You sure about that? You looked downright feral a minute ago. I don't want to provoke an animal in the wild."

She laughed and shimmied sideways, swiping away an errant chocolate orange and sending it careening across the linoleum, then patting the space beside her. "I don't bite."

I took up residence beside the stranger, giving her

enough space to feel comfortable, before reaching into the bag she held out and pulling out a wrapped square of chocolate. "Thanks."

She swallowed and nodded. "I really am paying for these. I promise." Her shoulders slumped as she unwrapped another piece and shoved the entirety of it past her pretty pink lips and into her mouth.

"Rough day?" I popped the square of chocolate into my mouth and tamped down the rogue curiosity of whether or not this was what her kiss would taste like.

She blew out a breath. "You have no idea."

I raised an eyebrow, encouraging her to continue.

She gestured at her flirty floral dress and tights-clad legs. "Blind date." She scoffed. "It did not go well."

I nodded. "Valentine's Day blind date? Risky move."

She laughed, and the sound was rich and warm. "Trust me, I have learned the error of my ways."

I shrugged, settling my back against the metal shelves and enjoying the soft lilt of her voice. "Tell me about it."

She cast a sidelong glance before tucking an errant strand of her dark-blonde hair behind her ear. It was wound into a tight bun on the top of her head, but my fingers itched to get the undone piece she missed. My hands stayed clamped on my lap.

"Um, so my mom set me up with a guy named Dickie Johnson—"

"Dickie Johnson?" The words were out before I could stop them. There was no version of any universe where Dickie Johnson was worthy of a date with this woman. Her stunned face gave me pause, so I cleared my throat before correcting myself. "I mean, isn't he kind of . . . old for you?"

She narrowed her eyes into little slits but didn't answer. Dickie was thirty-one, same as me, and *definitely* too old for someone as young and vibrant as this woman. A woman whose name I still didn't know. I wiped my palm against my pants before holding out my hand. "Whip."

She eyed my palm warily before setting the bag of chocolate aside and brushing her hands down her skirt. Her palm was dwarfed by mine. "Emily."

Sweet smile and bonus points for not being a townie.

My smile widened. "It's a pleasure to meet you, Emily."

A rosy blush stained her cheeks as her eyes moved over me. "So what brings you to this fine establishment?"

A grumbly laugh rumbled through me. I wasn't about to admit that it was *her* that brought me to the general store. "I had the day off and wanted to stop in to grab a snack before heading home."

Her eyes slowly raked over me beneath thick black lashes before darting away. "No hopelessly romantic Valentine's Day plans, then?"

A smile hooked at my mouth. I liked how shy and reserved she seemed. Even the somewhat modest, buttoned-up dress was doing it for me.

I shrugged, leaning into the playfulness of how my night was unfolding. "I don't know. I found a lonely librarian wolfing down half-priced chocolates. Night's still young."

Emily held out one finger as she lifted her chin. "Definitely not a librarian," she corrected with a smile and curt nod.

"Damn." I shook my head and frowned. "I really have a thing for librarians," I teased.

A shotgun of laughter rang out as she playfully shoved my shoulder with hers. I warmed at the contact. A warning scratched at the inside of my skull—there was something different about this girl.

Special.

Instead of bolting from the feeling like I should have, I let my shoulder settle against hers, and when she didn't ease away from the contact, I sank into the surprising comfort of our connection.

I shifted, holding out my hand for hers. "So . . . definitely-not-a-librarian Emily, would you settle for a Valentine's date redo?"

THREE

EMILY

I STARED at his outstretched hand, his wide palm and long fingers waiting for me to make a decision.

Do I do it? Oh my god, this is so unlike me.

A squeal threatened to tear out of me when I placed my hand in his. Whip gave it a gentle squeeze before standing and hauling me up with him. I flashed a quick smile to hide my nerves. Hand in his, I followed Whip through the deserted general store and out into the cold night. I shivered, and he dropped my hand to slip his coat off his shoulders. Before I could protest, he wound the large jacket around me and pulled it closed.

"You'll freeze," I argued, appreciating the way his biceps strained the long sleeves of his Henley.

"Nah." He shook his head. "I was built for the cold."

Whip towered over me—all broad lines and hard edges—as we walked. He was most definitely built and had the kind of body that screamed promises of warmed skin and protective embraces.

I swallowed hard as Whip led me down the sidewalk toward the muted sounds of music and neon lights. I shook away my wandering thoughts when my feet stopped short. "Shit! I forgot to pay for the chocolates!"

Whip grinned. "My cousin owns the general store. I'll be sure to square up with him before he starts printing the Wanted posters."

I sagged in relief. "Thank you."

"No problem." I couldn't tear my gaze away from him as he smiled. "Thief."

My laugh rang out into the crisp winter air with a puffy white cloud. Excitement danced under my skin as we walked.

My whole life I'd made the right choice. Been the good girl. It was exhausting, and for once I wanted to spread my wings—stop thinking twelve steps ahead in any scenario and *live*.

"I know a place just up this way." Whip continued up the sidewalk, shifting his position to be on the side closest to the roadway, and I followed, reveling in the subtly protective gesture.

When we stopped, I glanced at the neon sign next to the heavy wooden door. A jaunty skeleton grinned back at me.

"The Grudge Holder?" I asked. The muscles in Whip's arm rippled through his shirt as he leaned forward to pull the door open. I slipped past him as he held it for me. "Cute name."

He slid in next to me, and the warmth of the bar wafted over us. "Yeah, it's kind of an inside joke in this town."

I had started toward an empty high-top table when Whip's long fingers gently wrapped around my hip bone, stopping me. No man had ever touched me in such a benign way while exuding such raw masculinity. I willed my knees not to buckle.

His breath floated across the shell of my ear. "This way." With his head he gestured toward the opposite end of the bar. "My family only sits on the east side."

My eyebrows lifted. "Oh."

Whip helped me into the stool at a high-top table and rapped a knuckle on the wood. "Can I get you something to drink? My brother owns a local brewery, and they sell it here. It's pretty good."

"A beer would be great. Thanks."

Whip sauntered toward the large bar in the back, and I used the opportunity to stare incessantly at his ass. No man had any right to look that effortlessly put together in simple jeans and a long-sleeved Henley. *Totally unfair.*

I tore my gaze away from him before I got caught and took the opportunity to look around the bar. Music spilled from a jukebox in the corner, and posters announced various bands for the upcoming weekends. A pink-and-red banner was strung across the stage with loopy, romantic font. *Love is in the air—try not to breathe.* I laughed and soaked up the friendly, inviting atmosphere.

Curious, I looked across the dance floor toward the west side of the bar. A few wary glances were cast my way, and it seemed as though everyone really did keep to their own side. *Curious.*

Whip sidled up next to me and set down two beers, one light and one dark. "I wasn't sure of your preference." He pointed to the dark one. "Vanilla porter, one of my favorites." His finger moved to the other. "Hefeweizen with malty, caramel notes. Lady's choice."

My eyes danced with delight. "You really do know your beers."

He shrugged. "It's really Abel's deal, but I've learned a thing or two."

I smiled as I slid the porter in front of me. "Thank you."

Whip winked, and butterflies tangled in a riot inside my stomach. I took a sip to settle my nerves. "So you weren't kidding, were you?"

He slid onto the stool next to me. "About what?"

I deepened my voice and leaned forward. "My family only sits on the east side."

He chuckled at my impersonation. "Oh. No, definitely wasn't joking about that." He swiped a hand down his thick denim-clad thigh. "The name of this place, the Grudge Holder, comes from a long-standing feud between two families in town—the Kings and the Sullivans."

I leaned forward on the stool, resting my chin in my hand and widening my eyes. "Tell. Me. Everything."

The rumble of his deep laugh had heat pooling between my thighs, and I gently scissored my legs beneath the table to keep from squirming.

He shrugged. "Run-of-the-mill, small-town bullshit. Ages ago our families decided they hated each other, and now we spend ridiculous time and effort out-pranking each other. I guess we've never gotten it out of our systems." He paused, his beer halfway to his mouth. "Though my sister Sylvie has come the closest. She's with Duke Sullivan, so they sit in the middle now."

"Oh, I bet your parents loved that." My laughter died when Whip's shoulders stiffened at the mention of his parents. I also didn't miss the subtle twitch at the corner of his eye.

Apparently talking about parents is a no-fly zone. Noted.

I quickly redirected, grasping for the lighthearted mood we'd been enjoying. "So if your families hate each other so much, why not just go to separate bars? Avoid it altogether."

The mischief was back in Whip's piercing slate eyes.

"Well, that would kind of take all the fun out of it, wouldn't it?"

I laughed before taking a sip of my beer, letting the subtle vanilla and malt flavors melt over my tongue. "Yeah, I guess you're right about that."

I looked around the bar once more. If you didn't know about the feud, an outsider would likely see a typical dance hall, but upon further inspection, the divide in the crowd was pretty obvious.

"Okay, so give me an example." I sat up straighter. "Tell me about a prank that you've pulled."

He eyed me carefully, his lips gently pursing as he considered my question. "Hmm," he hummed. "How do I know you're not a Sullivan spy? Using your charm and beauty to unravel all our secrets?"

My cheeks warmed at his subtle compliment, but I feigned shock, letting my fingertips drag across my collarbone. "Me? A spy?" I blinked innocently.

Whip shook his head and scoffed. "You may not be a spy, but you damn sure are dangerous."

Pleasure thrummed through my veins. *When was the last time I'd been so at ease in a man's presence?* I had almost forgotten what it was like to flirt and *let go* for a minute.

I honestly couldn't recall the last time I'd felt so free. Whip was confident and sexy. Funny. And somehow his attention made me feel as if we were the only two souls in that run-down bar. He made me feel at ease. Comfortable in my own skin. *Electric.*

When the music changed to a popular country song that had been playing on repeat over the radio, I clapped my hands together and hopped from the stool. "Dance with me."

Whip took a sip of his beer before setting the glass down in front of him, but he didn't stand. I held up my hands. "Or does dancing go against some cool-guy code I don't know about?"

He chuckled and stood next to me, letting his fingertips drag from the inside of my elbow to my palm in one smooth movement as he leaned in. "Trust me. Being seen with a woman like you makes me the coolest guy in this shithole."

I laughed as Whip twirled me toward the dance floor. My feet stumbled, but he managed to guide me into a rhythm, and our unlikely two-step wasn't half bad. He held one hand out, the other banded around my waist as we moved with the music. As we danced, Whip whispered town secrets in my ear, sharing stories of the regulars —*townies*, he called them—as we wore a path on that old oak floor.

I wondered whether he would have a funny story about my parents if they had been there.

The music changed again, and a moody, bluesy number crooned from the speakers. Without missing a beat, Whip pulled me closer. His hard body pressed up against mine, and I stared up at his chiseled jawline. He rested my hand in the small space between our bodies, holding it close over his chest. His heart thudded against my fingertips.

Did he feel this too?

His warm, calloused palm grazed mine, and tingles swept across my skin. Minutes melted into hours, and I was drowning in this mysterious stranger.

Something about him was so familiar and comforting, yet all together exciting and intoxicating. By the time I came up for air, the bartender announced the last call—our drinks, long abandoned.

Whip offered me the extra warmth of his coat, and this

time I slipped my arms into it without hesitation. As I followed him out of the bar, I stared at his chiseled back and pulled the collar to my nose, filling my lungs with his masculine scent of soap and sage.

Once outside, I pointed in the direction of my car, parked only a block or so away. His arm banded around my shoulders, helping to ward off the February chill.

I shivered. "Are you sure you're not cold?"

He looked down at me, his eyes flicking to my lips for only a fraction of a second. "I'm perfect."

The walk was too short, and my stomach muscles tensed as I gestured toward my car. "Well . . . this is me."

Whip walked me to the driver's side, and I slipped off his coat before handing it back to him. "Thank you. I think this might have been the best, most surprising Valentine's Day I've ever had."

Whip scrubbed a hand across the back of his neck, and the grin he shot me wobbled my knees. "Better than Dickie Johnson?"

I grinned at him. "Dickie who?"

Intensity darkened Whip's eyes as he leaned in close, wrapping me in his heat. "Emily, do you think I could call you sometime?"

My insides were screaming. The last thing I wanted to do was go home to a lonely, still-unpacked apartment. Whip inched impossibly closer. I lowered my lashes, then gathered every ounce of courage before looking into his steel blue eyes.

I'd wasted so many years doing the good thing. The right thing with the wrong men. Whip may not have been the right man, either, but there was something about him that was pulling me in.

I didn't give a damn if it was wrong.

I wanted it.

Craved it.

"You know, I really appreciate you not calling the cops on me. I'm thinking I can thank you for that . . ." I swallowed hard and willed my voice not to tremble. "Maybe at your place."

FOUR

WHIP

My knuckles were white from my grip on the steering wheel. My eyes flashed to the rearview to make sure Emily was safely following me on the short drive away from downtown toward my house.

This woman is altogether surprising.

The last thing I expected was the shy, unassuming woman asking to take things back to my place.

I had struggled to keep my dick in check ever since feeling her soft curves as I swayed with her to the music. There was no way she didn't feel how hard her closeness had made me.

Just out of town, I pulled down the unmarked country road, watching in the rearview to make sure she made the turn. Dirt and gravel flew beneath my truck's tires. It had been a minute since I had been with a woman, and I willed my nerves to settle, but *god how I wanted her*.

Her car pulled next to mine, and I rushed to hold her door open for her.

Emily stood by her car, glancing up at my house. It had been built on the outskirts of my small town, and I prided myself on its function and design. It may be a bachelor pad, but it was classy, damn it. The Craftsman-style ranch home sprawled across three acres and was surrounded by woods and blueberry fields.

Away from the curious eyes of my neighbors, it was the only place where I could escape.

"I don't know, pal . . . the minute we pulled down that dark road, I thought maybe you were trying to murder me." A nervous giggle tumbled out of her. "I want you to know I don't usually do—"

In two long strides, I cut off her laugh as my mouth crashed to hers, swallowing up the rest of her sentence.

She moaned into me, her tits pressing into my chest as I pulled her closer. I bent at the knees and gripped the backs of her thighs, hauling her up against me. My cock ached and pressed against the fly of my jeans.

She moaned and moved higher, climbing me like a fucking tree as my hands roamed over her ass.

The harsh February wind didn't register as fire burned through my veins. I stomped up the porch steps and held her weight with one arm, digging my keys from my pocket.

"I never do this," she panted.

"I don't give a fuck." My tongue burned a path up her neck. "Even if you did, I wouldn't stop this."

Her gentle hums and moans as we kissed ratcheted the tension higher. Emily was soft and sweet. She seemed like the kind of woman who deserved a man who took his time and paid attention to every slope and dip of the curves beneath my fingertips.

"I told you I have a thing for librarians," I teased.

Her throaty hum was nearly my undoing. My blood buzzed in a frenzy. I couldn't get enough. I wanted to be over her, under her, around her, *in her*. A woman I had met only hours before was completely and overwhelmingly consuming.

Once inside I pressed her back into the wall, pinning her in place with my body as my hands explored.

"And I told you, *not* a librarian." She arched against me. "You sure talk a big game for someone named *Whip*. Is that a name or a promise?"

I chuckled. This quiet, unassuming woman had a hidden fire that I inexplicably found myself *craving*. I dragged my teeth along the thin skin of her collarbone. "It can be whatever you want it to."

Emily's desperate breaths brushed across my ear. "God, you smell so good. Why do you smell so good?"

My nails dragged down the back of her thighs, hating the tights that covered her legs. I lowered her to her feet, bracing myself on the wall behind her. "Take your shoes off."

Emily looked up at me, suddenly shy. Her teeth sank into her plump bottom lip. "You should know that I'm not very good at this."

I studied her face. "This . . . ?"

"Sex." Her blush deepened before she looked away. "It's just something an old boyfriend told me once or twice, and it kind of stuck with me. I don't normally do this with someone I don't know, and I just thought maybe I should tell you ahead of time." She rubbed her palms together, nerves rolling off her. "Shit. I'm sorry if I ruined the mood or whatever."

My fingertips toyed with the hem of her skirt, teasing her inner thigh. "You didn't ruin anything. Based on what I already know, that idiot didn't know what the fuck he was talking about." My hands inched higher. "Is this okay?"

Emily's trusting eyes met mine, and she nodded.

A sly smile twitched at the corner of my mouth. "Good. Now take your shoes off."

Her tongue swept across her lips as she looked up at me with wide eyes and complied. She kicked off her shoes, and I sank to my knees. My hands roamed up her legs, slipping beneath her skirt and finding the top band to her tights. With each breathy pant, I slowed my pace to a torturous descent down each leg, letting my fingertips rake down her thighs as I removed her tights.

Once her legs were free, my hands shoved the skirt of her floral dress upward. Only a thin swatch of silky black fabric covered her. I pressed my face over the fabric as she hitched a leg higher with a sharp inhale. From that angle, I could see the spot of wetness that had seeped out of her.

I pressed my thumb to the wet spot. "Already wet for me, Emily?"

Her knee came down as a shy blush pinked her cheeks. My cock throbbed beneath my jeans, hating every moment I wasn't buried to the hilt inside this gorgeous, intoxicating woman.

I looked up from my knees at her. "Don't be embarrassed. Not with me."

Her arms draped over my shoulders as her blue-green doe eyes gazed down at me. "If you want to know how wet I am . . ." Watching her confidence build was the sexiest thing I'd ever seen. I ached when her right eyebrow pitched higher. "You could feel for yourself."

My jaw flexed as I dragged the blade of my hand through her covered pussy. She was soaked.

I groaned a rough exhale. *"Fuck, Em."*

FIVE

EMILY

Fuck, Em.

Two words, ground out on a delicious, tortured moan, had been my undoing. Coffee in hand, I braced myself against the counter in the teachers' lounge as I stirred the creamer, remembering how those two words had sent electric tingles from my scalp to my toes before Whip hauled me over his shoulder, firefighter style, and stomped toward his bedroom.

That should have been my first clue.

We had hardly come up for air that entire night. He was assertive and attentive. He hadn't even minded the shocked expression that twisted my face when he had shed his jeans to reveal his piercing.

Yep.

Whip King had a pierced. Fucking. Cock.

I had only ever seen one in porn or random late-night Google searches, but being presented with a penis that looked like his—long and thick and veined—only to find out that he was also sporting a Jacob's ladder?

My thighs quivered at the memory, and I pressed my legs together, sucking in a long deep breath at how he'd—

"Earth to Emily."

I jolted at the feeling of a hand pressed between my shoulder blades, splashing coffee over the rim of my mug. "Ow! Shit." I shook off my hand, sending droplets of coffee flying.

"Are you okay?" Rachel assessed me from head to toe, concern pinching her eyebrows. "I was calling your name, but it looked like you were in a different world."

Yes. A world in which I was pinned beneath Whip King as he drove into me over and over with that glorious bedazzled cock.

I cleared my throat. "Yeah, sorry." I let loose a nervous laugh. "Just lost in thought, I guess."

Rachel flicked her short blonde hair back. "Well, the bell is going to ring in three minutes. We gotta get in there. *The Warden* can't be late."

I pulled down a handful of napkins from the dispenser and wiped away the spill and tried to hide the cringe from my unwanted nickname—as if being a teacher with *rules* was a bad thing. "Okay. I'll be right there."

I had better get my head on straight. I need this job.

The rumor floating around the teachers' lounge was that Mrs. Kirk wasn't planning on returning after her maternity leave. That meant there was a very good chance that this job at Outtatowner Junior High could turn into an actual career. For the time being, I was considering my long-term substitute job as her maternity sub as an extended interview of sorts.

I could nail this gig and get that job.

Oh god . . . but then I would have to face him again.

I clutched my coffee mug in both hands, letting the

warmth seep into my fingers before taking a steadying breath.

"Rachel," I called. She turned and smiled as I hurried to catch up. "Wait for me."

Side by side we walked through the corridors of the junior high school until we reached our doors across the hall from one another.

"Happy Friday." She clinked her coffee mug against mine. "Another week down. You know, a few of us are going to do happy hour after school. Are you in?"

"Sounds fun. Where are you going?"

Rachel smiled at Mrs. Kuder, the crabby, septuagenarian librarian who pushed her cart between us. I stifled a giggle, recalling Mrs. Kuder's beloved town nickname: *Scooter Kuder*.

I shook my head as she shuffled away. *You can't make this shit up, I swear.*

"We're going to the Grudge Holder. It's a local place. Do you want to come along?" Rachel looked at me expectantly.

The knot in my stomach grew taut. "Yeah, um. I'll think about it." I sipped my coffee to hide the slip in my smile. "I might come out tonight."

I wouldn't.

Rachel could see right through my bullshit as she tipped her head and raised her eyebrows in a look that said, *Yeah, fucking right.* "Come on. It's been almost two months since you took over Kirk's class. You're one of us now. You should come out. Given the students you wound up with this year, you have definitely earned it."

I chuckled as I glanced over my shoulder and through the classroom door. She wasn't kidding—my classroom of eleven- and twelve-year-olds was most definitely a handful.

There was even a rumor going around school that Mrs. Kirk had found out about the cluster of students in her class and had timed her pregnancy perfectly. The students were rowdy and rambunctious and needed a firm but kind hand if we were ever going to get anything done this school year.

They were perfect.

My eyes landed on one desk. "Hey, what do you know about Robbie Lambert and his family?"

Rachel's gaze followed mine. She was petite, but what she lacked in height, she more than made up for in gusto. Her short, light-blonde bob bounced when she tipped her head. "Not much, why? Is he a troublemaker?"

I shook my head. "No, the opposite. He's an angel—very sweet, but really quiet. I just get the feeling something is *off*. He came to school with no socks on last week and the other day forgot his coat."

She shrugged. "Kids are forgetful. It's probably nothing."

My lips pressed together, and I tamped down the unease in my belly. "You're probably right."

Rachel took a step toward her room. "Tonight. Please consider it."

I smiled at her. "I'll think about it. I promise."

She pointed one long manicured nail at me. "You better. Don't you lie to me, Warden."

I raised my hand in surrender. "I would *never*. I promise I'll think about it."

She lifted her coffee mug in salute to another day of shaping the future. I laughed, raised my mug with hers, and took another sip of my morning coffee.

Once inside, my gaze floated over the twenty-six student desks in carefully arranged clusters around my room.

My classroom.

I drew one resolute breath and exhaled, shoving down every unwelcomed thought of Whip King. "All right, let's do this."

~

My fingers tapped out a nervous rhythm against the outside of my thigh as my eyes swept through the Grudge.

This is a terrible idea.

For nearly two months I had successfully avoided this place, turning down any invite for a night out or drinks after work for fear I might run into him. Six of us had met outside, and I tucked myself into the middle of the clump of teachers, hoping to be invisible. People were already congregating in small clusters throughout the bar. A banner announced a live band, and it seemed others had the same idea we did about unwinding after a stressful workweek.

I shifted toward the east side, looking for a table big enough to accommodate our group.

"There's one over there," Rachel called out to us, pointing to a long table tucked against the wall of the west side. "Does that look good?" she asked.

"You chose last time," Becca, a seventh-grade teacher, chimed in. "Rock-paper-scissors for it?"

I watched in awe as two grown women pumped their fists and chanted, "Rock, paper, scissors, shoot!"

"Ha!" Rachel cheered when her paper beat Becca's rock. "Sullivan side for the win."

"Fine, let's snag it," Becca grumbled. "I guess it doesn't really matter anyway."

Oh, I think it very much matters.

Despite the heat prickling along my hairline, I followed

the group and took a seat with my back against the far wall so I could look out onto the bar and dance floor.

Rachel sat next to me, plucking a plastic menu from between the napkin dispenser and ketchup bottle.

"Have you ever been here?" she asked as she scanned the menu. "They've got great food and even better music. It's usually a really good time."

Becca leaned across the table with a smirk. "There's also amazing eye candy." She jerked her head toward the middle of the room. "The men around here are something else. I swear there's got to be something in that Lake Michigan water."

"Which is why"—Rachel waggled her eyebrows—"no one can ever agree on which side to pick. Once the tourist season picks up, the eye candy gets even better, if you can believe it." She shimmied her shoulders. "Nothing says school's out like a hot little summer fling."

A thin smile flattened my lips.

"I wouldn't mind having a fling with someone like *that*." Becca jutted her chin toward the far corner of the bar.

I knew those broad shoulders. The nip of his waist. My hands had roamed over every curve of his muscular ass. Heat clawed up my throat and cheeks as I tried to sink lower in my seat, using Becca's body to hide behind.

Whip stood shoulder to shoulder with another man, leaning over the oak bar and giving me a perfect view of his backside. When Whip's counterpart turned, I blinked in surprise. Whip had mentioned brothers, but the similarities between these two were striking.

When Whip had stripped out of his jeans and long-sleeved shirt, he had revealed beautiful tattoos that trailed along his arms and torso. This man next to him was extensively covered and held that same dangerous glint in his eye that had drawn me to Whip. Recognition from seeing him at the tattoo shop washed over me. He leaned in and said something to Whip. They both laughed as Whip turned to face the open space of the Grudge.

"Why are you acting weird?" Rachel leaned over to join me in my hiding spot behind the plastic menu.

"I'm not being weird," I whispered.

I was definitely acting like a fucking lunatic.

She pulled the plastic menu down. "And who do you keep looking at?"

"Shh!" I scolded. "Stop it. Nothing. No one."

"Is it the tattooed daddy over there?" Her eyes widened. "Or is it the lumber-snack next to him? Does the Warden have the hots for someone?"

I couldn't help but laugh. "Oh my god, stop it. And don't call me that." I looked again at Whip and prayed we hadn't drawn attention to ourselves. Thankfully he seemed oblivious to my ongoing meltdown in the back corner.

"They're Kings, you know." Rachel's voice held an air of awe.

"Everyone knows the Kings," Becca added. "Maybe you don't know all of them, but you've worked with one or grew up with another." She shrugged. "Who doesn't know the Kings?"

Rachel's pointed stare lingered after Becca's attention returned to the menu. She sucked in a breath as realization lit up her features. Her manicured finger poked my arm. "You *do* know him." She scooted closer, scraping her chair along the floor. "Tell me everything or I swear to you I will stand on this table and make a scene." The devilish grin and challenge in Rachel's eyes warned me she wasn't kidding.

For a teacher with a reputation of being a hard-ass, Rachel had a wild streak a mile wide. When I held her stare but didn't answer, she moved, planting one foot on the seat of her chair.

I grabbed her forearm and tugged her down, her butt landing with a plop. "Fine, I'll tell you, but shut up. Not the tattoo daddy, but the one next to him," I whispered, praying my colleagues were too engrossed in deciding what food to order for the table to pay any attention to me.

I tipped my head toward Whip. "We hooked up just after I got to town. I don't want him to see me."

She leaned back in her chair, crossing her arms. "Whip King? Why the hell not?"

Her head snapped back to me. "Is he terrible in bed? Does he have a micro-peen? Was he all jackhammer and no finesse?"

"No. Shut up." A giggle tumbled from me. "Honestly, it was really, *really* amazing." Even admitting that out loud felt forbidden and made me want to fan my cheeks.

"So what's the deal, then? Saunter up next to him and go in for round two." Her arms swept wide in invitation as if it would ever be that easy.

I pulled her arm back to her lap. "I can't."

"Why not?"

I exhaled a frustrated sigh. "He's a firefighter."

Rachel's eyes went wide. "Oh shit, that's right."

I sank lower in my seat. "Yep. And I didn't know that until after we . . ." My hand rolled in circles between us. "You know."

"He works for your dad? That is so freaking hot." Rachel stared at Whip across the bar.

I rolled my eyes despite the pressure building between my legs. "It is not hot, it's stupid." More than stupid—epically fucked up. My stepfather was the fire chief in Outtatowner and would definitely have *a lot* to say about me hooking up with one of his guys. Not only was Dad slightly overprotective, but I had grown up with all the behind-the-scenes stories about the reckless and dangerous tendencies of the men he worked with. I also had firsthand knowledge of the kind of men in his profession.

Rachel frowned. "And you didn't talk about your jobs before you let him go to Pound Town?"

My gaze whipped in his direction, and I lowered my voice. "We didn't exactly do a lot of talking."

Rachel hooted. "Oh, you dirty slut. I love it." She bumped her elbow into the side of my arm. "I knew you were a good egg."

A server came around, and I hastily ordered a vanilla porter before returning my attention to Rachel.

She squared me with a look. "You're a big girl. Your dad shouldn't have any say over who you fool around with."

I shrugged. "I know. He's just protective, and he's always warned me about firefighters. Plus, I know from experience that they're all either womanizers and cheaters or adrenaline junkies. Sometimes all three are wrapped up in an addictively hot package. Something about that type of man being caught up in the thrill of it all." I chewed my lip. "But really that's not the worst of it."

Rachel's wide eyes spurred me to continue. "I saw his uniform on the floor and I *knew*." I blew out a breath. "And instead of talking about it, I completely freaked out." I scrunched my face. "I gave him a *high five* and left." I buried my face in my hands.

"You did *what*?" Rachel's jaw hung open.

"Yeah, a high freaking five. And then I got dressed faster than I ever have in my entire life, left his house, and never looked back."

Rachel nodded and laughed, then sat back. "So you ghosted him."

My head reared back. "I didn't ghost him. I just . . . never spoke to him again."

"I'm guessing you didn't leave your number?" Her bland look was unimpressed.

I cringed. "I practically ran out the front door as he was still zipping up his pants." Shame coursed through me. I was a grown woman, fully capable of having a no-strings one-night stand, but I couldn't help but feel *bad* for Whip. He'd been charming and funny, and leaving him without any kind of explanation left a slimy feeling in my gut. The fact that my immediate reaction was to *run* spoke volumes for how closed off I'd become.

Maybe Craig was right about me after all. Damn it.

My only hope was that my stepfather was right, and a man like Whip wouldn't give me a second thought. Which, come to think of it, made my complicated feelings about the whole thing only *worse*.

I folded my arms and dropped my head to my forearms with a groan.

The server set down a round of waters for our table along with our drinks, and Rachel plucked it up and took a sip. "Well, there are worse things than a high five, you know."

I wanted to be *anywhere* other than hiding at a back table at the Grudge, letting the shame of my awkward exit wash over me.

Rachel bumped my shoulder. "Well, relax, Casper. It looks like you're off the hook."

I lifted my head and my stomach pitched. A pretty brunette playfully draped her left arm across Whip's back.

He laughed at something she said and smiled down at her. The look was full of friendliness and affection.

I shouldn't have cared. I was the one who'd bolted on him, after all, but nausea still rolled through me. My gaze was locked onto them as they engaged in what looked like friendly, comfortable conversation. Whip kicked off the bar and with his brother, along with the mystery woman in tow, headed toward the exit.

I had no right to wonder who she was or whether or not she was going home with him. It was none of my business, but a petty part of me hated her anyway. Between my fresh start and my father, any kind of future with Whip, a one-night stand or otherwise, was completely off the table.

As I watched the trio walk out of the Grudge, I couldn't help but wonder if things in my life could be different.

Just this once.

SIX

EMILY

"MISS WARD! Michael shoved my pencil up his nose, and now there's snot on my math page."

I paused, my nostrils flaring to stifle a grin, and turned to Samantha. "Michael shoved your pencil up his nose and you continued to use it?"

The redhead pouted. "Well, it's *my* pencil and I have the right to—"

I held up one hand. *I swear, some days it feels like first grade instead of sixth . . .*

"Okay. It's all right. Why don't you get a fresh pencil from the jar and throw Michael's booger pencil in the trash."

An incredulous look twisted her round features. "But it's a brand-new pencil. That seems awfully wasteful . . . are you okay with killing more trees?"

I blinked and offered her a gentle smile. "I think, just this once, we can sacrifice one fresh pencil."

She scowled but stood from her desk and walked to pitch her pencil into a nearby trash can. I turned back to my class, thankful Samantha's newfound righteousness hadn't escalated further—any other day she might have prepared a full-on protest.

I pressed the button at the corner of my desk, letting a doorbell chime ring out to alert my students. "Remember to manage your independent work time well. I will need group four in the back with your writer's notebook and a pencil." I raised an eyebrow in Michael's direction. "A clean one."

He blushed and gathered his supplies and headed toward the bean-shaped table in the back of the room. I smiled at the young man's back. With his floppy, unruly brown curls, Michael was one of those students who was tenderhearted, but full of mischief.

In my short time as their teacher, I had grown to feel affection for all my students. A few managed to hold a special spot in my heart, and Michael, with his mischievous grin, was one of them.

Time slowed as Michael stumbled on his way to the back of the classroom. His sneakers squeaked, and his hand landed on the corner of Talisha's desk before slipping from it. He crumpled to the floor.

My eyes immediately locked with Michael's health services assistant. "Get the nurse."

With a calm and commanding voice, I instructed my students: "Class, please line up outside of the classroom in the hallway immediately. Just like we discussed. Everything is fine."

Inside, everything was not fine.

Michael had documented medical concerns, including a history of seizures. According to his parents, who were lovely at his last meeting, he hadn't suffered from a seizure in over a year.

They were hopeful that his new medication would be a turning point in regaining some of his independence in the classroom. Being a preteen with a nurse following you around all the time had taken a toll on Michael's social standing.

I sucked a harsh breath through my nose as my mind went to work, and I stripped off my cardigan. I knew his seizure care plan backward and forward, and my body took over, positioning his head on top of my cardigan to keep him safe as I watched the clock to approximate the length of this episode.

Within moments the school nurse and health-care aide were at my side. The nurse's eyes met mine, and I grimly shook my head. "It's getting close. One minute forty-five."

I looked on helplessly as the seizure racked Michael's young body. As a part of his care plan in the event of a grand mal seizure, emergency services were to be called if his episode lasted longer than three minutes.

In so many situations three minutes feels like the blink of an eye—laughing over cocktails with friends, watching a sunset wrapped in your lover's embrace, a day on the beach where warm sunshine heats your skin.

Three minutes.

I watched helplessly as three minutes felt like three days. Michael's health-care aide stood at my desk with the phone in her hand, prepared to make the call.

I stared at the clock as the seconds ticked by. "It's too long. Call it."

She punched the final number to alert emergency services as we waited. Relief that medical professionals would be on their way to help him washed over me. I instructed Michael's care aide to bring the rest of the classroom to the library. I'd likely get an earful from the crusty old librarian, but I was attempting to provide Michael a sliver of dignity.

Thankfully Outtatowner was small enough that the whine of ambulance sirens in the distance came quickly. Adrenaline coursed through my veins as we waited.

My jaw dropped open when Whip King surged through the doorway with a commanding authority. Two emergency medical service workers, a man and a woman, followed closely behind him with a stretcher. Our eyes locked without even a flicker of recognition crossing his handsome features.

A mixture of relief and surprise filled my chest. Whip's attention was focused solely on his patient. He surged forward, pushing desks aside as he got closer. His navy tactical pants and short-sleeved shirt strained against his muscles. Whip crouched to assess Michael. Only inches away, I studied his profile as his gaze moved over Michael in what I could only assume was standard protocol to assess the boy's breathing.

My eyes squeezed shut. *Please help him.*

When I opened my eyes again, I saw how Whip's every movement was confident and assertive. It was clear he was calm amid the chaos as he worked swiftly. He clearly communicated with his team, instructing them on exactly what he needed, and they followed his orders without hesitation. His fingertips gently swept back a strand of hair from Michael's face, and my heart seized.

Another EMT slid a pad under Michael's head, replacing my cardigan.

"Skin coloration and airways look good."

I wasn't sure if Whip was talking to me or his crew, but I nodded anyway. The medical team continued checking his vitals as Michael's body slowly calmed.

"Did he hit his head?" Whip stared at Michael but was asking me.

"It's possible. He fell pretty hard."

The team continued their treatment as we looked on helplessly. Michael's mother had arrived at the school, and despite her experience with his seizures, tears streamed down her face.

Mrs. Marsh knelt beside her son and gripped his limp hand. I stood, giving a mother her moment with her child. The school nurse and Michael's health-care aide flanked me.

"He'll be fine." The confidence in my voice was hollow.

We stood as helpless observers as Michael emerged from the haze of his seizure. Whip and his mother helped him to a sitting position. Whip examined his head for tender spots. Michael had wet himself and slumped against his mother. Tears burned my nose as I moved to the coat closet in my classroom. I always kept a few sets of spare sweats and T-shirts on hand for the odd spilled lunch or muddy football debacle.

I gently placed a folded pair of spare sweatpants next to her. Tears shimmered in Mrs. Marsh's eyes. "Thank you."

A firm nod was all I could offer her. I was confident my voice would be thick with emotion. I turned and cleared my throat, discreetly patting the wet corners of my eyes.

"This is yours." Whip's deep rumble startled me, and I turned to him.

His clear blue eyes pinned me in place. Stunned, I searched for any ounce of recognition, but his features were hard and unmoving. I glanced over his shoulder, and Mrs. Marsh had stood with Michael, her arm wrapped around her son as the other EMTs chatted with her. Michael was nearly as tall as his mother, but in the aftermath of his seizure he looked slight and fragile.

Refocusing on the man in front of me, my eyes dropped to the cardigan in his hand.

When I reached for it, our fingers grazed, and electricity crackled across my palm and up my forearm. I tucked the cardigan under my arm as I folded them across my chest.

No recognition. Nothing. He doesn't remember me.

"Thank you." I couldn't even look at him. The single hottest night of my life and I was completely forgettable. I wanted to fold in on myself and dissolve before having to face him again.

Whip pulled a pen from his uniform and lifted the clipboard in his other hand. "He'll be released to his mother."

I nodded, unable to speak.

Without another word, Whip and his team strode out of the doorway and out of my life for good.

SEVEN

WHIP

I PRESSED the heel of my hand into my chest, willing the ache to let up. I was shocked to barge into a classroom for a medical emergency call only to find the woman I had been obsessing over gaping back at me.

Thankfully I stared for only a fraction of a second too long before instinct took over.

"It's always the worst when it's a kid." Lee Sullivan stared out the windshield of the ambulance.

I dropped my hand. "Yeah."

Lee and I were on opposite sides of the King–Sullivan feud, but when it came to work, it was the job that mattered. We typically saved our petty bullshit for the break room or outside of work. Plus, fucking with him held slightly less appeal now that I knew my sister would have my ass if we took it too far. Still, it hadn't kept me from gift wrapping Duke Sullivan's entire truck with dinosaur paper in honor of my nephew's impending birthday.

I chuckled quietly to myself. Our town flashed past the truck as we rolled down the road back to the station.

"What tickled your pickle, Bill?" Lee Sullivan gave me the side-eye from the passenger seat.

I clenched my teeth, knowing full well that if Lee knew I was behind the prank against his brother, he'd make it his personal mission to exact revenge. "Nothing—just remembering how funny it was to see you like a turtle on its shell when you slipped in that puddle."

During a house fire a few months ago, Lee was stripping siding off the building when he lost his balance and fell backward into a shallow koi pond. The weight of his air tank had made it so he couldn't roll himself over. He'd been stuck, like a turtle on its shell, moving his arms and legs and rolling around trying to right himself.

"Fuck off. You know those air tanks are heavy as shit, and it's not my fault the mud was too slick for me to flip over. You could have helped sooner, you know."

I grinned at the mental image of cocky Lee Sullivan stuck on his back, arms and legs moving in a desperate attempt to flip himself over. I watched and laughed for a good five minutes before hauling him up and out of that shallow puddle.

We drove through our small town, returning waves and smiles as we passed. Lee grinned and basked in the attention. In another town—another life—Lee and I might have been friends, but given who my father was and our family's history, there was little chance that would ever happen.

Too drained to continue our typical banter, I stayed quiet as I drove the ambulance the rest of the way to the station.

In our small town, the men and women on my team were trained as both firefighters and EMTs, and there were perks to serving my hometown—free coffee and congratulatory handshakes, kind smiles while waiting in line at the grocery store—but it also meant the people who needed your help would be family, friends, or neighbors. Every call carried the weight of knowing you could be arriving on the worst day of their life for someone you loved.

Once the fire truck and ambulance were parked, the team got to work restocking supplies and cleaning up. Back at the station I spent time preparing lunch for the crew and willing myself not to think about the soft shudders of Emily's breath as she came on my fingers or the pliant curve of her hips.

I dragged a hand down my face and sighed. *Damn it.*

The reality was she had consumed my thoughts for the past two months. Emily and I had danced and laughed and had what I thought was the most incredible accidental date of my life before she panicked and bolted out the door.

What the hell had I done wrong?

I went over every moment I could recall from the general store to the Grudge, to the hours tangled in my sheets, trying to find the exact moment I fucked it up. Despite my obsession with figuring it out, I couldn't pinpoint what it was about me and our night together that had sent her running.

Not even her hurried exit or the high five kept me from attempting to track her down. Despite her insistence she wasn't a librarian, I still made calls to nearby libraries and searched their websites, seeing if anyone named Emily was on staff. Of course, I had come up empty. I tried to ask around without raising too many questions, but in a tourist town, it proved impossible.

It wasn't until I came face-to-face with her that a tiny spark of hope ignited. The woman had disappeared like an echo on the wind, but somehow she was back in Outtatowner and teaching junior high.

Not a librarian.

I should have known. The shock on her face made it clear she had recognized me, but my gut told me she wasn't all that happy about it, so I didn't press the issue. I probably should leave well enough alone, but her immediate about-face rejection gnawed at me. Normally I was the first to bail when things started getting serious, so it was a blow to the ego for her to beat me to it.

Afterward, I had sat on my bed and felt so . . . *used.*

"William." Chief Martin's voice shook me from my thoughts, and I tossed aside the kitchen towel. "My office. Now."

"Yes, sir."

I followed behind my chief toward the row of offices in the fire station. Lee lifted his chin in my direction, and I flipped him my middle finger, earning a grin from him.

When we entered, Chief Joseph Martin stood behind his desk. He was on the shorter side, stocky yet strong, with white strands lightening his auburn hair. Chief was the kind of dude who took care of himself, even working out during our shifts if he had the time. He was a man who demanded the best from his crew, but never asked someone to do a job he wasn't willing to do himself. "Close the door, son."

I turned, ignoring the hot poker that jabbed my ribs anytime he called me that.

"I debriefed with Captain Jones about the call at the junior high today. I was glad to hear everything went smoothly."

I nodded. "Yes, sir."

His assessing eyes rolled over me, and I straightened, unwilling to let him see me squirm under his gaze.

"Jones said you took the lead, stayed levelheaded.

That's not easy when children are involved, but that's exactly the kind of leadership we need in a lieutenant."

Quiet buzzing filled my head.

"Truth is, you're not getting any younger," Chief continued. "But you have a real future here . . . *if* you want it."

My insides went tight. *Did I want it?* Moving up in the ranks would be so fucking satisfying, but every time I thought about it, visions of my father's own social climbing tainted the very idea. Having a son as a lieutenant would be the exact type of thing Russell King would exploit to his advantage.

I sat up. "I hadn't really considered it, sir."

Chief laughed. "Well, you should. My advice? Keep your head down. Don't let things like petty family rivalries or women distract you from what's important. Too many in our unit forget what's really important—they get caught up in the attention and ass-patting that comes along with the job. Stay focused and the promotion is as good as yours."

Having the respect of someone I held in high regard was unnerving. *Why the hell would he be considering me?*

I learned a long time ago that anytime I get my hopes up, people let me down. Still, I knew arguing with my chief was pointless. "Thank you, sir."

Chief tossed his pen onto the desk. "Very well. Now get out of here."

With a grin and a jaunty salute, I turned on my heels and headed back to finish preparing lunch.

Stay focused and the promotion is as good as yours.

For the first time in what felt like forever, hope for something better bloomed in my chest.

I TUGGED at the too-tight collar of my shirt. Standing in the banquet hall, the shiny black shoes of my Class A dress uniform pinched my toes.

The Outtatowner Emergency Services annual awards banquet was an excuse for everyone in our department to get together and celebrate our achievements for the year. Awards included firefighter of the year, meritorious awards, and Chief's Company—a hand-selected group of men and women received this honorary title as a reflection of exemplary service and reflected who Chief Martin would want in his company. These were the people our chief considered the best of the best.

The most coveted award, however, was saved for last.

A few years ago, my fellow firefighter Connor had been thrift shopping with his on-again, off-again girlfriend when he came across a replica of the marble Hercules and Diomedes statue. An homage to Hercules's strength and masculinity, the Italian statue portrayed Hercules wrestling with Diomedes and besting him . . . all while Diomedes is tugging on his dick.

The coveted Dipshit Award was reserved for someone who did a stupid thing that year. We all kept a running tally of humorous things that happened throughout the year. The caveat was that if you were a recipient of the award, you had to have the vulgar statue displayed prominently in your home.

The award itself added a bit of levity to an otherwise stressful career. While no one ever wanted to mess up on a call, knowing you had your unit behind you, rallying for you to shake it off, always helped.

You better believe Lee Sullivan's name was nominated more than once. I wasted no time and took great pleasure in nominating him for the Dipshit Award after the turtle-tank incident. Sure, I could have helped, but instead I laughed and, later that day, wrote his name in for the award.

"You look like you're about to crawl out of your skin. Relax and have a beer, dude." Connor stood next to me, handing me a beer and surveying the room. He was more of Lee's buddy, and I didn't have the energy to socialize tonight. He looked completely at ease in his dress uniform, his dark-blond hair cropped short and one hand casually draped in a pocket.

I shifted in my shoes. "Class A's are not my favorite."

He grinned. "Yeah, but the ladies love them." Connor tipped his chin, and my gaze shifted in that direction. Across the banquet hall, two women leaned in, whispering to one another, while shooting sidelong, hopeful glances in our direction.

The banquet was for firefighters and their families. I'd never extended an invitation to my family for fear my father would use it as an opportunity to deepen his connections in town. Plus, I never dated anyone long enough to warrant an invite either.

I eyed the women again. I was also careful to never shit where I ate. "They're all yours, man. I'm good right here."

I took a long pull from the beer bottle.

"You're missing out, bro." Connor chuckled. "There's something to be said about a woman who understands shift work and the demands of the job. There's no explaining or apologizing for being gone for long stretches of time."

I shrugged, accepting the truth of his statement. "I guess."

Connor bumped his shoulder into mine. "But I'm feeling spicy tonight. I think I'm going to hit on the chief's daughter."

My face twisted. "Chief Martin's daughter is like

twelve." I knew this for a fact given the prominent school picture displayed in his office of a young, braces-clad girl deep in the throes of her awkward preteen years.

Connor turned to me. "Dude, what the fuck are you talking about? Chief Martin's daughter is a smoke show."

He gestured with his beer bottle across the hall toward Chief Martin, standing proudly next to his wife, conversing and shaking hands with a semicircle of people. As the crowd shifted, Connor's voice faded to a dull echo in the background as the whoosh of blood hammered in my skull after I spotted Emily. Her navy satin dress clung to her hips. Thin straps dipped into a neckline that draped below her collarbone in a way that was tasteful, yet subtly sexy.

"I heard she moved from Virginia. The rumor is she's nursing a broken heart, and I am not above helping her nurse those wounds, if you know what I mean."

From her gaze on the floor, Emily's smoky eyes shifted as a smile bloomed across her face.

"Goddamn she's pretty." Connor chuckled beside me.

I cast him an angry glare. "That's the chief's daughter. Have some fucking respect."

I had disrespected her enough for the both of us. Many, many *times as the clench of her inner walls milked my cock.*

Connor laughed off my pissy mood, and his chuckle grated on my nerves.

How in the hell was Emily Chief Martin's daughter?

Then it dawned on me—the way her gaze swept over my open closet only moments before she was pulling her floral dress back over her head and running out of my house like she couldn't get away fast enough.

She knew.

She fucking knew.

She could have said something then—explained why

hooking up was a bad idea, and I would have agreed with her.

Probably.

Instead I spent weeks beating myself up over moving too quickly with a girl who had seemed to be plucked from my fantasies. I'd spent sleepless nights trying to figure out how I'd managed to fuck it up so quickly.

Typically women stuck around long enough to realize a King wasn't worth the trouble before they bolted, but Emily hadn't lasted even that long before she'd had her fill of me.

I drained my beer in two deep swallows. "I need something stronger."

I didn't wait for Connor's response before stomping toward the bar. The lanky bartender greeted me with a tip of his chin.

"Whiskey, neat." I rested an elbow on the bar and turned back toward the crowd.

Emily was still by her father, laughing and enjoying the conversation as it flowed around her. Her features were animated as she gestured. The entire clutch of people hung on her every word. She was radiant and alluring, and it pissed me right the fuck off.

After the bartender slid my whiskey across the counter, I deposited a generous tip into his jar. I planned to have a few more and wouldn't mind the preferential treatment a decent tip would earn me. The first sip of whiskey burned down my throat and warmed my gut.

I knew my stare was dark and intense, but I didn't care. I wanted her to see me.

As if she could hear my thoughts, her pretty eyes shifted and locked with mine. Shock flickered over her delicate features, but in a moment it was gone.

Emily leaned in, whispering something to Mrs. Martin

before excusing herself from the group with a small smile. I stayed planted where I was, letting her come to me. She ignored me as she stood at the bar and ordered a white wine. She thanked the bartender with a genuine smile, dropping her own generous tip into his jar, and turned to face the banquet room.

With a tight smile locked in place, she gently cleared her throat. "Um . . . hello."

I scoffed and decided to fuck with her. "Is that— Is that a ghost?" I stood tall and let my gaze go unfocused as I looked over her head. "Speak, apparition."

An exasperated grunt pushed through her lips. "Really? Quoting kids' movies? Stop being ridiculous."

Irked that she caught my *Megamind* reference so easily, I turned my back to her.

She cleared her throat more aggressively this time and gritted through her teeth, "I'm surprised to see you here."

I shook my head, taking a generous sip of my whiskey before turning to face her. "Bet you're not as surprised as I was." I drained the remainder of my whiskey and signaled the bartender for another.

Emily's eyebrows lifted. "I don't know what you are so pissy about. You came into my classroom and didn't even remember me."

Remember her? I had obsessed over her for weeks, but I wasn't about to give her the satisfaction of admitting that.

"Would you have rather I ignored the emergency medical needs of a sick child and struck up a conversation with you instead?"

A disgusted noise rattled from her pretty throat as she rolled her eyes. "Of course not, but I saw your face. You had no idea who I was."

A disbelieving hum was my only response. I wanted to let it go, but I couldn't.

"So when did you know?" Irritation simmered just below the surface. "When you stared into the tattoo shop and saw me for the first time? Or maybe at the general store? Did someone at the Grudge tell you about us Kings while I was getting our drinks? At what point did you know *exactly* who I was?"

Emily's shoulders shifted toward me. A defiant glint shimmered in her eyes. "You sure remember an awful lot about that night for somebody who treated me like I was utterly forgettable."

I shook my head. "You ghosted *me*, Prim," I seethed.

"Prim?"

I bit back a smile and leaned in. "You act all prim and proper, but I got to see how much of me you could take before your eyes watered."

Anger and desire flared across her features, sending pink flooding into her cheeks. My crudeness had probably crossed more than a few lines, but I liked this riled-up version of her. It planted her squarely into enemy territory, extricating her from the tiny cracks in my chest she had previously tried to burrow into.

"I'm not sure what your last name has to do with it, but I swear that I didn't know you were a firefighter." Her voice wavered, but only slightly before she hardened it again. "But then I saw your uniform in the closet, and it wasn't hard to put two and two together. My dad is your *boss*."

"I guess that explains your graceful exit." At the time, her awkward high five had been hilarious and endearing. Now it just poked at a pressure point between my ribs.

Across the hall I spotted Connor chatting up the two women he had pointed out earlier. I finished my whiskey, enjoying the dull, hazy numbness filling my brain. "Well, this has been fun, Prim, but I gotta run." With a smart-ass look on my face, I held up my hand for a high five. Emily's nostrils flared, and I chuckled. "No? Cool."

I strode away toward Connor but felt the chill of her pretty sea-glass eyes on my back.

EIGHT

EMILY

Apparently Whip King is an asshole.

A well-built, pierced dick, get-on-my-knees-and-beg-for-another-taste grade-A asshole.

But goddamn did he look good in his dress uniform.

When I caught sight of him across the banquet hall, I sucked in a sharp inhale at the way my core clenched, instinctively missing the absence of being stretched around him as he gripped my throat and pounded into me.

I pinched the bridge of my nose. *My one night of rebellion and I fucked a walking red flag.*

I tamped down the irritation at my body's instinctual response. The logical part of my brain knew he would be at the annual awards banquet, but despite me feigning a headache and attempting to make other plans, my mother insisted that this was important for my father, and I was guilted into going. When our eyes locked across the room and recognition—in addition to shock—flooded his features, I couldn't stop myself from walking over to him at the bar and seeing if he really did remember me after all.

I should have let it go. A smarter me would have let him

win that round. He was crass and a jerk. He walked away, and that could have been the end of it. Clearly the cut lines of his body and his filthy mouth had made me stupid.

I set my wineglass down on the bar top with a snap and marched across the dance floor, politely smiling and side-stepping a group of firefighters doing the Macarena. Whip and another firefighter were laughing and commiserating with two women I hadn't met yet. The blonde tilted her head at me when I approached, while the brunette continued laughing at something the men were saying.

Lacking all decorum, I pasted on a bright smile. "Hi," I interrupted. "*So* sorry. Can I just have a minute with Whip?" I placed my fingertips on the inside of his elbow, and he stiffened.

The women looked on in confusion as Connor's eyes bounced between Whip and me.

Whip tried to shrug me off. "We're kind of in the middle of something."

The fuck you are . . .

I tightened my grip on the inside of his arm and breathed through a smile. "Chief Martin was hoping for a word." I pulled his arm closer to me. "Back in a jiff!"

With a grunt that should not have sent tingles racing down my spine, Whip followed me. As soon as we were walking in the opposite direction I dropped my hand from his arm.

"What do you want, Prim?" he asked flatly.

"Stop calling me that."

A lighthearted chuckle spilled from him. *He's enjoying this.* "Fine, *Miss Martin*, what can I do for you?"

"Shut up and get over here." I found the darkest corner of the banquet room and ducked into the hallway. "It's Ward."

"What?"

"My name. I'm not Emily Martin. I'm Emily *Ward*."

Whip blinked and scanned my features.

"He's my stepdad, but he raised me." I lifted my chin. "So even if I would have introduced myself that night as Emily Ward—but, honestly, who even does that?—it wouldn't have made a difference."

Whip's lips pressed together as he considered. His jaw flexed. "So why is the only picture that the chief has of you in his office from when you were a kid?"

Heat flooded my cheeks. "Oh my god, I hate that picture. It's from like fifth grade, and Dad always said it was his favorite picture of me—that I would always be his Melly."

Whip's eyebrows shot up. "Melly?"

"Smelly Melly." I pierced him with a pointed stare. "I was a weird kid, okay?"

His laughter rang out, and I shushed him. My teeth ground together. "Oh, I'm sorry. Did you have something to say about nicknames, *Whip*?"

His flat stare gave nothing away. "Did you want something from me?"

My eyes flicked to his full lips. What I wanted—what my body wanted, and my head knew was smart—were two *very* different things.

My exhale was shaky. "I just didn't want you to think that I knew . . ." I met his gaze. "Before."

His eyes found the point in my neck where I was certain my heartbeat hammered through the thin skin. "You should have said something."

"Like what, Whip? What was I supposed to say? 'Oh hey, by the way, say hello to my dad at work tomorrow?' Be real. I panicked and ran out." My hands lifted in emphasis. "As one might do in that situation."

His arms crossed and his gaze roamed over me. "Smelly Melly."

I pinched the bridge of my nose. "Oh my god, please forget I ever told you that." I exhaled and tipped my face to the ceiling.

"I think Prim suits you far better." His voice was velvet over gravel, encircling me in the protective darkness.

My body hummed for him. Like flames sparking and dancing around the other before merging into a blaze that destroyed everything around it, I was drawn to him.

Shadows darkened the intensity in his eyes, and I couldn't look away. His gaze held me captive against my own warring emotions.

He stepped forward, crowding my space and gripping my hips through my navy satin dress. "It can't happen again." His warm breath floated over my tingling skin.

"I know." The pull between us inched me closer, but I waved my hand between us. "You need to keep you and that *thing* away from me."

"Thing?" He laughed quietly, not disturbing our echo chamber of restraint and tension. "Why do you keep gesturing at my dick, Prim?"

I scoffed. "Oh my god, I am not *gesturing at your dick.*" I looked around to be sure no one could overhear us.

One corner of his mouth crooked up as his gaze floated over my mouth. "I mean . . . you kind of were."

I let loose an exasperated breath. "I swear, you are just like the men my dad always warned me about."

Whip shook his head. With his height, he towered over me, filling my vision with only *him.* "And you are exactly the type of distracting woman your father warned *me* about."

I straightened. "This"—I gestured between us—"is not a thing." My mind wanted to retreat, but my body locked in place as Whip erased the inches between us.

A grunt vibrated in his throat. "Not at all. I am not friends with you, Prim."

My chest was heavy. "I don't even like you. You're kind of a prick." The grumble of his soft laughter sent heat pooling between my legs.

"Good."

Another inch and his mouth could devour mine. I gripped his corded forearm—the hard muscles tightening and bunching beneath his suit jacket.

"Emily? Are you out here?" My mother's voice startled me, and I leaned past Whip's broad shoulder.

I went to push past him when his hand caught my upper arm. In the darkness his blue eyes formed intense, black pools. I raised my chin and willed my knees not to wobble. "This conversation is over."

A soft rumble filled the space between us as his breath caressed the shell of my ear. "I bet if I lifted the hem of your skirt right now, I'd find your panties soaked, just for me."

I tugged my arm free, annoyed that he was 1,000 percent correct. "You'd be wrong." I swallowed past the lump that clogged my throat and leaned in close. An evil smirk crept across my face as my lips brushed the shell of his ear. "Because I'm not wearing any."

I didn't risk a backward glance and prayed that Whip—and the secret we shared—stayed hidden in the shadows.

NINE

WHIP

THE BUZZ of the table saw filled the air as sawdust floated out the door to my workshop. New wood was arranged in neat piles, but my favorite pieces—reclaimed barnwood, old beams, a centuries-old table with a missing leg—waited patiently while I decided how to use the materials. The early-morning May air still held a chill, but stacking boards and ripping planks for my next project had worked up a sweat.

I had learned early in my career as a firefighter that while the flexibility of my shifts was nice, it also meant increased downtime—downtime that made me feel itchy and stagnant.

Fishing was too boring, paddleboarding left winters unproductive, and a second job somewhere else lacked the freedom and flexibility I craved. I didn't have artistic talent like my brother, Royal, nor did I have the passion for operating my own business like Abel. I had fallen into furniture making by accident after my house had been built. Once I moved in, I realized the Swedish particleboard end tables and milk crate stools wouldn't do the house justice.

So I read books, followed Instagrammers, and YouTubed every episode of *This Old House* to teach myself a new skill. It required patience and fine-tuning, and the attention to detail necessary ensured that my thoughts wouldn't wander.

It meant I didn't have to think about keeping up appearances to meet Dad's expectations or irresistible women with dark-blonde hair and eyes that promised to see past all your bullshit.

Nope.

Definitely not thinking about her.

Instead, I imagined my sister Sylvie's eyes when I dragged my latest finished piece over to the home she shared with Duke Sullivan. My project was a gift for my new nephew and the heritage farmhouse-style trunk was made from handcrafted oak. Little Gus could pile all his toys inside, or maybe it would become the world's best hide-and-seek spot for him. Wanting to test my hand at a new woodworking skill, I'd used tulipwood to make a contrasting border inlaid across the top.

It was functional and timeless and gave me the opportunity to share a bit of myself with my nephew without having to actually have a conversation with my sister regarding her relationship with a Sullivan. Their relationship should never have worked, but there was no denying the love in Duke's eyes when he looked at my little sister. The fact that I couldn't even manage to hate him on principle alone made me want to punch myself in the face.

Or maybe it was just the realization that a love like that wasn't meant for a man like me.

Ah, fuck it.

I let the wood plank slap against the concrete floor. I

swiped a frustrated hand across the back of my sweaty neck, gripping the tension that resided there.

"Still haven't reined in that temper, I see." My father's voice filled the empty workshop, and I found him standing in the doorway. Time and stress had aged him. His shoulders were powerful and square, but the beginnings of a paunch exposed a life behind an expensive desk rather than that of his blue-collar father. Russell King had done everything in his power to escape his working-class roots.

The tips of his shiny loafers didn't breach the threshold, as if the mere act of entering a working man's space was beneath him. His hands were shoved in the pockets of his navy slacks as he rocked back on his heels.

Unexpected visits from Russell King were always a sign of trouble—if not for you, then most certainly for someone else.

"Hey, Dad." I reached for a rag and attempted to scrub the remnants of stain from my fingertips.

Russell King was a ruthless businessman, exceedingly smart and cunning. There was very little that didn't move the tide in his favor. People in town saw him as a shrewd businessman. He was cunning enough to know where to spend his money in a way that shed the best possible light on the King family.

If he fucked someone over or a deal went ass up, he'd simply make a huge donation toward renovations at the public library, garnering him a nice article in the Outtatowner news and completely overshadowing any misdeeds.

He had lived his life in such a way that no one would believe a bad word said about Russell King, but his children knew the truth. So did the Sullivans, which I suppose is why the generations-long feud had not only persisted but deepened when my father took the helm of the King family businesses.

"What is all this?" Disgust was evident on his face as he looked at the toy chest.

I moved to obscure his view of my work. "It's nothing important."

His lips pursed. "You shouldn't want to be anything other than a firefighter. That's honorable work. Makes the family look good to have a hero. Don't waste your time on things that don't matter."

I nodded, unsure if I was agreeing with him or at a loss for what to say next.

Everything Russell King did was about optics, never about the long-lasting impact his actions had on his children. It was a marvel only one of us had ended up in prison, and even then, with the help of our father and some hard work, Abel had managed to land on his feet.

There was no world in which a King failed.

The only person who had ever bested Russell King was our mother, and she was the smartest one of us all. She beat him simply by leaving the game—and her children—behind.

"I saw the article in the paper about the Chief's Company being selected. Congratulations."

My shoulders bunched. I had been among the few selected for the Chief's Company award. I was pleasantly surprised, and the pride of being selected only swelled when I locked eyes with Emily. I had sneaked a stolen wink and savored the flush of her cheeks as I shook her father's hand and accepted the award.

But as he did, my father had a unique way of leaching the joy out of any accomplishment. My stomach soured. "Thank you, sir."

It was important to stay on the good side of a man in power.

"Perhaps one day I might be able to say that my son is a lieutenant in the fire department rather than a lackey."

My lips pressed together. I didn't have the energy to feed into stroking his ego by telling him about my conversation with Chief Martin.

My father adjusted the cuff of his cashmere sweater, his gold pinkie ring glinting in the light. "You know, Chief Martin's wife is on the board for the Remington County Historical Association."

And there it was.

He was always angling for something.

"JP and I are working on a deal, and they've become a bit of a problem."

I lifted an eyebrow but didn't contribute to the conversation.

"The building I have my eye on would be an asset—an asset I plan to acquire." On the outside he appeared calm, but I could see the annoyance ripple through him before he tamped it down. "Problem is the historical society is hell-bent on declaring it a historical landmark."

"Is it?"

My father's lip curled. "Does it matter? It's going to be mine." His dark eyes looked me over. As the years passed I had mastered the art of not squirming under his assessments, but my skin still went hot. "Women have always had a soft spot for your charm. Perhaps applying a little pressure is in order."

I bit back an oath. "That doesn't really have anything to do with me."

Dad's nostrils flared, but he remained steadfast and

offered a small smile. "What's good for the family is good for you, William. Don't ever forget that."

Good for the family.

My whole life was an endless loop of choices and decisions made in the best interest of the King family—to increase our wealth, to save face. Never once because it was anything that any of us wanted or needed in our lives.

I should be disgusted at his manipulation, but the truth of the matter was, my father had been the only person in my life who had never left.

And for that, I owed him.

I tossed the rag on my workbench. "Chief Martin's wife isn't typically around the fire station." Marilyn Martin was a sweetheart, always smiling and bringing treats into the fire station. When she looked at you, her eyes held a maternal warmth that was fascinating.

Dad smiled. "Ah, but I'm sure there are times when you see her." He shrugged. "Just a small conversation if you find the time. That's all."

That's all. Yeah, right.

I knew my father meant for me to dissuade Mrs. Martin and the historical society from claiming the building so he could purchase it. With me, he saw an opportunity and wasn't afraid to exploit it.

Defeated, I met his gaze. "Sure."

I stood, still unsure of where to go next with this conversation. I had known this man my entire life and had yet to find a way to truly connect with him.

My father finally broke the silence. "Well, I'll let you get back to"—he waved a dismissive hand over my workshop—"whatever this is."

He turned and my shoulders slumped. I had done so

much to ensure I was nothing like Russell King, only to never have the balls to truly be any different at all.

~

You working late tonight?

ROYAL

Checking in on the new apprentice but then I'm free. What's up?

I was thinking of having a few at the Grudge. Want to join me?

ROYAL

Can't get your own dates?

Fuck off.

ROYAL

Maybe you're hoping to run into a certain librarian?

I never should have told you.

ROYAL

But you did . . . meet you there at 9.

Nine.

Fuck, I was getting old if my body screamed at the thought of going out at nine o'clock on a Saturday night. Royal was used to late hours at his tattoo shop, but I'd be lying if I didn't admit that being a firefighter fucked with my sleep schedule. Not only was I wired at odd times, but I could also fall asleep nearly anywhere when fatigue hit.

For the past few days, I had been dog tired.

I was attributing my fatigue to the new workout routine Brooklyn had started for our shift and not the mental gymnastics I'd been doing regarding Emily.

Chief was right—I didn't need any distractions right now, and a spitfire woman with kissable lips and a bad attitude most certainly qualified as a *major* distraction.

Still, the chance she might be out tonight had crossed my mind. Her being a distraction didn't stop me from putting in a little extra effort by pairing my scuffed boots with a new pair of denim jeans and a T-shirt that I was well aware was about half a size too tight in the biceps.

Hoping to clear my head, I parked my truck in the public lot near the north beach. Though the beach was technically closed, I could walk the pier toward Outtatowner's historical lighthouse and let the crash of Lake Michigan's waves drown out the thrumming in my skull.

On my way back up the hill toward town, I spotted Lee Sullivan's obnoxious black truck. With tourist season starting earlier and earlier each year, traffic through downtown was still steady even at this time of night. I glanced around but didn't recognize any faces or seem to be drawing any attention.

As I passed the driver's-side door, I tested the handle. To my surprise, the door popped open. I stifled the giggle that bubbled up from my gut.

"Fucking idiot." Nerves and excitement danced through me.

I had been waiting for the perfect opportunity to get back at the Sullivans for their latest prank, and Lee was always my favorite target. He loved his lifted truck and was always careful to ensure it was locked up or parked under a streetlight, making it nearly impossible to fuck with.

But tonight he had messed up, leaving his truck

unlocked and making it an easy target. I cast one last look around, ensuring I wasn't drawing attention before slipping the multi-tool from my pocket.

In under a minute, I had the fuse box in his dash open and made a few minor adjustments before closing it back up and shutting the driver's door.

When I stood to my full height, I startled at Miss Tiny, standing in the middle of the sidewalk, hands on her hips and scowling at me.

My eyes went wide. Ms. Tiny was crotchety, but her alliances stood firmly in King territory.

I nodded and suppressed my grin. "Ma'am."

"Didn't see a thing." She smiled sweetly before whistling and shuffling away.

I exhaled in relief. Part of the fun was getting away with our ridiculous antics and never letting on who pulled which prank. That way your opponent never knew which angle you were going to attack from. A skill I had undoubtedly learned from my father.

I hurried up the sidewalk and passed King Tattoo, peeking in only briefly and continuing on to the Grudge when I didn't spot Royal.

The kick drum from a live band thumped through the large wooden door as the neon skeleton smiled down at me. Inside, the dinner crowd was long gone, and the shift from family eatery to dance hall had begun. The band was well into their set of country classics as I scanned the bar.

My brother's bulky, tattooed frame stood out among the gathering, and I made my way toward him.

"What's with the shit-eating grin?" Royal clamped his hand into mine.

"Nothing, man. Best if you've got no knowledge of it." I squeezed back.

"You see Sullivan's truck parked up the road?" Royal asked before taking a sip of whiskey on ice.

I suppressed my grin. "Yup."

"You take care of it?" he asked slyly, his eyes never leaving the dance floor.

"Sure did."

Royal's wide palm slapped against the high-top table. "Well, all right, let's get you something to drink then."

The band was good. Kings, Sullivans, and tourists alike melted onto the dance floor. A rowdy bachelorette party caught Royal's attention, but I wasn't in the mood to flirt. With a shake of his head, he shrugged me off in search of a good time while I sulked into my beer.

When he returned a while later and I was still nursing the same beer, Royal frowned down at me. "Are you feeling all right?"

I sighed and rolled my neck. "Yeah, just wound a little tight tonight. That's all." My middle finger scraped against the chipped wood of the high-top table. "Dad stopped by today."

Royal shook his head and drained the last of his drink. "Yeah, that'll do it."

"Do you ever wonder sometimes why we do it?"

Royal's brows knit down.

I continued, unable to look at my older brother. "Why he says jump and we ask how high?"

Royal sighed. "What else are we going to do, man? Leave him like Mom did? He's done a lot for us."

My teeth ground together. *He's taken a lot too.*

I wasn't brave enough to voice the traitorous thought, so instead I swallowed it down with a gulp of beer.

"You sure are mopey for someone who asked me out

tonight." Royal's assessing eyes never left my face, and I shifted under the attention.

"Just been a long week."

A low, disbelieving grunt vibrated through him, but he didn't call me out on my outright lie. "Thought maybe you caught wind that Charles Attwater was sniffing around your librarian."

My head whipped up, catching his gaze, and he gestured toward the dance floor with his chin.

Sure enough, on the edges of the marred, wooden floor, Emily was politely smiling at Charles. Charles Attwater was a transplant relatively new to Outtatowner, but in a tourist town like ours, it was no wonder his boutique wine shop was a hit.

In all reality, JP and my father were just pissed they hadn't thought of that business venture first. Word around town was Charles's business was making money hand over fist.

Quiet, lean, and seemingly meek, Charles hadn't made any particular impression on me, and I had never viewed him as any kind of threat, business or otherwise. That was, until I saw the way Emily peered up at him, her blue-green eyes holding every bit of his attention. Her pants were a soft hunter green and cropped at the ankle. Her white top had delicate black stripes and was tucked into the waistband of her bottoms. Compared to the skimpy bar clothes most women at the Grudge were wearing, it was tasteful and unassuming, but no amount of modesty could hide her curves. Her sandy-blonde hair cascaded down her back in soft waves. I knew exactly what that hair felt like around my fist, and my hand itched to touch it again.

Fire burned in my gut as I watched them. The guy was clearly born with two left feet, and in a town where your only bar was a honky-tonk, we had all learned to dance circles around any tourist who passed through.

Charles was struggling, and Emily's tan, open-toed heels were no help against his fumbling. More than once he crushed her toes as he led them in an off-beat bounce that no one in their right mind would call dancing.

Still, Emily smiled up at him.

I wrenched my gaze away, stuffing down the tightness in my chest. Somehow Emily had become a hostile squatter, occupying every inch of my brain.

It didn't help that her pants were painted on. The soft material stretched over the curve of her ass, and my palm itched to grab another handful.

Royal's low whistle drew my attention. "You are so fucked, brother."

My face twisted, and I shrugged him off. "She's the chief's daughter. Not my type."

Royal's hearty laugh rumbled through the loud bar. "Is that why it looks like you're about to rip the guy from limb to limb and beat him to death with his own arms?"

I laughed at Royal's ridiculous—though not really a bad idea—comment. The last time I'd been face-to-face with her, I may have acted like a jerk, but she ghosted *me.*

I had zero interest in giving in to the temptation of her.

Despite all that, when she left the dance floor and disappeared down the back hallway, I followed.

TEN

EMILY

Charles Attwater was a terrible dancer.

I was fairly certain he would be a terrible kisser too. When I had accepted his invitation to dance, I had no idea the smooth-talking sommelier would be so utterly hopeless on the dance floor. There would be a zero percent chance I would be confirming my suspicions regarding his ability to kiss.

My poor toes were rioting in protest, desperate for a break.

"I'll be back." I held up my hands and smiled politely.

"Are you sure? This is a good one." Charles bit into his lower lip and shimmied his shoulders in what could only be described as bad, White-man dancing.

I held up my fingers. "Two minutes."

I swiveled on my heels, needing a moment alone. My shoulders sagged, and a deep exhale soothed my bunched muscles as I turned from him, escaping toward the darkened hallway that led to the ladies' room.

Despite the run-down honky-tonk vibe of the Grudge, the women's bathroom was spacious and bright. The gods of the ladies' room must have been smiling down on me, because it was also blissfully empty.

If my date wasn't so sad, it would have almost been hilarious. My mother and I had stopped into Charles's wine shop after she'd eagerly encouraged Charles and I to "go out and have a little fun." I had tried to laugh it off, but Charles agreed and called to set up a date the very next day. Knowing I needed to excise a certain rugged and infuriating firefighter from my brain, I had reluctantly agreed.

Charles's initial enthusiasm had been flattering, but I had quickly learned he was about as exciting as a cold, wet blanket.

I've really got to stop letting her set me up on dates.

The heavy bathroom door swung open, and my eyes flicked to the entry to offer a flat, polite greeting. My eyes widened when Whip sauntered in looking like hot sex on a stick. His chest strained the cotton of his shirt. His jeans molded to his thighs, and my eyes paused, only a fraction of a second, on his front, where I knew all too well that a thick, pierced, glorious cock was residing.

I straightened, my lips parted in shock as he made no move to leave the restroom.

Heat and desire rippled through me without warning as Whip's cocky grin hooked the corner of his mouth.

The silence was fraught with tension. I gave Whip my coolest expression, hoping like hell he couldn't sense the nerves jittering out of me. "You lost?"

Whip leaned against the bathroom door, blocking anyone from entering and breaking our cocoon. "I came to find out why."

My brows furrowed. "Why what?"

Whip shook his head and threw a thumb over his shoulder. "Why that guy?"

His jeans hugged his trim hips, and his thighs filled them out in a way that sent warmth buzzing through me. His arms were covered in intricate tattoos that disappeared into his too-tight shirtsleeves. Our late-night romp hadn't offered me the opportunity to really study them, but in the bright lighting of the bathroom, I could see how simple, yet detailed, they were.

My eyes flitted to his, and he stood, patiently waiting for me to answer his question.

I blinked, swallowing down the tension that had stolen my voice. "He called and asked me out on a proper date."

Whip scoffed but made no effort to move. "I would have called if you hadn't bolted."

I rinsed my hands for no other reason than to give myself something to do and reached for a paper towel, which was a mistake because I caught the irresistible, masculine scent of Whip's cologne. "You work for my dad."

Whip kicked off the door to tower behind me. I went still and caught his gaze in the mirror. His nose brushed against my hair, and he inhaled. "Do you always do what Daddy tells you to?"

Sizzling currents rolled down my back. "You're being ridiculous. This is the ladies' room. Someone could walk in."

Whip chuckled behind me, his rumbling laugh vibrating my back. "We're just talking. Is that against the rules?"

I resisted the urge to arch backward and rub against him like a cat in heat. "You're *flirting*."

Whip King was cocky and stubborn and knew exactly how to push my buttons. It annoyed me that I was beyond intrigued. The air between us grew thick and heavy. The thumping bass continued just beyond the door to the bathroom. At any moment someone could barge in and catch me melting over a man I had no right to be craving.

In the mirror, I could see Whip thinking, weighing his options as carefully as I was. He stared for a beat, and I could see the humor in his eyes melt away and be replaced with something darker.

Possession.

He reached up and cupped my jaw, tilting my head back and exposing the column of my neck. My thighs pressed together as my breath hitched. His wide hand tilted my head to the side, pulling my face to his.

My eyes adjusted to get a glimpse of how painfully handsome he was. His cut jawline, sharp cheekbones, and full lips were making my insides *scream* for him. All he had to do was inch forward and *take.*

"Do you want me to kiss you?" His breath was hot and minty across my parted lips.

My lips opened for him. Pinned between his hard body and the sink, I sucked in a breath.

Unlike any man I'd been around before, Whip knew how to lead. Melting into him was effortless and aching.

My hesitation was his answer, and he relaxed his grasp on my jaw.

His nose ran down the edge of mine, and his mouth hovered above me. "When you're finally ready to be kissed again, I'm going to make you beg for it."

Instead of kissing me, his thumb ran across my bottom lip. A hot bolt of arousal shot between my legs. His words were infuriating. Arrogant. Spoken like a dirty secret in the hidden shadows of a bar bathroom.

I could barely breathe, and defensiveness coursed through me. Rippling with pent-up frustration, I shouldered past him. "Get over yourself."

I yanked open the bathroom door just as another woman was entering. Her shocked stare flicked between Whip and me before a sly, appreciative smile overtook her face.

He's exactly like Craig, and you fell for it.

Again.

Embarrassment flooded my cheeks, forcing my voice to tick up several octaves higher than necessary. "Excuse me!"

The woman huffed and stood to the side as heat prickled my scalp and I hurried into the safe anonymity of the crowded bar.

Charles may be a dud, but Whip King was nothing but trouble.

"REMIND me again how this is for charity?"

Rachel stood next to me with her arms crossed and cocked her head in my direction. "You're going to tell me you wouldn't throw your hard-earned money at a group of firefighters just to get a peek at what's underneath all that turn-out gear?" She pursed her lips and shook her head.

"And you call yourself a feminist." I playfully rolled my eyes and bumped a shoulder into hers. "I just think that there are classier ways to beg people for money."

She laughed. "That may be true, but when this car wash starts in about twenty minutes and you see the line of vehicles down the block, you'll change your tune. The car wash makes big bucks, baby."

My eyes swept over the growing crowd. Rachel had a point. The car wash wasn't set to start for another few minutes, and there was already an eager line forming.

My presence was merely a fact-finding mission. Part of

my scheme to prove my worth at Outtatowner Junior High was volunteering to head the Outtatowner Education Foundation. The foundation was previously governed by the school librarian, Mrs. Kuder, but when her idea of the third seniors' bingo night of the year wasn't embraced with much enthusiasm, she'd been asked to step down as chairperson. Rumor was the grouchy old lady had egged the principal's car. Given her surly demeanor, that was a tall tale I wholeheartedly believed—Scooter Kuder was a wild card.

I needed some ideas—good ones—that encouraged the residents of town to open their hearts, and their wallets. The foundation's funds also hadn't been managed well, so there were very few dollars left for things like new books for the outdated library, extra school supplies for kids who couldn't afford them, or much-needed after-school enrichment programs. It didn't matter that I was the new girl in town. I was confident I could make a difference and help the principal see that I would be the perfect full-time addition to his staff.

Ideas were already percolating. I just hadn't settled on exactly *how* to get the town behind my ideas.

"I haven't seen him yet," Rachel said, leaning down to whisper. Pulled from my thoughts, I turned to her frowning, and she shot me a bland look. "Whip. I know he is who you're looking for, but I haven't seen him yet."

I set my shoulders, determined not to let the mere mention of his name send ripples down my spine. "I'm only here to find my *in*. I'm not a townie, so I need to see what makes this place tick. I'm not looking for anyone, least of all him."

A dimple popped in Rachel's cheek when she gave me a disbelieving smile. "If you say so."

I raised my eyebrows at my friend, hoping to nudge the

attention off myself. "Maybe it's *you* who is looking for him."

Rachel chuckled, and her delicate fingers covered her lips. "Uh, no." Her fuchsia manicured finger pointed at one of the female firefighters with long black hair, slicked into a high, braided ponytail. "She's more my type."

I raised my eyebrow in surprise and nodded once. "Oh. Nice."

In my short time knowing Rachel, she hadn't shared with me her interest in women, and a tiny pang of guilt poked my insides. I resolved to be a better friend to her from here on out, worrying less about my own disaster of a love life and more about getting to know the woman who had been nothing but kind and caring since I had arrived in Outtatowner.

"She is beautiful." I toyed with the ends of my own lackluster dishwater-blonde hair. "Her hair is so shiny."

"Right?" Rachel popped a stick of gum into her mouth before offering me one. "So fucking hot."

We leaned in and giggled like a couple of grade school girls with crushes, which in all reality, we kind of were.

"Ladies." Whip's deep velvety voice snagged my attention.

I cleared my throat and stood taller, praying he didn't see the blush crawling across my warm cheeks.

When you're finally ready to be kissed again, I'm going to make you beg for it.

My traitorous eyes flicked to his full lips before finding a spot in the middle of his forehead and burning a hole into it with my stare.

"Oh, hey, Whip." Rachel smiled sweetly. "Didn't know you would be at the car wash today."

His wide arms spread open. "Come on, it's for charity. I wouldn't miss it."

"Did you hear that, Emily?" She bumped me with her elbow. "A philanthropist."

I pressed my lips together and made an unladylike grunt before smiling sweetly. "A real bleeding heart."

Whip smirked. "I'll pay extra special attention to your car, of course."

My eyes bored into his as heat clawed up my chest. "I would literally pay for you to stop talking."

Humor sparkled in his silvery eyes, and my dismissal only seemed to goad him on as he took a few steps backward, holding my stare. When he winked and turned away, a disgusted noise shot out of my nose. "Ugh, he is so annoying."

Rachel smirked and stared at his ass as he walked away. "Annoyingly hot, maybe."

My face twisted. "What the hell, Rach? I thought you were on my side."

She only shrugged. "What? I'm bi, not blind."

I crossed my arms and pouted. "I wish I were blind. Then I wouldn't have to be reminded of all"—my arm gestured wildly in front of me—"that."

As if on cue, Whip reached behind his neck, pulling his navy T-shirt off and tossing it aside, putting his muscular back on full display.

My body went rigid and my mouth went dry. I let out a slow, steady stream of breath through my lips.

"No kidding . . . ," Rachel agreed.

"What the hell am I gonna do?" I was asking myself as much as I was asking my friend.

Rachel shrugged, popping her gum. "The way I see it, you've got two options. You give up on all that and move on.

Or you say *hell yes* to more orgasms and hope dear old Dad doesn't find out."

My core clenched at the mere mention of the word *orgasm*, as if it were begging—*yes please!*—demanding option two.

As the cars started filing in, Rachel stood tall and smiled at me. "All right. Time for me to get in line and see if I can finally get Brooklyn's number."

I waved. "Good luck."

"You coming?"

"No. I mostly came to see what it was all about. If I can't figure out a way to raise some money for the foundation, Principal Cartwright is going to give it back to Mrs. Kuder."

"Have you considered senior bingo?" Humor danced in Rachel's eyes.

"Huh." I giggled. "I hadn't thought of that one!"

Rachel's bubbly laugh mixed with mine. "I think you need to talk with the Bluebirds."

"Who?"

"The Bluebird Book Club. They're the women of Outtatowner who meet at the bookstore on Wednesday nights. You want anything done in this town, those ladies can make it happen." Rachel left me with a wave over her shoulder, and I walked in the opposite direction, refusing to look back at Whip.

Fine. I totally looked. Sue me.

Tan firefighter pants molded to his trim hips. The red suspenders hung at his sides. His bare chest and arms were smattered with rich, fluffy bubbles. It reminded me of a porn video I'd watched once, and I made a mental note to see if I could find that one again. Whip's bright smile dazzled driver after driver as they all lined up and paid for the men and women of the Outtatowner Fire Department to wash and scrub their vehicles.

It was amazing to see how many cars waited, and, if my math was even close, the fire department would make a killing for their chosen charity.

If Whip and his stupid smile and ridiculous pecs could do it, then so could I.

I needed the full-time position at the school. There was no other option. If the foundation was the way to make that happen and some women's book club could help me, then count me in.

ELEVEN

EMILY

Bluebird Books was nestled among the quaint storefronts in downtown Outtatowner. The wooden sign that hung above the glass door looked hand carved, and it hearkened back to a time before smartphones and Kindles and other modern technology.

I peered through the glass. The bookstore held promises of whispered secrets between stacks of old books, of discovering new favorites among cherished classics. Through the large front window, I saw plush seating arrangements nestled between tall stacks of books. Along the window seat, overstuffed pillows invited visitors to take a break from the beach and bustle and simply sit and relax with a good book and a cup of hot coffee or tea.

I hadn't even set one foot inside its doors, but the Bluebird Book Club had already become my favorite place in Outtatowner. Though the lights were low, I could see figures milling about at the back of the store. I stood, feet planted in front of the entryway door, and smiled at the sign that stated *Closed for the Bluebirds*.

Rachel assured me that this unique group of women

would be the *oomph* I needed to push my fundraising ideas forward. With their support, I might be able to rally the members of my new town and impress my boss, proving to him I was worthy of a full-time position on his staff.

I am confident.

I am capable.

I am charismatic.

I closed my eyes and repeated my mantra, and when I opened them again, a sense of calm settled over me. I nestled my laptop case deeper into my armpit and set my shoulders. Energy hummed under my skin.

The metal bell clinked against the glass door, announcing my arrival. I followed the murmur of hushed voices as I wound my way through wooden shelves toward the back.

The overhead fluorescent lights had been turned off, and the entire space was illuminated by candles and a smattering of table lamps, casting the space in a warm and inviting glow.

As I got closer, my heartbeat ticked higher. Excitement rather than nerves danced through me. I gently cleared my throat and lifted my chin, prepared to insert myself into what Rachel called a super-secret not-at-all-about-books book-club meeting, when my toe clipped the corner of a bookshelf, throwing me off balance.

I crashed to the floor. My laptop skittered across the thin carpeting with a sickening crunch and bounce. My knees and wrists caught the brunt of my fall, and a chorus of gasps rang out, followed by deafening silence.

I stared at the hunter green and mauve fibers of the Berber carpeting. My breaths sawed in and out of my lungs.

That did not just fucking happen.

My knees throbbed and my head ached from the jolt.

"Emily?" My mother's voice drew closer, and I was shocked to find her crouching at my side. One arm banded across my shoulders, and the other dipped into my armpit in an attempt to hoist me up. "Honey, are you okay? What are you doing here?"

I allowed her to pull me to standing. My stomach wanted to fold in on itself as I took in the curious faces of the women in front of me. I rolled my sore wrists and glanced down at my laptop.

"Hey, Mom. I could ask you the same thing."

"Are you all right, dear?" An older woman stepped forward, concern furrowing her brow.

I plastered on the calmest, fakest smile I could muster to keep from crying. "I'm embarrassed, but otherwise just fine. Thank you."

"Did you need me for something?" my mother asked.

I smoothed my hands down the front of my slacks before jerking my head. I looked out into the small group of onlookers. "I'm here to speak with all of you, actually. I had heard that the Bluebirds were who you turned to when you were desperate and in need of help."

"Told you word was getting out." Another older woman looked annoyed as she topped off her coffee.

"Oh, stop fussing, Bug," the first woman tutted before turning back to me. "That's exactly what we do. I'm Tootie Sullivan." She jerked her head toward the woman at the coffee maker. "That old grouch is Bug King. Don't mind her surly attitude. There's a kind heart in there somewhere." She looked at me and winked. "We think."

Bug King.

Thoughts of Whip flooded my mind as his resemblance to the woman started to take shape.

My mother's hand rubbed up my spine, snapping me

back to the present moment. "Let's get you settled, and then you can tell us about the kind of help you're looking for."

"Thank you," I whispered, still reeling from the embarrassment of my entrance.

Mom ushered me toward a console table that was made up as a makeshift bar. Coffees and teas were littered among a host of alcohol.

"Coffee, or do you need something stronger?"

I looked over my options. "I think that entrance calls for tequila."

A laugh erupted over my shoulder as my mom poured me a margarita into a glass cup that appeared handmade. "That's my kind of girl!" I turned to see a woman who looked to be around my age smiling at me. She stuck out her hand. "Hi, I'm Julep, but everyone calls me MJ."

I took her hand in mine and shook. "Emily."

MJ turned her body, opening herself up to the room. "You've met Tootie Sullivan and Bug. Over there is Mabel, Big Barb, and Martha." As she pointed, women waved or saluted with their drinks. "Then there's my sister Sylvie sitting by Lark, Kate, and Annie."

"Hi." I offered a wave, and my mom handed me the drink, topped with a hot-pink paper umbrella.

"Go sit with your new friends," Mom whispered, and I suddenly felt like the new girl in middle school, hoping someone would let me sit at the lunch table. I followed MJ to the group of women around my age and hoped none of them were like Amy Winters, who in seventh grade pretended to be my friend but then spread a rumor that I wore boys' underpants when the kid she had a crush on asked me to the eighth-grade dance.

As I approached, the women smiled up at me and shuffled around to make room for me on the plush velvet couch.

The woman I was seated next to—Lark, I think?—leaned in. "At the Bluebirds, Kings and Sullivans don't *really* matter, but we still have to ask. Are you a Sullivan or a King?"

My mouth went dry. "Um . . ."

Five pairs of eyes waited for my answer.

"If it makes you feel any better, I'm both." Sylvie smiled.

Sylvie.

Recalling Whip's mention of his sister and how she'd fallen for a Sullivan came rushing back. He'd claimed she'd come the closest to ending the feud with her relationship and the baby she shared with her husband.

Heat flooded my cheeks. "I . . . I think I might be a King?"

MJ whooped and laughed. "Yes!" She playfully stuck her tongue out at the other women. "Now we're even, three–three."

"Sylvie's one of us. Four–two," Annie teased.

"Nope," Sylvie playfully laughed. "I'm *both* so I count on both sides. Four–three. Sorry, MJ."

"Whatever. Close enough." MJ pulled my hand so I would sit next to her.

"What is happening?" I asked.

MJ waved her hand. "Just a little friendly competition. Like I said, at the Bluebirds, we're just friends."

I sipped my margarita, and *holy shit* it was strong. I coughed as it burned down my tightening throat.

Annie laughed. "Sorry about that. I think I was a little heavy handed with the tequila tonight."

"It's great," I squeaked and sipped again.

Playful conversation folded over me as I took in my surroundings. The bookstore had been transformed from a frumpy run-of-the-mill bookshop to a place where the women of Outtatowner relaxed and laughed. Chairs and settees were mismatched. One woman told a story while she knitted something in her lap. All walks of life were represented among the Bluebirds.

"The Bluebirds can pretty much come through with *anything* that needs doing in this town," MJ said. "What do you need our help with?"

I looked around again. My knee bounced. "I don't want to take away from whatever you were doing. Were you talking about a book or something?"

Kate laughed. "Not a chance. We only tell people it's a book club." She turned toward Annie. "What was the book for tonight?"

Annie grinned. "*The Conqueror of Desire*—some bodice ripper Mabel found." She shrugged. "It's actually pretty good."

Sylvie leaned in. "We always get our story straight just in case anyone asks what book we're discussing."

I raised my eyebrows and nodded. "Smart."

"So let's hear it. How can we help?" MJ asked, her question drawing the curiosity of the entirety of the Bluebirds.

I straightened. "Well, I had a whole presentation ready." I looked down at my laptop and prayed it would boot up after the tumble.

Bug King gestured with her crystal cut glass of sweet tea. "This really isn't a presentation kind of a group. Just lay it on us."

Bug was straightforward. No nonsense. I didn't know quite how she was related to Whip, but I liked her already.

"Yes, ma'am." I cleared my throat. "You may know that I am new to Outtatowner. My mother"—I gestured toward my mom, who offered an encouraging smile—"and stepdad moved here a few years ago. I was living in Virginia, but after some time I decided I needed a fresh start."

All eyes were on me. The group of women were listening intently as if my story was riveting. They didn't need to know about how I'd hung my hopes on a man who'd turned out to be the worst kind of liar—the kind that twisted the truth and made you believe *you* were the problem. For a long time I'd thought if I was just pretty enough or smart enough or perfect enough that I would be everything Craig ever wanted. As it turned out, he wasn't even looking for my kind of perfect. He wasn't looking for a square peg, and no amount of contorting who I was would fit into that round hole.

I realized then I would always be the one who cared the most. I'd shown my true feelings, and he'd used them against me. I had been too stubborn to accept the obvious and leave. *Never again.*

"Outtatowner is that fresh start," I continued, gathering my courage. "I have family here and fell in love with the coast on the short visits I've made. Right now I'm substitute teaching sixth grade at the junior high school. I'm doing everything I can to make a good impression, and I'm hoping it can transition to a full-time position." I willed my voice to stay steady. I hated the feeling that I was baring my soul, but I needed their support. "There's nothing left for me in Virginia."

"And what can we do for you, dear?" Tootie's soft eyes made the lump in my throat grow larger.

"I've been put in charge of the Outtatowner Education Foundation. There are a lot of areas that are severely in need of fundraising. We need money for extra school supplies, after-school enrichment programs. The school library is an area I'd really like to focus on. The books are quite literally falling apart, technology is nonexistent, and we aren't providing for the children in a way that will prepare them for how rapidly things in our world change. Without this money, nothing will improve. And if that's the case, what are we even doing?"

Bug King's eyebrow lifted. "That's quite an impassioned speech for a tourist."

I bit back a grin. Her bold personality didn't deter me in the slightest. My chin lifted. "I plan to be a townie before too long."

Her chin dipped slightly, and I took that as a win.

Tootie's hands clapped together. "I, for one, love a proper fundraiser. I'm sure we can come up with some ideas that will impress your boss and bring a little excitement to our town."

Lark walked toward the small counter that held the register, then bent over the counter with her butt in the air as her feet lifted off the ground. When she settled back on her feet, she turned and smiled, holding a pad of paper and a pen. "I'll take notes."

"Okay, Bluebirds," MJ announced, gathering the group together. "Let's hear your ideas."

"A plant sale?" Mabel offered.

I looked around, and no one—including myself—seemed particularly enthusiastic about it, but it was a start.

"No bad ideas." MJ smiled. "Write it down, Lark."

Lark nodded and started writing.

One by one, ideas started filtering in, the women calling out ideas both big and small.

"A bake sale."

"The car wash usually does well . . ."

"A silent auction."

"A cake walk through the historic houses in the area."

Finally, after idea after idea was written down, Bug King stood. "What are we, amateurs? Come on, ladies."

"Let's think about what's coming up. Something that will really excite people." Kate Sullivan brushed aside a wisp of her silky brown hair as she tapped her foot.

"Mother's Day is around the corner," Lark offered.

"Mother's Day *off*. How about that?" Sylvie laughed, but my wheels were turning.

"I love that!" Mom chimed in.

A soft blush stained Sylvie's cheeks. "I was kidding."

"I'm not," Lark added. "If Wyatt gave me a day of zero responsibility? I'd give him another baby just to say thank you."

MJ laughed. "That literally makes zero sense." She pointed at Lark. "But I like the way you think."

I tapped a finger against my lip. There was something there, something we could use. "What if we do catered meals? 'Mother's Day Off' where you can buy some delicious food—something like a main course, a few sides, maybe a salad? No cooking and no mess."

Mom smiled. "I would have loved that on Mother's Day."

A hum of excitement buzzed through the crowd as the women nodded and agreed.

"This is perfect." MJ smiled at the group, gathering consensus.

"What else do we have?" Lark was furiously taking notes.

MJ shrugged. "We could ask our brother Abel about a trivia night at the brewery. Those are always fun."

"I also think we can end with a bang." Tootie smiled and swept her hand in an arch. "A carnival. There's not much going on around here between the Fourth of July and the autumn Fireside Flannel Festival. It could be an end-of-summer carnival. Like a last hurrah push before the new school year."

Annie squealed and danced her feet. "I *love* the idea of a carnival. The lights and music and silly little games. I think it's absolutely perfect."

"It's settled then." Bug nodded. "Mother's Day Off, a trivia night if Abel gives us the okay, and a carnival. Does that work for you?"

Tears pricked my eyes as I saw with perfect clarity how the Bluebirds showed up for and stood behind one another. "Yes, ma'am. I can work with that." I swallowed the glass in my throat and looked around at the smiling faces of the Bluebirds, landing on my mother. "Thank you."

I may have never been the girl to fit in, but if there were ever a space where I had wished I could, it would be with the Bluebirds.

TWELVE

WHIP

"WHAT THE FUCK ARE YOU WEARING?"

My brother Royal looked down at his black apron. The words *I Heart MILFs* in bold, white letters and a glittery red heart were emblazoned across his chest. He'd even "forgotten" to wear a shirt underneath.

A smile crept across his face. "What?"

My eyes rolled and I shook my head, then lifted the black steel door to one of the smokers various residents had lent out for the Mother's Day Off event. Plumes of white vapor carried the mouthwatering smells of perfectly smoked barbecued chicken.

"Don't you mess up my chicken, young man." Mama Faye pointed her long, bony finger in my direction as she walked past. "I don't care who your daddy is, I'll take the spoon to you." She extracted a long wooden spoon from her apron and swirled it in the air as proof.

"Yes, ma'am." I smiled at the woman. Mama Faye had been cooking up Remington County's best smoked barbecue since before I was born. She was bird-boned, with leathery wrinkles across her dark skin, and had one of the most genuine laughs I'd ever heard. If Mama Faye was around, people were having a good time.

Much to my father's dismay, she had declined his offer to move her from the silver Airstream trailer she cooked out of and allow her to rent one of the Kings' many storefront properties. Despite his assurance that it would be better for business—and his bottom line—Mama Faye had insisted that nothing could top the trailer her beloved deceased husband had built for her when she dreamed of opening her own barbecue restaurant. In public Dad had acted as if he was happy for Mama, but in reality he'd been dissatisfied with her *independent spirit.*

Dad abhorred anything and any*one* he couldn't control.

"Okay, boys"—Mama Faye smiled and winked at our female firefighters—"and ladies. I'd like to thank those of you who donated your time or equipment. We've got lots of orders to pack, and I expect more walk-ups than usual. Let's get some food on the table."

Whoops and hollers rang out. In the open field behind the fire station, Mama Faye's Airstream stood proudly, and the banner announcing her business flapped in the breeze. Chief Martin had approached several of the shifts at the station, hoping for volunteers to assist in a fundraising project for the local school district. Once people got wind that Mama Faye would donate a platter of food in exchange for the help, others—like my brother—were all in.

Just before three o'clock, our first customers started walking up. You couldn't blame them either. For ten dollars per container, you could get half a smoked chicken, potato salad, smoky baked beans, and a side salad. For Mama Faye's barbecue, it was the steal of a lifetime.

When Chief Martin walked up, I busied myself with stacking empty containers, ready to complete the orders as the food was prepared.

"Sure smells good around here."

I grinned at him. "Mama Faye's is the best."

"Thank you for volunteering your time. It's good for the crew to see their own stepping up. That's the kind of leadership we're looking for." Pride swelled in me. I was a grown man, but the chief's approval still tended to hit me in the center of my chest every time. "It also means a lot to Emily," he added.

My brows pinched. "Sir?"

"My daughter, Emily. She's the new chair of the educational foundation, and she and a few of the women in town came up with some new ideas to raise money for the school." Chief shook his head. "She's hoping to impress the principal over at the junior high, but he's a fool if he can't see how resourceful and stubborn she is."

That's Prim, all right. I bit back a grin.

"You'll meet her today, I'm sure."

Not wanting to deceive my chief, I offered a tight smile.

Chief Martin clapped his hands together. "Well, I suppose I better make myself useful. But before I forget, the missus asked me to invite you to supper tomorrow evening."

I wanted to refuse. There was no way I'd be able to be that close to Emily and not screw it up, and the last thing I wanted was Chief Martin knowing I'd fucked his beloved daughter. The very same daughter who got under my skin and somehow turned me into a version of myself I barely recognized.

A nod was my only response.

I stared at his back as he walked away. He was

completely unaware of the history between his daughter and me.

My hand flexed as irritation rolled through me. The last time I'd been face-to-face with Emily, I'd been unhinged—jealous of Charles fucking Attwater and his two left feet.

Though she mostly looked down her nose at me like a bug under her shoe, there were moments—like in the bathroom when I caged her against the sink and her round ass pressed into my cock—when the fire in her eyes melted into something hungrier.

I shook away the image of Emily's lush body pressed against mine as my first customer walked up. Wyatt Sullivan was Outtatowner's golden boy—hero quarterback who went on to the NFL and returned to coach at a university not far from here.

His cocky swagger was every bit a Sullivan as he stepped in front of me. "Whip," he said and nodded.

"GB," I shot back, knowing full well he'd fought long and hard against his *Golden Boy* nickname.

Unfazed, Wyatt said, "I've got five orders for pickup."

I scanned my list and placed a check mark next to his name before accepting his payment. As I stacked the premade containers into bags, I got curious. "Your little girl hit a growth spurt or are you feeding a few more these days?"

Wyatt smiled. "Pickle can eat a linebacker under the table lately, but we also have a player who lost his mom spending the weekend with us . . . so he doesn't have to be alone." He shrugged. "Plus, Lark likes having the players around."

That was the thing about Sullivans—they were so fucking perfect. Unlike the Kings, they'd been raised to fight fair and work things out with words rather than fists. I had no clue what that would have been like.

I handed the bags across the table.

Before he turned, Wyatt paused. "You got him pretty good."

My eyebrows raised.

"Rewiring the fuse box in Lee's truck so the horn blared anytime the turn signal went off," he continued with a laugh. "It was a damn good one."

My lip twitched. I had laughed my ass off when Lee rolled through town and couldn't figure out why his horn was honking in time with his blinker. "No idea what you're talking about."

Wyatt raised the bags in silent salute. "Still. It was entertaining."

The afternoon flew by. There had been no sign of Emily—a fact I found mildly annoying since I had been looking forward to ruffling her feathers a bit. It was probably for the best. I ignored my begrudging disappointment and did what I could to make the event as successful as possible. I was attempting to put my best foot forward, and Chief didn't need to catch me mooning over his only daughter.

An endless stream of families picking up their platters and even donating extra funds for the foundation made Mother's Day Off a resounding success. After the final orders were picked up, the rest of the barbecue was sold out in under an hour. Mama Faye had set some food aside just for the volunteers, and we greedily accepted.

My back was tight, but we hoped to make quick work of stripping the white plastic tablecloths from the long tables and cleaning up after the event. Rounding the corner, a hunched figure caught my eye. I instantly recognized the bunched shoulders and shuffling gait of Bootsy Sinclair.

Bootsy and his deceased twin, Bowlegs, were born and raised in Outtatowner. Though they often lived on the fringes of our town, they were still part of us. I glanced at my containers of food, and my stomach grumbled. With a sigh, I swiped the containers off the table and headed toward the back of the fire station.

"How you doing, Bootsy?"

He startled at my greeting. "Oh, hello. Hi." He tipped his head. "Good to see you, Whip."

His eyes snagged on the container in my hands, and I held it up. "There was an extra platter of food. It would be a shame to go to waste. You wouldn't want it, would you?"

Bootsy was a proud man, and I assumed someone like him never wanted to be viewed as a charity case. Bootsy licked his lips and stepped forward. "If it's just getting thrown away, I could take it."

I handed him my platter and nodded.

When I went to turn, he called out to me. "There is one thing . . ."

I turned and waited, my stomach jumping.

"Your father kindly asked me to check in on you. He wanted progress on the historical society."

My jaw flexed and I sighed. My father often used Bootsy's circumstances against him, offering money, food, or housing in exchange for keeping an eye or ear on people in town. Apparently that also meant his own children.

"You can tell my father that if he has something he needs to ask me, he can do that himself."

Bootsy shook his head. "Oh no, young man. Can't do that. Mr. King is a good friend, and I made a promise to talk with you."

Some friend—one who requires you to call him Mr. King.

I gently placed my hand on Bootsy's slight shoulder. "You're right. I'm sorry. I've just had a long day. You can tell him not to worry and that I'm taking care of it."

He grinned up at me. "I did good then?"

My smile faltered, but I did my best. "Real good."

With more pep in his step than before, Bootsy clutched my dinner and walked away. Exhaustion washed over me. Russell King had the special talent of draining my energy even when he wasn't in the room.

My boots stomped across the grass but stopped short when Emily's round ass came into view. Bent over, she was fighting with the folding legs of one of the tables. Denim stretched over her lush curves as she bent at the waist. My dick twitched, and I bit back a groan when she wiggled.

I hated the way her presence unearthed something carnal inside me. Everything about Emily Ward was wrong, but my body didn't care. My traitorous mind had a field day with flashes of her face down, ass up in that exact position as I felt each row of my piercings slowly slip into her tight pussy.

I growled and suppressed the memory before stepping beside her. "You're going to break it."

Her face whipped to the side, sending her soft hair cascading over her face. She blew the strands with an annoyed breath. "I'm fine and don't need your help."

I crossed my arms. "I wasn't offering it."

She huffed and stood tall. "Figures."

"Can't even show up to your own fundraiser?" I poked.

Her eyes betrayed her by snagging on my uniform and lingering for a second too long. Her hands settled on her hips with a huff. "Well, I can't cook, and Dad said there were plenty of volunteers, so I decided I'd be best put to use with cleaning up." She glared at me. "Not that I have to explain myself to you."

Damn. That makes a lot of sense.

I lifted a shoulder in indifference. "Fine. You can explain to Mama Faye how you broke her table."

Emily glared at me, and I smiled broadly, just to piss her off.

"Hey, Prim!" Brooklyn walked past us toward the parking lot, raising her container of food. "Great idea for a fundraiser. Seemed like a hit."

Emily swiveled in her flats and glared at me. "You did *not*."

I held my hands up innocently. "You wanted to be a townie. A nickname is just part of the gig."

Emily turned her back to me and lowered to her knees to continue fussing with the table leg. I distinctly heard her grunt and mumble something over her shoulder about me and my *glitter dick*.

A laugh threatened to burst from my chest, but I tamped it down, not wanting her to permanently detach it from my body. After letting her struggle for another minute, I decided to put myself to use loading the smokers onto the truck beds of their owners, but not before ruffling her feathers one last time.

"Hey, Prim." She glared up at me, and I bent low so only she could hear. "Figure it out yet?"

She sat back on her heels, sizing me up as I peered down at her with an amused look on my face. She pointed her finger at me, motioning up and down the length of my tactical cargo pants. "Are those functional pockets where you store all of your audacity?"

I laughed and her scowl deepened. I turned to walk away. "You know . . ." I turned back, rubbing my palm against the stubble on my chin. "I forgot how good you'd looked on your knees."

Blush flooded her cheeks as fire ignited in her eyes. A coy smile spread across her face as she looked up from under her lashes and raised her middle finger. "Enjoy it, because this is the last time you'll ever get to see it."

THIRTEEN

EMILY

"MOM. WHAT DID YOU DO?" My teeth ground together as my mother arranged another place setting at the table. Despite a casual cookout, she gently placed a thick, white paper plate in front of the proper seat.

"What do you mean?" She blinked and tried to play innocent, but I could see right through her.

I sighed. "Who is coming for dinner?"

Her shoulder raised, causing her light-brown hair to fall in a lovely cascade down her back. "Just a friend of your father's. He's up for some promotion, and I thought it would be hospitable to invite him to supper."

My eyes tracked my mother as she scurried around the farmhouse-style table. I toyed with the inside of my lip. "As long as this isn't another one of your setups. After Dickie and Tall Chad, your matchmaking privileges are permanently revoked."

"Other Tall Chad," she said.

"What?"

"I tried to set you up with *Other* Tall Chad." She waved a hand in dismissal. "Totally different person."

I shook my head and tried not to laugh at how bizarre this town was. I shot my mother a pointed look. "Please just tell me this dinner isn't you trying to arrange another date for me."

"Of course not." She batted her lashes as a smile teased the corner of her lips. "Our guest works with your father. That would be *scandalous*." Mischief glittered in her eyes as her eyebrows waggled.

I pressed the heels of my hands into my eyes. I looked over my dusty-pink blouse that was french-tucked into a simple pair of ankle-cropped jeans. "Just tell me who it is so I at least know whether I need to hurl myself off the roof before or after dessert."

My mother's soft laughter filled the dining room despite my total lack of humor regarding the situation.

"His name is William, and he is very charming. I'd wait until after dessert, at least." Her blue eyes swept over me. "Maybe do up your hair a bit?"

My head tipped back, and I audibly groaned to the ceiling. Nothing made me feel more pathetic than being twenty-five years old and relying on my mother to resuscitate my love life. "I really wish you'd stop trying to find me a boyfriend, Mom."

Her eyes softened as she stepped closer. "I just want to see you happy."

"I am happy," I insisted. "If I get a full-time job here, I'll be even happier." I swallowed hard, giving voice to the words I'd rehearsed over and over in my mind. "That's what I need to focus on. There are goals that I have every intention of achieving. I can do this."

My mom's arm settled across my shoulder as she pulled me into a side hug. Her soft, floral perfume filled my nose, and I sank into her hug. "You can do anything. I only know how deeply you feel, but that you're afraid to show it. I just hate that he took that from you."

Emotion clogged in my throat. Feelings were something that could be used against you. It was the most important lesson Craig had ever taught me. "It has nothing to do with him."

I hated lying to my mother, but she let the small untruth go without an argument. "Sometimes I think you're all action and you forget to remember that the best parts of life aren't line items to be checked off, but moments you can only *feel* your way through."

"That sounds awful," I deadpanned as my mother squeezed.

Her bubbling laughter broke the tension, and I touched my head to hers. I knew she meant well, no matter how misguided her matchmaking attempts were. "Just . . . try leaning into your feelings. For me," she pleaded.

I pouted. "Fine. But only because I'm going to steal a brownie before dinner!" With a laugh, I escaped her hug just as I took off like a shot toward the kitchen.

"You better not!" She whipped a dish towel in my direction and chased me into the next room.

My laughter died a slow, squawking death, and my feet came up short. My mother's body propelled me forward from behind as I stared at Whip, standing in my parents' kitchen.

"There are my girls." My father beamed at us as he shoved the remainder of a brownie into his mouth.

"Joseph Martin. I told you those were for dessert. I swear, you and Emily are cut from the same cloth."

Dad wiped his hands as I continued to stare at Whip. Heat prickled along my hairline, and Whip's eyes stayed locked with mine.

Mom moved past me in one graceful motion, opening her arms wide. "William, it's so good to see you."

My jaw came unhinged as I watched Whip envelop my mother in a comfortable, familiar embrace. His eyes stayed on me as he hugged her. Clearly she'd left out a few details regarding *William*—specifically that she had a soft spot for him and that outside of her and my father, everyone seemed to call him Whip.

Her hands came to his biceps. "I hope you're hungry. Joe bought far too many hamburgers, as usual. I'm afraid you'll have to carry the leftovers to the firehouse."

Whip's laugh was warm and laced with familiar affection. "I doubt anyone is going to complain about that. Especially if there are any of your famous black-and-white brownies left."

"That will be up to these two." She laughed, gesturing between her husband and me.

"Mom . . ."

Mom turned to me. "What? Why are you standing there?" She motioned toward Whip. "Come on over here and say hello."

I took one wooden step forward. He was dressed casually in dark denim and a white T-shirt. My stomach flipped at how his shirtsleeves strained against his muscles.

"William, meet my daughter, Emily. Emily, this is William."

Whip held out his wide palm. "Emily."

Manners took over as I slipped my hand into his. "*William.*" I tipped my eyebrow up, acknowledging his name with my steely gaze.

The corner of his mouth hooked up as he squeezed my hand. Heat unfurled in slow waves up my arm, liquefying my bones under his touch. I snatched my hand back.

"Can I give you a hand outside, sir?" Whip turned his attention to my dad, who held up a platter of thin round hamburger patties to be grilled.

Dad smiled. "Grab a few beers and meet me outside."

Sir. What a kiss-ass.

An image of me bent over Whip's bed, bare ass in the air as he burned a path of hot, wet kisses up the back of my thigh flashed through my mind.

NOPE. Thinking of literally *anything other than that . . .*

I growled and watched from the safety of Mom and Dad's kitchen window as my stepdad and the man I was determined to forget laughed over beers in the backyard. This house may not have been where I grew up, but somehow my mom had made it feel like home. Pictures of our happy, simple lives dotted the hallway, and she'd decorated the kitchen with framed recipe cards written by her grandmother.

It was cozy and safe, and Whip's presence was fucking it all up. It was clear my dad was in love with him, and the more they joked and laughed, the more annoyed I grew.

Whip's eyes moved, catching mine through the window. Deep and intense, he held my stare. His mouth eased into a satisfied smirk after he must have realized I was trying to steal a peek at him.

My fingers dug into the granite countertop as I glared a hole into Whip's forehead from the window.

Cocky prick.

Mom hummed beside me. "Mmm. Heck of a view, don't you think?" She smiled as she took a sip of her sweet iced tea.

"Mother," I deadpanned and turned away from the window.

A content laugh floated from her. "What? I'm happily married, but I'm not blind."

"He's a jerk. I don't know how Dad doesn't see it." I continued studying Whip from the corner of my eye as he leaned in closer to my father. It looked as though my dad was teaching him something about the grill or the food. Whip nodded, asked a question, and listened.

Mom moved to finish making potato salad as a side for dinner while the men grilled. "I've met William at a few of the firehouse functions. He's always been polite and respectful. He looks up to Joe."

I frowned. "Doesn't he have his own father? I heard his family has more money than God and practically runs the town."

My mother mixed in the dressing and stirred. "When we moved to Outtatowner, Russell King was one of the first people to welcome us. On the outside he comes across as charming and, admittedly, we were fooled. But there's something off there—something darker. I've always had a strange, uneasy feeling when it comes to him. Russell is always angling for something, and I can't put my finger on it." She shrugged. "I keep it to myself since it's the role of the fire chief's wife to remain neutral. But it's something I noticed working at the police station too—if there's trouble, somehow Russell King seems to be at the center of it."

I mulled over her words. My mother's intuition was rarely wrong. "What about the mother? What's she like?"

"As far as I know, she's not in the picture. I heard a rumor that she up and left all six of those kids when they were pretty young. Apparently starting a new life without them was better than staying with her husband. I can imagine that's hard on any child."

My stomach soured. I didn't want to feel pity for Whip

and the shit hand he'd been given, but it was there, lurking on the edges, nonetheless.

My mother pushed the bowl toward the center of the island and wiped the countertop. "It's a wonder, but those kids all seem to be thriving in their own ways."

"Maybe they're all rotten on the inside like their father, but know how to put on a good show." I studied her as I leaned against the counter and popped a rogue cherry tomato into my mouth. "What do the Bluebirds say about the Kings?"

Mom's shoulder lifted. "Not a lot. Bug is Russell's sister, and she'd never let anyone speak ill of her family. She's tough and loyal. Though the Bluebirds try to stay out of it, with the King–Sullivan feud, it seems you pick a side and stick with it."

I lifted my eyebrows, eyes wide. "So you're saying you're Team Sullivan?"

She pointed the potato-covered spoon at me and winked. "I'm Team Let's Eat. Finish that salad."

I shot her a playful look and finished topping the lettuce with tomatoes, cucumbers, and a sprinkling of cheddar cheese.

Once the burgers were done, Dad and Whip joined Mom and me in the dining room. My stepdad sat at the head of the table, with my mother to his left. I sat across from her, and to my dismay, Whip took the seat next to me. I subtly angled my body away from him and did whatever I could to ignore his presence.

Heat radiated off his body, and tiny hits of his clean, masculine scent distracted me from the conversation more than once. I participated in the conversation when directly spoken to, but otherwise spent my time shoveling food in my face to hasten my mother's disastrous attempt at a love connection.

When Whip's knee grazed my outer thigh, I nearly choked on a chunk of cheeseburger. I coughed and sputtered in an attempt to not die at the dinner table.

"Are you okay?" Mom half stood from her seat, concern thick in her voice.

I coughed again but managed to hold up my hand and nod between hacking coughs. A hard thump on my back rattled me, and I glared at Whip. His wide palm stayed planted on the center of my upper back. His fingertips stroked the base of my neck.

I swallowed hard and cleared my throat. "I'm fine," I reassured my mom, then turned to Whip. "Thanks."

"No problem." His eyes roamed over my face, and heat licked up my spine. His hand was heavy on my back.

I shifted my shoulder, hoping he'd remove his hand, but it stayed planted. He leaned in and I sucked in a breath.

"You've got . . ." He gestured toward his own face with a gentle smile.

Heat flooded my cheeks as I snatched my napkin from beside my plate and furiously wiped at my mouth. Sure enough, a streak of mustard stained the white paper.

Whip finally removed his hand, and I glanced around the table. Everyone was amused by my mishap, and I wanted to crawl under the table and die.

Dad leaned back in his seat and patted my hand that was clutched around my napkin. "She's all right. Melly's in good hands here if she needs the Heimlich."

Whip laughed in agreement. "Yes, sir. I know what to do if she chokes." He turned to me with devious, knowing eyes.

Take it. Choke on it.

The memory of the deep rumble of Whip's voice as he spoke those deliciously dirty words hummed through me.

I stood abruptly, rattling the table after bumping it with my knee. "I'm good. Thanks. Can I take your plate?"

I scooped up Dad's plate before he could answer and escaped to the kitchen.

I stomped across the kitchen floor. It was impossible. How could I be so turned on by someone I couldn't stand? Whip was *everything* I didn't want or need, yet somehow every word out of his mouth liquefied my insides and turned me into a needy puddle.

I tossed our used paper plates in the trash and paced in the kitchen. Maybe it's just hormones. Maybe in some sick way I'm trying to get back at Craig for cheating on me with my supposed best friend and blaming *me* for being boring in bed when I didn't want a threesome with her. Maybe Whip bewitched me with his gigantic pierced dick, and none of this is my fault.

Yes! Love this for me. It's his fault—definitely the magical penis.

I bent and touched my toes, stretching my back and trying to refocus. I tipped my face toward the ceiling and exhaled. "Fuck."

"Emily," Mom admonished from behind me.

I straightened and offered a sheepish smile. "Sorry." I rolled my shoulders and sucked in a deep lungful of air. "I'm just having a weird day."

"I can see that." She waited for me to explain myself, but I stayed silent. Finally, she sighed. "Dad is taking Whip to see the Chevelle, though I know it's really a ploy to sneak a cigar." She unwrapped a white platter. Piled high were her black-and-white brownies—a favorite of Mom's. Half were dark chocolate fudge brownies with little hearts cut out of the middle, which were replaced with a blondie heart. The other half were blondies with fudge brownie hearts. "Give them a few minutes to think their secret is safe and then take these out to them, will you? I'll start cleaning up."

My molars ground together. The last thing I wanted to do was offer up a heart on a platter—brownie or otherwise—to Whip King.

FOURTEEN

WHIP

"Now, my wife doesn't know these are out here, but there's no harm in a bit of solitude."

He stared down at the glowing cinnabar ember of his cigar, then chuckled. "Ah, who am I kidding? I can't keep a thing from Marilyn." He tapped the side of his nose. "That woman's got a nose like a bloodhound, but she lets me think I'm getting away with it."

I hummed in acknowledgment despite the fact I found his relationship with his wife curious. It was clear even after the years spent together, he was still wildly in love with his wife. Whether it was the long shifts away from home, media influence, or the general hero worship, it was a widely accepted misconception that firefighters were heartbreakers.

In some sick way it was probably what led me to become a firefighter in the first place. When given the choice, people will always choose someone else over me. I didn't need to get attached only for them to decide I wasn't worth the effort after all. The misconception that by nature

I must be a philandering womanizer made it easier to keep things light.

Noncommittal.

The real joke was on me, though. In my experience the men and women on my crew were some of the most loyal humans on the planet. Joe Martin was a prime example. I'd heard him tell the story of how he met his wife and was instantly captivated. Despite the crew occasionally cracking jokes and bemoaning their spouses, Chief had never once whispered an ill word about his wife.

I couldn't remember a single positive thing my father had uttered about my own mother.

Leech.

Thankless.

Whore.

Those were the broad strokes in which my father painted my mother—the woman who'd disappeared under the cloak of night without so much as a goodbye to the children who had loved her.

But we'd all done what we could to survive my father's rule. We became achievers to earn his approval. Praise wasn't doled out sincerely like Chief did. It was hard-earned.

I looked at the man I had often secretly wished was my father. He was on the shorter side—unassuming, yet a powerhouse. He had kind eyes and an easy laugh. He was tough, but it lacked the slicing edge of malice under which I had grown up. No, Joe Martin was tough because he saw the potential in everyone.

And you went and fucked his darling daughter.

Shame rippled through me. I had sat at the Martins' table, eaten their food. Jesus, the things I had done to their sweet little Melly. It was a wonder I could look them in the eye.

Unaware of my internal tailspin, Chief held out a fresh cigar. "You're sure you don't want one?"

I swallowed around the hard lump that had formed in my throat. "Not tonight, but thank you, sir."

Without pushing he simply nodded and tucked the cigar back into its box. "Outside of the station, you can call me Joe."

I smiled and shook my head, my eyes not lifting from the concrete garage floor. "I'm sorry, but I don't think I can do that."

His brown eyes were smiling. "Maybe someday."

I returned his kindness and shrugged. "Maybe."

Three sharp knocks on the entrance to the garage startled us. Chief tapped out his cigar and flipped on a fan, dispersing the thick plume of smoke out the open window. It was no use. The entire garage reeked of tobacco.

Chief's shoulders softened when Emily appeared in the doorway.

"Just me," she announced, maneuvering the heavy door and carrying the platter that held Mrs. Martin's famous brownies. She gestured with the platter before unceremoniously depositing it on a workbench to her right. "Mom says 'don't forget to close the window,' because otherwise it'll get buggy."

The tips of Chief Martin's ears grew red, and he smiled. "Thanks, Melly."

Her smile softened as she looked at her stepdad. "You bet." Her face morphed into a snarl. Turning to me, she plucked a chocolate brownie with a vanilla blondie heart off the plate. "Night!"

She waved over her shoulder and blew out of the garage just as quickly as she'd come in.

Chief Martin's chuckle drew my attention. He took a generous bite of his brownie and shook his head. "I swear," he mused, "I have never seen a more stubborn woman. Even as a child she was headstrong. Always liked things *just so*, and if they didn't go her way, she could dig her heels in and move mountains with sheer stubbornness. I don't know what you did, but you're in it."

"What do you mean?" Panic ratcheted up my heartbeat.

Shit. Was he on to me? Did he know?

"Something's got her hackles up."

I plucked a perfectly square brownie from the plate. "I'm not sure either"—*I was*—"but I think it may be the general profession that irritates her."

He took another bite and considered with a shrug. "She wouldn't be wrong. There's still a sensitive little girl beneath her grit and strong will, and our type makes it hard on a person like her."

"Our type, sir?"

"The kind of person who can endure the stress of the job. The unknowns. The long hours. Dealing with death and trauma day after day." He gestured vaguely toward his skull. "Makes a lot of us internalize our pain instead of dealing with it in a healthy way. Emily has always craved order and quiet predictability."

I couldn't disagree with his assessment of *our type*, so I offered a quiet harrumph.

He was probably right.

Prim was a rule follower by nature, but I'd gotten glimpses of a hidden rebellious streak that I knew her father knew nothing about. It was a simple fact that she deserved so much more than a man like me, but I'm nothing if not a glutton for punishment, so I couldn't help but poke the bear.

I wasn't looking to be anyone's husband, but if she ever offered another late-night fuck, I wouldn't have the willpower to refuse.

It was bad enough I couldn't stop thinking about how desperately I wanted to touch her again. I couldn't stop thinking about the intensity of our connection that night, and I had stopped myself a dozen times from falling to my knees and begging her to let me worship the smooth angles and lush curves of her body.

I exhaled a sharp breath through my nose. It was time to finally concede that I was more like my own father than I wanted to admit. I was willing to sacrifice my standing in the eyes of a man I respected to get what I wanted . . . and I wanted only *her*.

I leaned forward, hand out. "Thank you for dinner, sir. Please tell Mrs. Martin that the meal and the company were lovely. I look forward to another invitation soon."

Chief Martin clamped his hand into mine, placing his other on my shoulder with a squeeze. "You're welcome at my table anytime, son."

I tried not to let his casual turn of phrase burn a hole through my chest. I had accepted his invitation with the intention of bringing up the building my father intended to purchase. Only problem was I was utterly charmed by Marilyn Martin and didn't have the heart to spoil such a nice meal with underhanded business dealings disguised as small talk.

The fact Emily was also at dinner was an unexpected bonus. I also couldn't worry about what my chief might think of me if he ever found out about the history between Emily and me.

I was on a mission.

Closing the garage door behind me, I spotted Emily striding across the lawn toward the driveway. I lengthened my strides and called out to her. "Hey, Prim." She shot an annoyed glance over her shoulder. "Wait up," I called.

Despite irritation flashing in her eyes, she paused, hand on her hip. I bit back a smile, admiring her commitment to despising me.

"What do you need? Would you like to know what other family functions we have coming up so you can ingratiate yourself with the chief?"

I shook my head. "Careful, Prim. You know us hero types struggle with the big words." I furrowed my brow and thumped a fist against my chest. "Fire bad. Water good."

She shot me a dead stare, but I could see the shimmers of a smile hinting at the corners of her pert little mouth.

Determining that subtle twitch to be a win, I popped the fudge heart out of the center of my blondie. "You want my heart?"

I'm sure she assumed I was simply messing with her, but the question hung in the air.

I stretched out my hand and dropped it in her open palm. In one quick movement, she tossed it into her mouth, chewing aggressively.

I winced. "Savage."

Emily planted her hands on her hips. "Cut the shit, Whip. Why are you really here?"

I blinked, feigning innocence. "I was invited."

She huffed, eyes narrowed. "Are you using my dad to try to get that promotion?"

The accusation poked at me. I may have the sick urge to bend his daughter over the hood of my truck, but I would never accept a job in the department that I didn't earn.

Her teasing had been amusing, but now I was pissed. "The job wasn't even on my radar until your dad brought it up to *me*. But I deserve that promotion." My finger pointed to the ground between us. "I'll get it because I've earned it, Prim."

Her chin lifted, proving my nickname for her accurate. "Don't call me that."

The sun hung heavy in the western sky, slowly sinking behind the trees in the distance. Summer days were rapidly approaching, leaning into yawning afternoons that whispered promises of heated summer nights. The blaze of orange and fuchsia played with the muted blues and greens in her eyes.

I risked a step forward. "What would you prefer I call you?"

She sucked in a breath, hoisting her perfect round tits higher in the air. I held her fierce gaze. "I *prefer* for you to call me nothing at all."

Excitement danced through me as tension crackled in the humid coastal air. I crowded her space, feeling her pert, hard nipples graze my chest. "You sure about that?"

Fury laced with indignation flared in her eyes, and my dick swelled in my jeans.

I struggled to keep my eyes off her—the thump of her pulse in her neck, the flush of pink in her cheeks.

The worst thing was the way my body eased toward her as if an invisible tether tugged us closer. I ached to touch her.

Who wouldn't be attracted to Emily? She was funny, strong willed, whip-smart, and gorgeous. Aside from the fact her father was my boss, I had fun provoking her. She could take a smart remark and toss one back with her razor-sharp tongue. What I really wanted involved that tongue wrapping around my cock again. My dick twitched just thinking about it.

Damn it.

I knew exactly what I was doing when I grabbed her wrist. I was fully aware it was a terrible idea, and I had a pretty good feeling it was bound to bite me in the ass eventually.

Still, I yanked her arm, pulling her into me until she was so close the peppermint on her tongue mingled with my breath.

I held her wild stare for a moment. Then two. "Do you want me to kiss you?"

Emily swallowed hard but didn't answer my question.

My attention raked over her features, her hazy aqua eyes nearly black with desire. "I told you I was going to make you beg for it."

Emily sucked in a sharp breath. "Whip . . ."

"Beg, Prim." My blood was white-hot. My fist gripped the back of her shirt.

"I—" Her eyes fluttered closed. "*Please . . .*"

Sick satisfaction washed over me with a wolf's grin as my stomach clenched. "That's my girl."

I devoured her, surging in with confidence as I took her mouth. My hands slid up her back, then down over her ass. I pressed her into me as my hips jutted forward. I wanted her to *feel* what she did to me.

She looped her arms around my neck, inching higher up my body as she rose on her tiptoes. Our tongues clashed, rolling over one another as I tasted her. Mint and chocolate made her irresistible. I couldn't get enough.

It was wrong and we were in the middle of the driveway. Chief could walk out of the garage at any moment and find me with my tongue down his daughter's throat, but I didn't care.

That kiss alone was worth my entire career.

Emily was all-consuming and forbidden at the same time—everything I'd ever craved and couldn't have rolled into one provocative little package.

My mouth traveled across her jaw, and I sucked on the pulse point at her neck. "Tell me to stop."

"Whip," she whispered.

My hand coasted up her back, burying into the hair at the nape of her neck as I pulled her head back. I grazed my nose along the column of her neck, committing her scent to memory.

I held her face in my hands. "Tell me to go to hell. That you don't feel this. Tell me to stop and I'll walk away."

Her breath floated across my cheek as her eyes searched mine. "I can't."

I groaned as I planted my mouth on hers, taking whatever she was willing to give and praying I survived it.

I needed that kiss to last. If it was the last one I was ever going to get from her, I would make it worth it. I delved into her mouth, exploring and tasting and devouring her. At any moment her father—my *boss*—could walk out and catch us. Emily didn't need a man like me interrupting her life, and I sure as hell didn't need to get fired for dry humping the chief's daughter.

My head was spinning.

With one last taste, I gathered my resolve and gripped her shoulders. I peeled us apart, our breaths mingling as we panted. I ached for more. If she couldn't walk away, then I would have to.

"We can't do this. It's not worth it."

Hurt flashed across her face. Emily's hackles went up

before I could explain I didn't mean *she* wasn't worth it—hell, I'd been seconds away from igniting my entire life for a taste of her. I only meant that we shouldn't expose our connection in the driveway like a couple of horny teenagers. We needed to be smarter than that.

Her puffy lips taunted me before she pressed them into a flat line. "Fine," she ground out. "I couldn't agree more."

She turned, storming up the porch steps.

"Prim—" Her eyes flashed and I lifted a hand. "Emily. Please. I only meant—"

Her chin lifted and her features iced over. "I know what you meant, and I agree. Good night."

Without another word, she entered her parents' home, letting the screen door slap against the frame.

It's for the best.

The words rattled in my skull, but were hollow. I glanced back at the garage, where I had left my chief. I didn't have the balls to face him either. Resigned, I chalked it up to yet another thing in my life I had managed to fuck up.

FIFTEEN

EMILY

I PRESSED a finger to my lower lip and closed my eyes, remembering the way Whip had kissed me in my parents' driveway. Days later, I was still dazed from the kiss and had no idea how I had managed to drive back to my tiny apartment across town after being so thoroughly rocked.

Tell me to stop.

His charged words echoed in my mind as I counted, then recounted, the stack of still ungraded essays in front of me.

I wouldn't have been able to stop him if I'd tried—my body would never have allowed it. Whip King ignited something bone-deep and feral inside me. It was like my feminine energy was screaming *I know what his dick feels like and I need more of it!*

I pressed a hand against the flutter that danced low in my belly. Desire entwined with hurt clouded my memory of his kiss.

It's not worth it.

I ground my teeth together. How does a girl not take those words personally? Whip wasn't the first man to say I wasn't worth the effort. Still, the words were like a slap in the face, and anger burned in my cheeks.

I glanced at the clock, noting only a few short minutes until my students would come streaming in.

"Focus, Em." I blew out a breath, acknowledging that my little pep talk was utterly useless. Ever since Whip pulled me against him and fervently kissed me—*after he told me to beg for it*—I couldn't think of much else.

When the bell rang, the chatter of students floated down the hallway. I set the essays aside as I rounded my desk, determined to greet each student before he or she entered my classroom.

In addition to algebraic expressions and cultural context in literature, the bulk of my time at Outtatowner Junior High was spent building a community. Each student walked through my door with different strengths, and we worked together to honor and celebrate each other's uniqueness.

As each student began finding their place in the social hierarchy of junior high, some days were a challenge. I greeted each of my students with a smile and cheerful "Good morning!" Most of the time I received smiles and mumbled greetings back, but the occasional scowl also helped me to understand the kind of morning each of my students was having.

As the last students walked down the hallway, I spotted Robbie Lambert trudging across the blue-and-white-checkered linoleum with his head hung low and a sad expression.

My heart sank.

The subtle shift in his attitude over the past few months had not gone unnoticed. His sweet and shy demeanor had slowly morphed into something withdrawn and sullen.

As he approached, I offered my sunny greeting, which he completely ignored.

Concerned, I gently placed my hand on his shoulder, but when he winced and ducked from beneath my touch, I quietly pulled my hand back.

"Hey, Robbie." I kept my smile locked in place. "Everything okay?"

He paused, but his eyes stayed planted on his feet. "It's fine."

"Oh, okay." My attention snagged on his shoes, whose white leather was stained and dingy. Parts of the upper were separating from the sole. I frowned. Just last week I had gifted Robbie a brand-new pair of sneakers.

My brows knit tighter. "Did the new tennis shoes not fit? We can figure something else out if—"

Robbie's jerky movements as he flung his backpack off his shoulder stopped me midsentence. He unzipped his bag, pulling the new shoes from his backpack.

He shoved them toward me but still hadn't looked me in the eye. "I can't accept these."

I carefully took the shoes from him. "Oh. Okay."

I remembered how excited Robbie was when I had presented them to him one day after school.

I was sure to make it seem like the new shoes were just some extra pair of men's shoes I happened to have lying around, when in fact I had specifically gone out and purchased them for him. During an after-school tutoring session, Robbie had made a self-deprecating comment about not having a decent pair. Kids his age were brutal, and his worn-out shoes hadn't gone unnoticed.

Later, I casually mentioned that I found a random pair lying around that I planned to get rid of and he could take them if they fit. At the time, his eyes lit up, and his wide toothy smile had squeezed my heart.

He'd even leaned over and given me a quick hug before dropping to his butt in the middle of my classroom to put them on. This sudden one-eighty from him was concerning.

Robbie still hadn't looked me in the eye. "I'm not a charity case." He shouldered past me, leaving me stunned in the hallway.

I blinked away the sudden surge of emotion as I stared into the near-empty hallway. Walking with his secretary at his side, Principal Cartwright headed straight for my room. I swiped the moisture from my eyes and lifted my chin.

I perked up and gave him my attention. "Good morning, Mr. Cartwright." I nodded at his secretary. "Miss Austin."

The principal offered a flat-lipped nod. "Miss Ward. Miss Austin will look after your classroom for a few minutes. I need a word with you in my office."

My heartbeat fluttered, but I kept my composure. "Of course." I stepped aside to gesture toward my classroom. "Right this way, Miss Austin."

Principal Cartwright waited at the entrance to my classroom while I briefly walked Miss Austin through our typical morning procedure, adjusting slightly for the fact someone other than myself would be opening today's math lesson.

Once I was satisfied the children were in good hands, I met Principal Cartwright at the doorway. He nodded and together we made the silent, uncomfortable trudge from my end of the hallway to his office.

"I've got to say," I started, laughing. "I can't remember ever being called down to the principal's office."

My small chuckle was weak, and the joke landed flatly.

Once at the doorway to his office, he gestured toward the small table and chairs. "Please have a seat, Miss Ward."

"Emily, please." I smiled up at him. My hands were jittery, so I clamped them together in my lap to maintain my composure.

Principal Cartwright sat across from me. I guessed he would have been around Whip's age—older than me, sure, but by no means an old man. The stark contrast between the two men was almost laughable. The overhead fluorescent lighting illuminated the male pattern baldness on Principal Cartwright's scalp and disappeared into the halo of hair that circled the back of his head.

He shifted in the chair. "I'm sorry to interrupt your morning routine, but I needed to speak with you about an incident that came to my attention this morning."

"Oh?" I lifted my chin, proud that my voice was clear and strong.

"Is it true that you gave Robbie Lambert a brand-new pair of gym shoes?"

The angry, near-tears expression on Robbie's face this morning flashed through my mind.

I took a quiet breath and steeled my spine. "I happened to have a pair of shoes in his size, and I offered them to him, which he accepted."

Yes, not a total lie, but Principal Cartwright didn't need to know that I had spent hours obsessing over whether the Nikes were on trend enough to purchase.

Principal Cartwright scribbled something on the notepad to his right. "I see. And have you purchased gifts for other students in your class?"

A tendril of panic seized my chest before calm settled over me. "I wouldn't really call them a gift. His shoes are steps away from falling off his feet while he wears them. He needed new tennis shoes, and I happened to have a pair. I view it the same as if a student needed a new notebook or pencils. I wouldn't refuse a child in need."

More scratching and scribbling on his notebook. I wished I could read his chicken-scratch writing to know what the hell he was writing down.

He frowned. "But you agree that a brand-new pair of expensive tennis shoes is a bit different from a pencil. Do you not?"

My temper flared, but I tamped it down and took a calming breath. "'Fair treatment doesn't necessarily mean equal.' That was the statement you made in the staff IEP training last month. Is it not?"

His upper lip twitched as I smiled sweetly across the cheap cherrywood table. He sat forward, his hands smoothing down the bulge of his belly. "Yes, I mean, we did discuss that . . . but that was in terms of students with special needs."

I nodded. "I agree. And I also believe that Robbie had a unique and special need for footwear." I smiled sweetly across the table. "I apologize if I had taken your presentation and its intent a bit too literally."

Principal Cartwright let out an exasperated breath and pinched the bridge of his nose. A thrill of victory zipped through me. It wasn't often someone could defeat calmly presented simple logic.

"Look, Mr. Lambert stormed into my office this morning, going on and on about how this school views his son and his family as a charity case. He threatened a discrimination case against us." My brows furrowed and he continued: "I know, it doesn't even make any sense, but he's noisy, and I don't need the headache. Do not go around me on this."

I clenched my jaw. "I understand." I almost added *it*

won't happen again but decided flat-out lying to my direct supervisor was probably a bad idea.

Principal Cartwright wrote one last scribble on his notepad. "Good. Thank you, Miss Ward."

Dismissed and utterly pissed off at the entire situation, I stormed down the hallway to my classroom.

~

Abel's Brewery stood proudly on the outskirts of town, hugging the rugged Lake Michigan coastline. After running with the Bluebirds' idea of trivia night, MJ managed to convince her brother Abel to host the event, and when I'd made a visit to check the space out, I couldn't believe my eyes.

The brewery itself was upscale, with the outside highlighting heavy wood and iron accents. The back wall, which faced the lake, was lined with glass garage-style doors that opened during the spring, summer, and fall months. The view was breathtaking. Firepits with cushy seating dotted the exterior. Inside, a large double-sided fireplace could add warmth during winter months. It was the perfect location for townies and tourists to spend money.

The response to the trivia night fundraiser had been overwhelming, and I was relieved when Abel assured me they could open the rolling doors on the side of the building to accommodate additional tables. Over the phone, Abel was efficient, if not a bit surly, and reminded me a touch of Whip's aunt Bug.

It had taken me the better part of the week to shake off the conversation I'd had with Principal Cartwright. I hated feeling as though I had done something wrong, especially in the eyes of the principal who held the key to my future employment. Surely he wouldn't be keen on hiring me full time if he didn't feel like he could trust my judgment.

Still, I had only tried to do right by Robbie. The pained look in my student's eyes still nagged me.

There had to be a better way.

My phone rang, and Rachel's name flashed across the screen. I shook off my sour mood before answering.

"Are you there already?" She was frazzled.

I glanced at my watch, relieved I was earlier than planned. "I just pulled up. I'm going to make sure everything is ready and that the DJ is able to get set up. What's going on?"

"I am having a crisis. I don't know what to wear. I finally got the guts to ask Brooklyn on a date and figured trivia night would be the perfect opportunity. She agreed to be my plus-one."

"I love that idea," I responded. "Casual, but fun."

"I think it's a great first date, which brings me to my problem of having nothing to wear. What are you wearing?"

I glanced down at my own outfit and shrugged. "Jeans and a cute top."

Rachel sighed. "Can you please be more specific? This is imperative."

I smiled. "Fine. Ankle-cut distressed jeans with light-brown Western-style booties and a silky mushroom-colored camisole top. I couldn't figure out my bra situation with the thin straps, so I opted to go without, but I brought a cardigan in case it gets chilly in there. I don't need my nipples broadcasting the temperature of the brewery to the entire town."

My over-the-top description earned a laugh from my friend. "Are you serious? No bra? I didn't think you had it in you. I'm proud of you, kid."

I laughed, glad the tension had eased out of her voice. "What can I say? I hate strapless. It was really just me being practical."

Rachel's hum buzzed over the phone. "Of course it was. Okay, I was thinking of going with a skirt, but since you're going more casual, I think I'm going to do the same. But I need to hurry! She's going to be here in a few minutes. Thanks, friend." Rachel ended with a smacking kiss noise on the other end of the phone.

"Good luck and have fun!" I encouraged. "I'll see you when you get here."

I smiled as I ended the call and slipped my phone into my brown leather cross-body bag. I glanced around and noticed a few cars had already started to fill the parking lot. An excited giddiness hummed through me.

As expected, the Bluebirds had pulled through and helped generate more buzz for the fundraiser. I gave polite smiles to a few familiar faces as I entered the brewery and stepped inside. MJ had arrived before me and was barking orders with a smile. I headed straight toward her.

"Am I late?" I grinned at MJ. It wasn't often someone beat me to an event.

"I didn't have a shift at the nursing home today. I got bored, so I opted to come early and make sure Abel wasn't terrorizing the staff."

I softened. "It was so kind of him to let us host the fundraiser here."

A crash startled us both, and we turned toward the bar. A blonde woman had dropped a glass, and it shattered across the pecan-colored wood floor. "Shit!"

"You good, Sloaney?" MJ asked.

The blonde's head whipped up, and she blew a strand

of hair from her face. "Yep. Just bobbled it." She was wiping splatters of liquid off her jeans with a white rag.

MJ squeezed my arm as she moved past me. "I'll find a broom."

Sloane, a server who worked at Abel's Brewery, laughed as she straightened. "Maybe try pulling the giant one out of Abel's ass."

MJ's eyes floated over Sloane's shoulder and went wide. In slow motion, Sloane turned to find her boss standing behind her with his arms crossed.

"I think I'll start checking people in," Sloane chirped and scurried away.

"I'll be on cleanup duty," MJ added with a laugh.

She bumped my elbow lightheartedly as she walked past in search of the broom.

I sized up Abel King. He had his brother beat in both height and bulk. There was a darker edge to him that hinted there was something a bit dangerous about him.

Never one to be intimidated, I smiled brightly and stuck out my hand. "Mr. King. I'm Emily Ward. I believe we spoke on the phone. I wanted to thank you in person for the use of your facility for our fundraiser."

"It's fine." His voice was quiet yet commanding as he briefly shook my hand.

Oookay . . . apparently he was also a man of few words.

"Well, it was very generous of you to donate the space. The foundation would have happily rented it, but we appreciate it nonetheless."

His hard eyes looked me over. "I said it's fine. It's for the kids, and extra traffic is always good for business."

Silence and tension hung in the air. I opened my mouth to speak but was unable to come up with anything to move the conversation forward. I landed on "Great."

Without so much as a nod, Abel turned and disappeared down a darkened hallway toward the back of the brewery.

"Don't mind Abe," MJ whispered from behind me, holding a broom. "There really is a good guy hiding beneath his gruff exterior." She looked affectionately at her oldest brother and shrugged. "At least I think so."

Her face scrunched, which broke the tension, and I laughed alongside her. MJ was funny and bubbly, and I felt a kinship developing between us.

It was kind of a shame I couldn't stop thinking about her brother and whether he might show up to the fundraiser. It seemed as though the whole town might turn out, but despite scouring the list of names, Whip's had not been one of them.

Refocusing, I smiled at MJ, who made quick work of sweeping up the broken glass. "Thanks for your help. I really couldn't have pulled this off without you and the Bluebirds."

She lifted her shoulders as if it were nothing at all to ask this of them. "It's what we do. Oh shoot, my brother is my plus-one, and he just walked in. I've got to get him his bracelet. Be right back!"

My pulse quickened, and my eyes went wide as she moved past me. I didn't actually know how many other King brothers there were, but I couldn't risk turning around and seeing Whip for the first time since he kissed the fuck out of me in my parents' driveway.

Instead, I chose the coward's way out and found the DJ so we could get the fundraiser started.

SIXTEEN

EMILY

Forty minutes in and the Forrest Grumps were absolutely *dominating* the competition. The team of eight elderly gentlemen looked unassuming, but their combined knowledge of pop culture references was astounding.

I hadn't intended to join a team, but MJ and Rachel insisted that I sit at the table with them, Brooklyn, and Whip. Rachel and Brooklyn sat next to each other with MJ across from the duo. I quickly took the seat next to Rachel to avoid any kind of proximity to Whip. I figured he would opt for the seat at the head of the high-top table. Instead he, of course, sat in the stool directly across from me.

The man was utterly confusing. First, he grabbed me in my parents' driveway and absolutely destroyed my panties with a soul-searing kiss; then he told me I wasn't worth it. Instead of stuffing it down and acting like it never happened like a *normal person would do,* he was staring at me. Sneaking glances and eyes that flicked from my eyes to my mouth to my tits and then back again. It was like he was interested but also beating himself up over it. I didn't have the energy to keep up.

I massaged the side of my neck and gave it a stretch as we waited for the next round to begin.

Rachel's forehead creased. "Something wrong with your neck?"

I stretched my neck from side to side. "Just a bit of whiplash, I think." I shot a pointed look across the table, and Whip ducked his gaze as he took a sip of his beer.

"You should see my masseuse, Ricardo. He's amazing with his hands," Rachel offered.

"That sounds perfect. Thanks." I flashed a demure smile, and when Whip shot me a fierce look, a hot rush moved down my thighs. My body hummed with awareness at his attention. Intentionally, I ignored his presence and focused my attention and enthusiasm on the rest of our table.

Whip scowled into his beer, and I allowed myself a smirk of satisfaction at pissing him off a little.

I bet Ricardo wouldn't tell me I'm not worth it.

The crowd around us was completely oblivious to our petty, silent bickering. They were engaged and rowdy, calling above the DJ, whooping and hollering as their teams earned points for correct answers. Abel King and a few servers worked the bar and ensured participants were never without a drink.

Sloane had worked our table, and her cheerful wink made me smile. She was sweet, and I promised myself I would ask MJ if she and Sloane would like to go out for coffee or drinks sometime. Making friends as an adult was awkward as shit, but if Outtatowner was going to become my home, I needed to get past any hang-ups of rejection.

As the night wore on, my competitive streak bloomed in full force. More than once I had to catch myself from glaring at tables that weren't taking it seriously. It became pretty clear that Phil and the Blanks were a team mostly there to pick up women. But I didn't care, because the purchase of their ticket only benefited the foundation.

When a break between rounds finally came and MJ disappeared for a bathroom break, I focused my attention on assessing the room. For each table, I had included a handwritten thank-you card detailing how their donations benefited the children of Outtatowner, along with other ways they might be able to help. Even the empty Cheese Balls tub used for additional donations was filling up quickly. Each group had also been given a small basket of snacks, provided by the foundation.

Across our high-top table, Whip caught my attention as his eyes flicked from me to the center of the table, where I had my eye on a small bag of pretzels. His hand reached out and snatched it.

What a jerk.

His eyebrow tipped up as he opened the bag and slid it across the table to me without a word. I scowled at him despite my growling stomach. Reluctantly, I plucked the bag off the table and diverted my attention to the DJ, who was announcing the next question just as MJ returned to her seat.

"First question of the round . . . What is the only planet to rotate on its side?" The music, which served as our timer, played in the background.

I perked up and spoke around my mouthful of pretzel. "Uranus."

Whip sat straighter and planted his hand on his chest. "My anus?"

I didn't *want* to laugh, so I concealed my cackle with a clearing of my throat. I shot him a bored look and flicked a pretzel in his direction as Brooklyn's laugh cracked above the crowd.

I swallowed down my mouthful of dry pretzels. "It's pronounced Yoor-ah-nis. Not *your-anus*." I shook my head. "Child."

Whip sent a playful look my way, and I coughed into my elbow to hide a grin.

Rachel narrowed her eyes on me as she wrote our answer on a slip of paper. "You're sure?"

"Sure. Sure." I nodded. In fact, I'd once had to talk with a few of my students about a particularly tasteless joke on the very topic.

"If you say so." Rachel folded our slip of paper and held it up. "Runner!" MJ hopped off her stool and took the paper toward the DJ as he counted down the last thirty seconds over the microphone.

Under the table, Whip's knee bumped mine, and I shifted in my seat to avoid contact. It was bad enough he smelled as good as he did and wouldn't stop looking at me with danger sparking in his eyes.

When the DJ announced the correct answer, our team cheered, and I added our points to the running total on the slip of paper I was using to keep track. "Okay." I looked at our team, imploring them to get serious. "If we get the next few correct, we might pull off second place. We'll need a miracle to beat the Forrest Grumps." I scanned the crowd, pleased everyone seemed to be having a great time. "And Victorious Secret is hot on our tails."

The team across the room included Tootie Sullivan and five other women, a few of whom I recognized from the Bluebirds meeting.

MJ laughed and reached across the table to steal my paper. "Relax, Emily. This is supposed to be fun."

"The *Warden*?" Rachel teased as she bumped me. "Have fun?"

I playfully snarled in her direction. "I know how to have fun," I insisted, signaling for MJ to hand the paper back. "I just don't want the Smarty Pints to win. *Smarty* my ass," I grumbled with a scowl. "I saw them using their phones to look up answers. That's cheating."

Whip's rumbling laughter filled the air, but I didn't get the sense he was laughing *at* me. It was more like he was enjoying himself despite the frosty attitude toward him I'd be harboring all evening.

"Shh, shh. Next question is coming." Brooklyn wound her arm around the back of Rachel's chair, and my cheeks pinched tight with a smile. It looked as though their first date was going really well, and I was so happy for my friend.

"Okay, teams, next question. What is a group of flamingos called?" The music started up again, this time an electric synth-pop song I didn't recognize.

I racked my brain but couldn't come up with a plausible answer.

"A murder?" MJ offered, but frowned at her own answer. "No, that's crows."

"Flock is too obvious, right?" Rachel asked the group.

"Forty seconds. Let's get those answers turned in!" the DJ crooned.

I opened my mouth, but no sound came out. My palms went up in defeat. "I got nothing . . . maybe just write down *flock*. A guess is better than not answering."

"It's a flamboyance." All eyes turned to Whip, who took a sip of his caramel-colored beer. He shrugged off the attention. "What?"

"You're sure?" I pressed, leaning forward across the table.

He set the glass down and twirled a finger in the air. "The songs. They're clues. If you listen to the lyrics, this one keeps saying something about being flamboyant."

We paused just long enough to hear the singer warble *you're so flamboyant* in the chorus.

Skepticism laced with angered disbelief in my voice. "The songs have been clues the entire time?!"

"Twenty seconds, ticktock!" The DJ clucked his tongue like a ticking clock.

"Who cares? Just write it down!" Brooklyn urged with a laugh as Rachel furiously wrote down our answer. MJ sprinted toward the DJ table, making it with a mere second left.

Sure as shit, Whip was right. A group of flamingos was, in fact, called a flamboyance. Which, when you really think about it, makes a lot of sense given their stylish pink feathers and statuesque, bendy legs.

After a few more rounds using Whip's correct assumption that the songs were subtle clues, our team—Four Gals and a Random Dude—eked out a respectable second-place finish.

To my surprise and delight, the Forrest Grumps not only donated their $100 first-place winnings, but matched it with an additional donation as well. Then Abel refused my offer to help clean up, assuring me that he needed the setup, given the influx of customers who were staying after trivia ended.

Rachel and Brooklyn's first date didn't seem to be ending anytime soon, and I had zero interest in being a third wheel, so I finished my drink and slid from the high stool. Whip had wandered off to mingle, and I forced myself to not track his movements.

I didn't care what he chose to do with his time. Not one bit.

With an exaggerated yawn, MJ stretched her arms above her head. "I'm hosed. Time to call it a night."

"Already?" Rachel asked.

MJ smiled. "Early shift tomorrow, but I'll text soon."

She slipped her purse over her head.

"I'm heading out too," I said, then waved goodbye to Rachel and Brooklyn. "Night, guys."

"Good night!" Rachel singsonged. She smiled, and as Brooklyn turned to face the bar, she let out a silent squeal and an *Oh my god!*

I held my hand to my head like a telephone and mouthed, *Call me!*

Together MJ and I walked into the darkened parking lot. Overhead lights illuminated the space, and the lulling crash of waves could be heard behind the building. Inky indigo clouds loomed above the water.

MJ wrapped me in an unexpected hug. "It was a great night."

Surprised, I laughed and hugged her back. "Thanks for your help."

"Anytime." She beamed at me as the first fat raindrops started to fall. "We should do this again sometime."

I smiled back, shielding my head with my hands. "I agree."

I quickly dug my keys out from my purse as I hustled to my car, hoping to dodge the bulk of the rain. Up to that point, the weather had held off, but it looked as though the storm was coming in strong.

My car beeped when I unlocked it, and I sat in the driver's side with a huff, shaking the droplets from my cardigan. I sighed into my seat.

It really was a good night.

When I went to start my car, nothing happened. I sat straighter. "What?" I leaned over to check and be sure nothing looked wrong, but when I pressed the ignition again, nothing happened. I stomped my foot on the brake and tried again. And again.

Still nothing. Just when things were looking up, the universe dragged me back to reality.

Defeated, I slumped my head back in my seat and let out an aggravated growl. A loud rap on my window had me clutching my chest and screaming.

On the other side, MJ held up her hands. "Sorry!" She laughed despite the sprinkling of rain falling onto her head. "Sorry. Everything okay?"

I tried to lower the window, but because my car was being a dick, nothing happened. Instead, I rolled my eyes and hauled my sorry ass out of the vehicle.

"I don't know what's going on. It won't start."

MJ's typically sunny features turned down into a frown. "Shoot. Well, I don't know anything about cars. Like, at all."

I laughed. "Me neither." I dug through my purse to find my phone. "It's fine. I can call someone to give me a ride."

Her hand clamped onto my forearm. "Don't be silly. Whip!"

My head shot up as MJ's arm waved wildly across the parking lot.

Hell. No.

"Hey!" she called out again. "We need some help over here."

My cheeks flushed, and I was thankful for the dim lighting in the parking lot. I stayed behind the open door of my car, the metal and glass acting as a form of protection against the way he swaggered across the pavement.

"Something's up with Emily's car. Can you help out?"

His brow furrowed, and I frowned at myself for the visceral reaction his grumpiness immediately caused.

"What's wrong with it?" he asked as soon as he was within earshot.

"I'm not sure," I offered reluctantly. "Won't start." Whip stared at me for a beat, so I scrambled. "It's fine. I'll call my dad and get a ride."

"Don't be silly." MJ laughed. "Whip, you can get her home, right?"

I stared a hole into the side of my new friend's face. Why couldn't *she* offer to drive me home? I swallowed hard as I waited for his answer.

He scrubbed a hand on the back of his neck, causing his biceps to bunch. "Uh, sure."

I shook my head. "I'll be fine, really."

He tipped his head toward the east end of the parking lot. "I'm parked over there," Whip ground out.

Unaware of the simmering tension between us, MJ grinned. "Thanks. I'll call you in a few days, Em. Night, guys!" When she turned, I swore I saw her wink, but dismissed it as the low lighting playing with my senses.

I closed the driver's-side door and relocked the car. Whip started across the parking lot, now dotted with moisture from fat raindrops, toward his pickup truck. When he moved toward the passenger side rather than his own driver's side, I paused.

He yanked the door open. When I didn't move, he let out an exasperated breath. "Get in the truck, Prim." His words were rough, like sandpaper gliding over my skin.

My bones melted, nearly sliding to the pavement in a puddle of hormones and *knowing*. By sheer force of will, I pulled myself into the cab of his truck. The door rattled as it closed, and I watched him as he rounded the hood in the rain and climbed behind the wheel.

Without a word, Whip started his truck, and the engine growled to life. After flipping the wipers on, he offered a three-finger wave over the steering wheel as he waited for a twosome to cross the lot. In silence we bumped along the road toward the main thoroughfare through town.

When the truck took an unexpected turn, I shifted in my seat. "Where are you going?"

"My place. Your car battery is probably dead, and I have a portable jumper in the shop."

Like a petulant child, I folded my arms in defiance, mostly to cover the fact that my nipples had formed into hard pebbles thanks to the chill of the rain. "You could have left me in the parking lot to wait for you to come back."

Whip scoffed but didn't take his eyes off the shadowy, winding road. "I'm not leaving you in the dark parking lot of a *bar*, Prim."

The protective edge in his voice sent a shiver down my back, and I pulled my cardigan tighter around my middle.

My movement caught his attention, and he switched on the heat, fiddling with the vent and pointing it in my direction. "Cold?"

"I'm fine," I lied. I was very much *not* fine. I was crawling out of my skin being so close to him. The cab of his truck shrank into a tiny bubble filled with his masculine scent and my needy, achy nipples.

His place.

Despite only ever being there once, it was chock-full of delicious, haunting memories. Memories I wished I could forget but at the same time didn't mind using to get myself off from time to time. I shifted in the seat as pressure bloomed between my legs.

Good grief.

I needed to get myself under control. Half the time we couldn't stand each other, and the rest of the time we were in the presence of my father.

The short drive to his home was spent in strained silence. When he pulled down his driveway, I exhaled a sigh of relief. I could get through this. As we pulled up to his house, Whip opened the large bay doors to the detached garage on his property rather than the one attached to his house.

Rain pattered against the windshield as he pulled into the open bay. After he put the truck in park, he glanced at my lips, then quickly darted away. "Be right back."

Warm light flooded the garage, illuminating the large space. I realized it wasn't a typical car garage, but rather a workshop of some kind. Exposed beams and wooden rafters framed the space. Wood projects—what looked like furniture mostly—were in various states of completion. I tried to marry the carefree, indifferent nature of the man I thought I knew with someone who could create something so beautiful and with such an attention to detail.

Curious, I exited the truck as Whip looked for the car battery jumper thing. The scent of freshly cut wood mingled with the earthy fragrance of varnish and filled my nose. The shop was bright and clean. Every tool was neatly organized on a huge workbench that ran the entire length of the back wall. In the center of the room stood a gorgeous table that looked as though it had been freshly sanded. It was long, big enough to accommodate at least eight, and had beautifully turned wooden legs.

I ran my hand across the pale, glass-smooth surface. The warmth of the wood seeped into my fingertips.

When I heard his footsteps behind me, I didn't look up. "It's gorgeous."

"Sure is." His deep voice caressed my skin.

I turned to find him staring at me. As if my attention startled him, he quickly turned and set a small machine in the back of his truck.

Awareness settled over me. Night and rain enveloped us in a cocoon of solitude. Here, on his property, there was no one to see us. No father or boss or ghosts from our past.

Just us.

I ran a hand down the unbuttoned edge of my cardigan, brushing the back of my fingertips across my nipple. I stared at Whip's chest as I gathered the courage to look him in the eye.

When I did, the fire in his burned back at me. His chest rose and fell with measured breaths.

"I don't understand you, Whip King." I surprised myself at how low and sultry the words came out.

He took a step closer to me—a predator stalking his prey. "What do you mean?"

"Just when I think I have you figured out, you surprise me." I took a step toward the workbench at the back of the shop and ran my hand over the cool metal of his tools. I shot a hot look over my shoulder. "I don't like things I can't figure out."

I turned, leaning against his workbench. Heat sizzled through me, and rain battered against the metal roof, drowning out the rest of the world.

"I never asked you to like me." He took another step forward, closing the distance between us.

My stomach quivered, and I lifted my chin in challenge. His hand moved to my hip and squeezed. I slid my palm up his chest. Another step and his body was flush against mine.

His hard length pressed against me as I was pinned between him and the workbench.

"No. You just asked me to beg." I lifted an eyebrow and watched his blue eyes darken.

His right hand slid from my hip up my chest and clasped around my throat. My head tilted back to maintain eye contact as my skin ignited.

"I like the way you whimper when I finally give you what you need." His hand faintly flexed around my throat. "You don't have to like me to let me praise how well you take my cock."

The tether of my control snapped at his promise. My grip on his shirt tightened as I pulled his mouth to mine.

SEVENTEEN

WHIP

THAT GODDAMN WOMAN made me lose every ounce of control. My mouth took hers, hot and savage. The whimper that escaped her throat only stoked the fire inside me as my tongue swept inside her mouth.

Hours sitting across from her at trivia night were pure torture. Anytime she wasn't looking, I was staring at her. My head knew it was a mistake to even *think* about Emily Ward, but just being in her presence was like a shot to the chest.

I couldn't think straight around her, and it pissed me off. I poured that anger and frustration into my kiss. Days —*weeks*—of pent-up frustration overwhelmed me. My hands roamed over her clothing. My head reared back, and heat coursed through me when I realized she wasn't wearing a bra beneath her silky top.

A sultry smirk flashed across her face as she licked her lip. A growl ripped through me, and I swiped a hand across the workbench, sending wood blocks and tools clattering to the ground. I gripped her hips, hauling her on top of the wooden surface.

My lips pressed against her neck, nipping and licking at her hammering pulse point. Her legs wrapped around me, digging her boots into my back and pressing me into her. I palmed her ass and ran a hand down the outside of her thigh.

I straightened, leveling with her. "Are we really doing this?" My thumbs strummed her hard nipples beneath her silky top.

She was breathless and keyed up. A hot flush crept across her cheeks and neck. "Yes. You can hate-fuck me if that's what you're asking."

My brows knit together. "Hate?" My palm ran down the column of her neck and gave it a testing squeeze, and her hips bucked forward. "Can't we just call it strong dislike fucking?"

Her breath hitched as her leg inched higher up my back. "I don't give a shit what you call it, just fuck me."

I leaned forward to growl in her ear. "Only if you say please, Prim. You know I like it when you beg for my cock." I nipped at her earlobe, earning me a small yip.

She reached between us, palming my erection through my jeans. "Oh my god, please. *Please.* I need you to fuck me."

I towered over her, standing tall to reach behind my head and pull my shirt off. Her nails raked down my chest. Her sandy-blonde hair fell over one eye as her hungry gaze roamed over my bare chest. Her cardigan had slipped off her shoulders and hung around her elbows. The dainty straps of her top looked thin enough to break, and I resisted the urge to slip a finger beneath one and tug.

Instead, I grabbed two handfuls of ass and hauled her against me. Her arms looped around my shoulders. Swiveling, I shifted toward the unfinished table at the center of my workshop. The freshly sanded surface would be gentler on her skin and give me ample room to worship her for as long as I wanted.

I was overwhelmed by her. Our hands tore at clothing—I pulled off her boots; she yanked at the button of my jeans; I peeled hers down her thighs. When we were both naked, my hand skated across her smooth skin. She braced her arms behind her, baring every inch to me. I moved my mouth down her throat. She tipped her head and sighed when I sucked the hollow of her collarbone.

Emily reached between us, gripping my hard cock in her hands. My dick pulsed, and she purred, sliding her fingers across the rows of piercings. She rubbed her thumb over the tip, and I groaned.

"I like this," she whispered as her fingertips skated over each barbell on the underside of my cock. "Is it for you or for me?"

I glanced down, giving her a smug look. "Both." Her gaze was locked on me as I continued: "There's increased sensation for me, sure. But the real treat is watching your pussy struggle to take all of me and still feeding you another inch."

"Jesus, fuck." Her hips bucked and her head lolled as I slipped my hand between her thighs. I caressed her with soft, gentle strokes but didn't enter her. Not yet.

Emily rocked her hips over my hand and whimpered. Her sex glistened, primed and waiting for me to fuck her. I slid one finger inside her and pressed the heel of my hand against her clit. She leaned back, bracing herself on her elbows as I slipped another finger in. My dick throbbed at the sight of Emily sprawled across my table while I finger-fucked her.

I ached to be inside her. "Don't. Move." My eyes flashed

a warning as I slipped my fingers from her and tortured myself with a taste.

Thankfully, she listened and stayed where she was while I strode to my truck to dig a condom out from the glove box. I'd stashed a few there after I'd almost lost control and nearly railed her against the car in her parents' driveway.

Still sprawled for me, she watched as I rolled the condom down my length. She was breathless and waiting. "It's annoying how fucking hot you are."

I panted as I took in the view of her. "How do you think I feel? I'm risking everything because I can't stay the fuck away from you."

Tension bunched in my back. I was going to die if I didn't bury myself inside her. Gripping my dick, I gave myself a few hard tugs to release some of the tension. She opened her knees wider.

My eyes flicked up to hers. "Don't tease me, Prim."

I lowered my mouth to her breast, teasing her with my tongue. My other hand dragged my cock against her spread legs, teasing her entrance. I sucked and gently used my teeth to torment her. Her arms trembled.

I pressed the head of my cock against her opening.

"Whip. Please." Her thighs clenched, begging for more.

I slid the head of my cock into her tight, wet cunt and paused. My breath hissed through my teeth as a shock wave coursed through me. Heat gathered in my spine. My body screamed to thrust deep and rail her fast and hard and angry.

Instead, I stilled and watched her stretch around me. "Jesus, this has never felt better. More?"

She swallowed hard and nodded. I gave her another inch, slipping the first set of barbells inside her. Her hips shifted upward, begging for even more of me. I dragged out, torturously slow before going deeper.

"Yes. Yes," she panted. "That's what I needed."

I gripped the base of my cock, willing myself not to come too quickly. "That's not even half, Prim. You need to relax so I can stuff you full. I need to go deeper." The rope of my control was fraying at the ends. I gritted my teeth as her pussy clenched and stretched around me. "You can take it."

Her breath hitched as her knees widened. She moaned and relaxed enough for me to feed her another inch. "Good fucking girl." I massaged her thigh as I eased the rest of the way inside her. I paused when I was buried to the hilt. "Fuck, Em."

"I'm so full. Holy shit."

Still gripping her thigh, I shifted my hips. Her body tightened before she began to relax. Her jaw hung open, and I could envision her just like this—sprawled open as I painted her pretty mouth and tits with my cum.

"I need to move, baby. Are you okay?" My hands moved delicately over her breasts and stomach. I used my fingers to tease her clit and feel where she stretched around me.

Her pussy throbbed. "Yes. Are you?"

"God, you feel so good."

Emily rocked her hips, and a wicked grin flashed across her face. Gone was the prim little librarian, and in her place was a sexy little tease who was begging to be fucked. A switch flipped inside me, and my body roared to life.

I surged forward, pressing my cock as deep as it would go, and covered her body with mine. I pinned her with my hips and grabbed her wrists, planting them above her head.

I drove into her with deep, powerful thrusts. I let her sharp intakes of breath and the grind of her hips guide my pace. I was rough and commanding, but she met me stroke for stroke.

Heat and tension built at the base of my spine. Fucking her hard and watching as her tits bounced in time was pure torture. I ground the base of my cock against her clit and felt her entire body tense. She tugged to free her arms, but I held them firmly in place. Her pussy was a vise around my cock, and my vision blurred with heat and intensity.

Then I felt it.

Deep and rhythmic pulses around my cock as her orgasm broke free. I let go of one wrist and pinched a nipple between my fingers, rolling and tugging every drop from her. She swore, cried out, and cursed my name. My name on her lips was all it took, and my cock thickened and pulsed. Two more hard pumps and I was exploding inside her. My entire body quivered as she milked every last drop from me. My hands slid over warm, sweat-slicked skin.

Emily hummed and went limp beneath me. Sweaty strands of hair clung to her forehead. My still-hard cock could have stayed buried in her for an eternity, but I gripped myself at the base around the condom and slowly slipped from inside her.

She exhaled and rested the back of her hand against her forehead. "What the hell was that?"

I chuckled and moved to grab some shop towels to clean her up. "Hate fucking, I guess."

Wobbly, she propped herself up, unashamed of her own nakedness. "Told you it was hot."

Charmed, I surged forward, gripping the back of her neck and kissing her swollen lips. I didn't have it in me to say it definitely was *not* hate fucking. Instead, I helped her clean up and disposed of the condom before redressing.

As I slipped my shirt over my head, I looked around the

shop. It was a total disaster. I sighed and raked a hand through my hair. On the table, in a light coating of sawdust, was Emily's ass print.

Her gaze followed mine, and her sharp peal of laughter filled the garage. "Oh my god." She laughed again and moved toward the table, hand lifted.

I caught her wrist. "Don't you fucking dare." I smirked down at the perfect peach-shaped mark. "That stays."

"Ugh. Why are you so in love with me?" She chuckled and rolled her eyes before shaking out her discarded cardigan. "I guess the sex was worth it after all," she teased.

My mouth went dry, and a lump formed in my throat. There was no universe in which I was allowed to fall for Emily Ward, but her words were a punch to my chest. Sure, she was hilarious and strong willed and the best lay of my life, but love? No fucking way. Not in this lifetime.

I looked at her with all the sincerity I could muster. She deserved to know it. "You're worth it, Prim."

Emily blushed and turned from me as though my words were too much, too soon. She stood at the threshold of the open garage door and looked out into the rain. Her hair was mussed, and her feet were bare, but there was no denying that she was the prettiest woman I'd ever seen.

She peered into the blackness as sheets of rain poured down. "I think this storm is here to stay."

I hadn't even noticed the flashes of lightning and low rumble of thunder in the distance. I had been too consumed with *her*.

I dragged a hand across my scruff. "Looks like it."

Her hand delicately rested on the bed of my truck. "I'm too keyed up to go back and figure out what's wrong with my car. Want to hang out for a while?"

I considered her proposition. "Hang out. Like . . . friends?"

Her laughter rang out. "Well, I don't know what kind of friends you have, but I've never done *that* with any of my friends." She circled her finger toward the table.

I grinned. "Fair enough."

"You know what I've always wanted to do?" She tipped her head in thought.

"What's that?"

"Sit in the back of a truck bed and look at the stars. Like in the movies."

I smiled at how in a matter of moments she could shift from intoxicating sex kitten to irresistibly cute. "I don't think you're going to see any stars tonight, but hang tight."

I quickly moved to the metal locker on the side of the garage and pulled out a large wool blanket. After removing the car battery jumper, I carefully laid the blanket in the back of my truck.

I tapped the bed twice with my hand. "Load up."

In a surprising and swift movement, Emily planted one foot on the tire of my truck and maneuvered herself into the truck bed, settling her back against the cab. I grabbed a second blanket for her legs on the off chance the rain made her chilly. Then I climbed in and sat beside her.

Her arm rested against mine, and she made no attempt to scoot away. I relaxed and watched the storm roll in. With Emily at my side, I felt good.

Too good.

And I didn't know what the hell to do about that.

EIGHTEEN

EMILY

LISTENING to the rain and thunder in the bed of Whip's truck was surreal. My body hummed with the kind of satisfaction that came only from incredibly good sex. At least, that was what I could *imagine* given I had never, ever had sex like that before.

Well . . . before Whip at least.

My body ached in the most delicious way, and despite the throb between my legs, I already itched for another round. Sex with Whip was making me delirious, especially given the fact I was somehow considering him a *friend* of sorts.

The musical patter of rain on the metal roof was soothing. My feet bounced to the faint rhythm. "So you're a . . . firefighter."

Whip chuckled at the way the word *firefighter* dripped with derision.

He glanced at me, unamused. "Glad you're able to keep up."

His gentle ribbing caused a giggle to bubble up inside

me. I nudged him. "No, I know you're a firefighter. Obviously. But . . . why?"

He shrugged. "Why not?"

My face twisted as I studied him. "Well, it's dangerous, for one. Plus, the hours are weird."

He nodded. "We're a small community, so we double up—firefighters and EMTs. That keeps things interesting." He shrugged. "I kind of just fell into it. And in a small town it's not as dangerous as you think. The weird hours give me time to do something else."

"Like making furniture?" I asked.

"Exactly." Whip stared into the darkness. It was obvious he didn't often talk about himself.

I tilted my head, genuinely curious. "Which do you like better—being a firefighter or an EMT?"

He scoffed lightly. "I guess no one ever asked."

I shrugged. "Well, I'm asking. Is it because you love the adrenaline of battling a blaze, or is it something else?"

Whip eyed me carefully as if he was measuring his words. Our relationship had been contentious at best, and I was his boss's daughter, directly asking him about his work.

Finally, he answered. "I wanted to become an EMT."

When I looked at him with hopeful eyes, urging him to continue, he crossed his bare feet and settled in. "I was on this snowboarding trip my senior year of college when I split from the group to try a side of the mountain I'd never boarded. It was risky, going alone, but I didn't care."

Whip's eyes stared into the rain as if he was lost in thought, recalling that day. "It was an epic run. The snow was fresh and deep in the backcountry. I was cruising through these narrow clumps of trees when something caught my eye. I stopped and looked back, and my stomach dropped when I realized it was the blue tip of a snowboard peeking out from the snow."

"Holy shit." My eyes were wide as I inched forward, entranced by his story.

"Yeah. It was bad. I knew in my gut someone was likely buried in the snow, but I had no idea how long they'd been there. I was pretty convinced I was about to uncover a dead body. My heart was pounding. I had a hard time moving through the deep snow, but I went as fast as I could, using my board to pull me forward. When I got to him, I just started digging."

My fingers pressed to my lips. "Was he dead?"

He shook his head. "Shockingly, no. I cleared snow from his mouth and nose, and he was conscious. Alive and alert. His friends had been radioing him on a walkie-talkie, but his arms were pinned by the snow. He'd fallen into a tree well, and the more he moved, the harder the snow packed around him."

"You saved his life." An ache in my chest bloomed. *Whip really is a hero.*

"Yeah, I did. But he saved mine, too, in a way. After we got him down off the mountain and my pulse went back to normal, I knew exactly what I wanted to do. I finished business school just to have the degree and appease my father, but then I turned around and figured out how to become an EMT."

I shook my head and smiled softly at my lap.

"What's funny?"

I shifted to look at him. Something was changing between us, and while I didn't know exactly what to do about it, I liked it. "It's just a great story. Full of danger and adventure and a really happy ending."

I sighed, closed my eyes, and rested against the back

window of the truck. I could still feel his eyes studying my face, so I peeked at him from under one lash before closing it again. "My life is not dangerous or adventurous, and based on how things have been going? I'm not sure if I will eventually get that happy ending." Embarrassed that I'd phrased things that way, I turned my head and smiled at him.

He lifted a shoulder. "The night's still young." A smile eased across his face. "Maybe after another orgasm or two, you'll think differently about it."

He leaned in, crowding my space. His lips were surprisingly soft and gentle as he peppered kisses at the corners of my mouth. My body hummed to life.

I pressed my hand against his chest. "What are we doing, Whip?"

His eyes searched mine, and he frowned. "Is this the *What are we?* talk?"

"No." I playfully pushed him. "Yes? Not really. It's the *How do we keep doing this without ruining both our lives?* talk."

He bit back a grin. "So you want to keep doing this?"

I shot him a plain look and then filled my lungs before putting on an air of nonchalance. "I mean . . . you're not *terrible* in bed." I shrugged. "I guess we could keep doing it."

He grinned and inched closer. "Oh, I'm not terrible? Is that right?"

I pressed my back into the cab of the truck, easing away. "I've had worse." Laughter threatened to spill out of me, but I reined it in.

His brows shot up. "You've had worse?" His fingers pressed into my sides, tickling me as he pulled me closer. A delighted shriek burst out of me, and I crumpled to the truck bed in a fit of giggles.

"Stop! No tickling! That's cheating!" I could barely breathe, I was giggling so hard.

His teasing laughter folded over me, wrapping me in warmth as his body covered mine. "Say it." His fingers danced over my ribs. "Say you think my dick is pretty."

The ridiculousness of his request sent me over the edge into a full-blown fit of raucous laughter. Tears pricked my eyes as I lost it. Trying to regain composure, I squirmed beneath him, feeling his cock thicken between us.

"Fine!" I shouted into the air. "You're better than average."

Whip maneuvered me under him, pinning me down with his hips. "You're a brat."

I rolled my lips together, defiance flashing in my eyes. When he motioned to tickle me again, I held up my hands. "I love your dick!"

With a satisfied smile, Whip sat back on his heels. He cupped a hand by his ear. "I'm sorry. What was that? I didn't catch that last part."

I propped myself up on my elbows but didn't move away. My hips pressed against him, and my thighs draped over his. We were both breathless and laughing. "I said, 'I love your dick.' Happy?"

Whip's grin was wide and white. "Very." He pulled my hips impossibly closer as his hands slipped up my top and settled on my ribs. "I think everything about you is perfect."

His eyes roamed over me. Tingling flooded my system. How many times had I been told by Craig that I didn't quite measure up? How many times did I nearly break to be the best student, the best teacher, the best *everything* just to feel good enough?

After a lifetime of not belonging, Whip had an effortless way of making me feel *seen*. It was unnerving. Addicting.

He was the kind of man I was certain could destroy me, but there was something about him that I couldn't stay away from.

The rational, overachieving part of my brain couldn't out-logic the hope that bloomed inside me whenever we locked eyes. I was always the woman who got shit done—the good girl who followed the rules. But for once I wanted to break every rule I'd ever put into place. The only good girl I wanted to be was *his*.

Emotions rolled through me, but I tried to play it off as casually as I could. "Let's just keep this between us, okay?"

A wicked grin spread across Whip's face. "I can do that."

I planted my hands on his shoulders. "We can't tell anyone—and I mean, *no one*."

Dark desire swirled in his eyes. "I'm good with that. Besides, a public spectacle isn't really my thing."

I cocked an eyebrow, hoping to hammer home my point. "So you agree, then? Friends?"

"I'd say friends is a stretch after what I just did to you but . . . yeah. Something like that." His words washed over me, sending tingles from my toes to my scalp. Then he growled as he hiked my hip higher and pinned me to the bed of his truck with a kiss.

NINETEEN

WHIP

I DIDN'T DESERVE a woman like Emily Ward. That was a fact. But when she looked up at me with a mixture of hope and desire in her eyes, I was a fucking goner.

It didn't matter that she was the sexiest woman I'd ever known. She was rigid and stubborn, but I was the lucky son of a bitch who got to see her unravel. It was the most beautiful thing I'd ever witnessed.

After we'd fucked—again—in the back of my truck, I tucked her into my side as we watched the rain clouds start to dissipate. I wasn't typically a cuddler, and it was unnerving how perfectly she fit into the nook of my arm.

I glanced at the clock in the garage, and Emily noticed where my attention landed. I looked down at her. "It's getting late."

The dreamy, half-asleep look on her face snapped to a hard frown as she stiffened. "Oh. Right. I guess I should go." She barely looked up at me as she shifted from my embrace. "I need to get my car."

I squeezed her shoulder, willing her to relax. "It's late.

Abel will have closed the brewery already. Your car will be fine in the parking lot until morning."

She toyed with her lip and met my eyes. "It's just . . . if someone sees it, they might tell my dad. He'll worry and likely send out the cavalry."

I considered her logic for a moment. In Outtatowner, gossip spread faster than butter on hot toast. Still, I wasn't ready for our night to be over. Emily was someone who appreciated directness, so I figured it was time to quit fucking around.

I frowned down at her. "I want you to stay."

"Oh." The tiny smile at the corner of her mouth gave her away. "Okay, sure."

With a nod, I carefully stood and hopped from the truck bed. I stretched my back, and despite the padding of the blanket, I could tell my back and knees were going to feel like shit in the morning.

I held out a hand for Emily. She slipped hers in mine and gracefully hopped out of the back of the truck. "What's wrong, old man? Can't keep up?"

My face twisted. "Old man? I'm not that old." Her brows crept up her forehead as she stared at me. I rolled my eyes. "Whatever. I am not old."

Her chuckle danced over my shoulder as I headed toward the main house. It was the prettiest sound in the world, even if it was making fun of me.

Emily trotted to keep up. "Well, how old are you, anyway?"

"Does it matter?" I looked down at her, fishing my keys out of my pocket.

She shrugged. "I guess not. Just curious."

I put the key into the lock and paused. "I'm fifty-two."

The shock flashed across her face, and I couldn't hold in my laughter. "I just turned thirty-one."

Emily let out a relieved exhale. "Oh. Cool. Great. I'm twenty-five."

"Relieved you're not banging an old man?" I teased as the door opened with a soft thud, and then I stepped aside for her to walk in.

Without missing a beat, Emily breezed past me. "You *are* an old man."

I slapped her ass as she crossed the threshold and was rewarded with a giggling yelp. Once inside, I flipped on a few lights. Warm light flooded my home. Emily took a few steps in, looking around as she went deeper inside.

The living room unfolded in warm hues and sturdy wooden accents that reflected my home's Craftsman style. Emily brushed her fingertips along the arm of a leather chair before walking toward the fireplace. It was masculine and simple, but it was home. I tried to read her expression as she turned in a circle, taking in my sanctuary.

"This is beautiful, Whip." She smiled in front of the handcrafted wooden bookshelves that flanked the fireplace. "Did you read all these?"

I enjoyed watching Emily take in my space as if it were the first time she was there—which, given her hasty exit the first time, I guess made sense. Humbled to have her appreciate my home, I tucked my hands into my jeans. "Not yet."

"This view." Emily turned toward the picture window that framed views of the wooded landscape barely visible in the darkness. She turned and grinned. "I did not expect this."

I narrowed my eyes at her. "What did you expect? Milk crate end tables and a mattress on the floor?"

She giggled. "I mean . . . kind of." She waved a hand in front of her. "That would be very on brand for a firefighter."

I grinned and closed the gap between us in two strides. "Well, maybe I'm not like every firefighter you know."

She tipped her chin to look at me. "And I guess I'm not like every librarian *you* know."

My eyes flashed with humor. "See. I knew there was a librarian hidden in there somewhere." I flicked the end of her upturned nose and smiled.

When her stomach audibly grumbled, I grabbed her hand and pulled her toward the kitchen.

There, the craftsmanship continued with custom oak cabinets and a meticulously tiled backsplash. The farmhouse sink, with its gleaming white porcelain, overlooked a garden where I had planted a variety of vegetables. Blueberry fields stretched beyond my property line and faded into the horizon.

A pendant light cast a warm ambiance and illuminated a handcrafted dining table surrounded by Craftsman-style chairs, each bearing the hallmarks of a woodworker in training. None of them matched, as I was testing out different styles when I made them, and they were far from perfect, but they were mine.

Emily surprised me by hopping up onto the counter. I moved to position myself between her knees. Her fingertips laced as her arms draped over my shoulders. "Make yourself at home," I teased.

"I like your place." She grinned. "It's so . . . you."

I nosed the column of her neck and inhaled her subtly sweet and feminine scent. "Thanks."

"Did you build it?"

She hummed when I gently kissed her heated skin. "No, but I've enjoyed remodeling it. Making it mine." I scraped my teeth against her collarbone, earning a delighted shiver. "I like making things mine."

Her breathy laugh shot heat straight to my groin. "I can see that."

I reared back to search her eyes, possessiveness surging through me. "Are you mine, Prim?"

Bratty defiance glimmered in her sea-blue eyes as her eyebrow arched. "For now."

My palms ran up her thighs and squeezed. "For now." I hated the sound of it but appreciated a good challenge. "Let's get you something to eat."

I turned from her, already missing the warmth of her skin, and examined what I had in the fridge. Without looking at her, I scanned for ingredients. "I know it's late but how does shrimp scampi sound?"

"Ha!" she barked. "I was expecting peanut butter and jelly or something. Scampi sounds incredible. It's not too much work?"

I pulled a few items from the fridge and dumped them on the large kitchen island. *For you? Of course not.* I leveled her with my gaze. "It's not too much work."

Emily hopped off the counter and joined me by the island, picking through the ingredients. "Okay, how can I help? I'm not much of a cook, but I can follow directions."

"Stop." I placed my hands on hers. "Just let me cook for you."

Her eyes softened and went wide. It didn't take much to see that Prim was always busy—hustling to be useful and at the top of her game. For once, I just wanted her to *relax*.

I gripped her hips and hauled her up onto the island. I pointed a finger. "Sit."

She threw up a jaunty salute. "Yes, sir."

I smirked and crowded her space. "Careful. I might like

that a little too much." Opening the drawer beside her legs, I lifted out a pair of tongs and clapped them in her direction. "Just talk to me."

Emily toyed with her lip as her eyes moved over the simple ingredients on the counter—shrimp, butter, garlic, lemon, parsley. Her hands itched to mess with them. "Talk to you . . ."

Clearly it was a challenge for her to sit still. Shaking my head, I pulled some orzo from the cabinet and smiled as I filled a large pot with water. "Tell me about work. How's Michael been?"

She relaxed with a sigh. "Michael has been good. No more incidents. Work is . . ." A furrow deepened between her eyes. "It's okay."

I paused and turned down the heat on my skillet. "Just okay?"

"I kind of got into a little trouble," she admitted.

I hummed as I added butter to the skillet and let it melt, then moved to salt and pepper the shrimp. Keeping my attention on the food rather than her seemed to help her feel more at ease.

"I did a thing," she continued. I raised my gaze to let her know I was listening. "There is this kid in my class, Robbie. He's a great kid—creative and kind, but a little bit of an outcast. Middle school is tough."

I turned the heat down on my skillet and inverted my plate so all the shrimp hit the pan at the same time. "What's his last name?"

"Lambert."

I frowned down at the shrimp and started flipping them.

"You know the family?" she asked. "The dad is—"

"An asshole with a chip on his shoulder," I supplied.

Emily chuckled. "Yep."

I focused my attention on her. "Did he do something to you?"

Her smile softened. "No, nothing like that. I just noticed that Robbie was coming to school with shoes that were falling apart. So I got him a new pair."

A pain poked me in the chest. "That was kind of you."

"Yeah, well, no good deed goes unpunished, apparently. His dad forced him to return them to me, and then he stormed into the office threatening my principal. I was accused of 'special treatment' and basically got a slap on the wrist for it."

I added garlic and let the shrimp sizzle. "That doesn't sound too bad then. It's a shame that the kid has to suffer because his dad won't accept someone else's help, though."

"Exactly! I just hate that this year isn't going as I expected, you know? I really want Principal Cartwright to see that I'd be perfect for a full-time position."

I carefully plucked each shrimp from the hot skillet and set them on a clean plate while I worked on the sauce. Adding lemon juice and chicken stock, I scraped a wooden spoon across the skillet.

Emily inhaled. "Oh my god, that smells good. Where did you learn how to cook?"

Pride swelled in my chest. Somewhere along the line I enjoyed Emily's praise just as much as I enjoyed poking at her. "Picked it up at the fire station. We all take turns making meals, and there are bragging rights involved." A thought sparked as I moved to drain the cooked pasta. "So you got in trouble because Robbie was the only one who needed the shoes?"

Emily considered. "I mean, there are other kids in the school who need things like shoes or clothes, but essentially because Robbie was the only one who *got* this so-called special treatment, I got reprimanded for showing favoritism or some bullshit."

"Got it." I bit back a grin as a plan bloomed in my mind. "Why don't you let me take care of it?"

She looked at me with an expression of skepticism mixed with disbelief. "What do you mean?"

I added the drained pasta to the broth mixture in the skillet, then tossed in lemon zest, a bit more butter, and the shrimp. I tossed the dish together before grabbing two pasta bowls from the cabinet. Mischief danced in my eyes as my plan solidified. "I don't want you to worry about anything other than eating."

I heaped a portion of shrimp scampi into a bowl and lifted it for her. "Deal?"

Her eyes fluttered closed as she inhaled the rich, buttery smell. Her eyes opened and she lifted a brow. "There's a lot of garlic in that. Are you still going to want to kiss me after?"

I laughed and planted a smacking kiss on her lips. "Honey, I plan to do a whole lot more than just kiss you, and I'm eating it too. Besides, I have an extra toothbrush if that will make you feel better."

Pink splotches bloomed on her neck and cheeks when I gave her a wink and clinked my fork against hers. Still sitting on my kitchen island, Emily devoured the shrimp scampi.

I watched her scoop portions of pasta and shrimp past her lips, the slick butter making them irresistible. We laughed and talked about everything and nothing in the warm glow of my kitchen.

I wondered if she felt the same shift I did—that somehow we'd gone from going at each other's throats to going at each other's clothing without missing a beat. I certainly wasn't mad at it.

Absently, I rubbed the ache that formed in the center of my chest, knowing it would only get worse when she finally walked out.

TWENTY

EMILY

WITH A BELLY FULL of the most delicious shrimp scampi I'd ever had, I dipped into the bathroom attached to Whip's primary bedroom. His room was masculine and held the scent of clean laundry mixed with his cologne.

Despite my teasing, I didn't really expect to see milk crate end tables and a mattress on the floor, but I definitely did not anticipate seeing how effortlessly put together his home was. Admittedly, the first time I'd been in his home, I hadn't really taken it in—we'd been too busy tearing our clothes off.

But now that I had the opportunity to really look around, it screamed masculine coziness. In the primary suite, the headboard of his bed was a work of art with its wood grains and elegant lines. It stood as the centerpiece beneath the vaulted ceiling lined with heavy wood beams. Muted tones and carefully chosen textiles created an atmosphere of quiet strength, while the rhythmic creak of a ceiling fan echoed the coastal breeze that filtered through the open windows.

I inwardly groaned at the thought of my own budget

linens and haphazardly chosen duvet. It was *fine* but certainly not curated like Whip's house appeared to be. While I brushed my teeth, I made a mental note to update my bedding on the off chance Whip and I spent some time at my apartment.

Looking around the gleaming, oversize bathroom vanity, I doubted that was necessary. Going to my place would also mean risking someone seeing his truck and finding out about us—something I was still unwilling to do.

This was supposed to be fun. Casual. I couldn't let the sexy way his eyes darkened when he saw me derail my entire life.

You can do casual.

I stared at my reflection and fluffed my hair before adjusting my boobs in my top. All I needed to do was focus on having fun, and sex with Whip was a *whole lot* of fun.

I stopped at the doorway to the bathroom and looked into his room. He'd lit a few candles and pulled back the navy sheets on his bed. Whip was removing his watch and placing it on a tray on his dresser when he turned to me.

My heart stuttered.

Casual. Casual. Casual.

I swallowed hard and offered a sultry smile before closing the space between us.

~

I LOOKED at the neat rows of empty desks in my classroom, and my eyes filled with tears. I had done it. The kids had lost all interest in school the last few weeks, but we'd limped along and made it to the end of the school year. While my students were in PE, I prepped for one final hour with them as my students.

My classroom was quiet—no scuffing shoes, no scrape of a chair against the linoleum, no raucous laughter interrupting my lesson. My first assignment as a teacher in Outtatowner was officially coming to a close.

"It's amazing, isn't it?" Rachel's voice startled me, and I dipped my head to hide the wave of emotions I was feeling.

I grunted to unclog my throat and swiped under my eyes. "Hey." I offered her a watery smile, and she kicked off the doorjamb and walked toward me. Her arms wrapped around me and squeezed.

"It's always a wonder how we make it through, wishing summer would come, and as soon as it does? I immediately miss them." She squeezed my shoulder and sucked in a breath. "At least the smell is still with us."

I let my head fall to her shoulder and released a weak laugh. The stench of pubescent teens was *ripe*, and from April until now, we had practically needed gas masks to survive.

"It really is something. They were driving me bonkers all week, and then today I found myself wishing the clock would slow down."

"When you see them next year, they'll be a foot taller."

An ache pinched in my chest. Hedging my bets, I had put in several applications at schools in the surrounding area, but it was slim pickings given the low turnover in small towns. Worry flashed through my mind. *Where will I be next year?* "I hope I get the chance to see that."

Rachel released me from her hug. "Didn't you hear?" My brows pinched. "It's official. Jenny Kirk isn't coming back."

I searched her face for the truth. "Seriously?"

Her grin expanded. "Seriously. Rumor is that she told Principal Cartwright this morning that she plans to stay home with her kids. Her resignation is official as of today."

Hope and excitement sparked under my skin. My gaze flitted around my classroom.

Rachel bumped my shoulder as children's voices grew louder in the hallway. "So maybe don't pack up the classroom quite so soon."

I swallowed hard and smiled. "Maybe I won't."

"Bro!" Michael Marsh stopped midway through the door and gestured toward the whiteboard where I had written their final assignment. "What's this?"

I arched an eyebrow. "Bro?"

His sheepish grin nearly made me smile. "Miss Ward." He tipped his head. "Come on." His charming smile didn't work on me, but that didn't stop him from trying. "An essay? It's ninth period and practically summer break!"

I glanced at my handwriting on the whiteboard and smiled. "We've spent all semester building our classroom community. A part of that is expressing gratitude. Once we finish the assignment, we'll do one last exit dance party, and you'll finally be rid of me."

I winked at Michael, and he grinned. My throat grew tight as I tried to find excitement in the prospect of the school year ending. The students filed in, and I took my position at the head of the classroom. I pressed play for gentle background music to softly flow from the classroom speakers.

"Please take out your gratitude journals and flip to a fresh page." My eyes roamed over my students, doing my best to commit each one to memory. I pointed at the prompt. "Sit quietly with yourself. Take a deep breath. Close your eyes if that feels good to you." At this point, nearly every student closed their eyes and relaxed. We had come so far in such a short amount of time. "When was the last time you felt truly peaceful? Who were you with? What were you doing? Take two minutes to let the memory play in your mind like a movie."

I glanced around. Even Michael's health-care aide was standing in the back of the room with her eyes closed. I allowed mine to shut. I took a deep breath.

Warmth washed over me as the memory of Whip's embrace flooded my mind. I had been surprised to discover he was a cuddler. I was not. By nature anything that kept me from moving forward was inherently uncomfortable, but somehow the strength and warmth of his arms around me allowed me to melt into him and just *be*.

"Now open your eyes and try to capture that moment on your paper." Dreamy expressions and soft smiles morphed into concentrated furrows as my students followed my instructions. Gratitude journaling had been something that was outside of the curriculum, but I'd woven it into our lessons, and I hoped it had made a significant impact on my students, even if they didn't continue the practice after this year.

Movement at my doorway caught my attention. Mrs. Kuder scowled at me. I paced toward the door. "Afternoon. Can I help you?"

She gestured toward the rolling cart behind her. "You have a delivery."

I glanced at the cart. Boxes were stacked on it. "I do?"

"Every classroom is getting a delivery, but there are special instructions that this box goes to *you*."

Curiosity piqued, I gestured for her to enter. "Come on in. Thank you."

She grumbled, undeterred by my friendliness. Apparently she was still salty about me taking over the educational foundation.

Whatever.

She could be mad all she wanted. With my help—and that of the Bluebirds, of course—the foundation had raised more money in a few short months than they had in the last four years *combined*. Plus, we hadn't even hosted the carnival yet.

The top box on her cart had the words *Miss Ward* written in neat, blocky handwriting. I looked at Mrs. Kuder. "Where did these come from?"

The deep wrinkles around her mouth deepened. "The firehouse did a charity drive. Each classroom in the whole school is getting something." She shook her head in disbelief. "Every kid. Can you believe it?"

My heart flopped over with a splat. *Why don't you let me take care of it?* Whip's words echoed in my mind. Could it be?

I blinked and refocused my attention as my excitement grew. "Thank you."

With a harrumph and a swat of her hand, our grumpy librarian exited the classroom. I took the box marked with my name to my desk. Using scissors, I carefully cut open the tape. On top, there was a white envelope with the word *Prim* written with the same masculine handwriting.

I looked around and despite a few curious glances, my students were still working on their journaling. I slipped my finger under the seal and pulled a note from inside the envelope.

Prim,

I told you I'd take care of it, and I did. The Outtatowner Emergency Services Department is happy to provide various items to make each student's summer a little brighter.

You can thank me by meeting me at Trawler's Cove at 7 p.m. tonight.

The note was unsigned, but I knew exactly who it was from. My face lit up. Beneath the note, on top of the pile of items, were a pair of men's size 9 Nikes—an exact match to the pair I had attempted to give Robbie.

How in the world had he . . . ?

The gentle trill of my timer went off. My head whipped up, and I stuffed the note into my desk drawer. Several students continued to finish their journaling while others sank back into their chairs.

I stopped the timer and music, glancing at the clock. "Well, class, we have an unexpected development. Before we do our final exit dance party, it seems as though our local fire department has a few parting gifts for us!"

Excited murmurs and titters rolled like a wave through the room. "Robbie, can you meet me at my desk?"

Michael's health-care aide smiled at me. "Can I help pass things out?"

I grinned. "That would be great. Thank you. I guess . . . organized chaos is the best we can hope for. I'll be there in one second."

She nodded and started opening the remaining boxes as Robbie approached my desk.

From the box in front of me, I pulled out the Nikes. His eyes went wide.

"These are for you."

He didn't look up from the new shoes. "I . . . I can't accept a gift from you. My father—"

"These aren't from me," I interrupted. "Like I said, the fire department generously donated a few gifts. *Every* student gets something."

His fingertips grazed the white leather before he picked up one shoe. "They're even my size." When his eyes shot up, I winked at him.

Robbie leaned across my desk, pulling me into a hug. My breath caught in an *oof* as he squeezed. "Thank you," he whispered, voice thick with emotion.

I straightened and squeezed his shoulder. Grabbing the box, I moved to the front to help manage the excitement.

Fire department swag, T-shirts, gift cards—there was truly something for everyone, but somehow Whip had managed to make sure Robbie had been taken care of.

Whip King was full of surprises.

I glanced at the clock. "Oh! The bell is going to ring. Let's circle up for one last exit dance party."

Rowdy whoops and hollers rang out, but I didn't care. I queued up the music we'd selected as a class and let it flow out of my speakers. Kids bounced and danced and circled as we sang along. Several girls from my class walked up to me, offering watery smiles and tight hugs as we said our goodbyes.

For someone who'd gone her whole life never quite feeling part of the group, those twenty-six kids shifted something inside me. I would always miss them, and they would also hold a special place in my heart.

After the last student waved goodbye, I finally broke

down and sobbed behind my desk. After school, Rachel found me hiding behind my desk, puffy eyes, snotty nose, and all.

She sank down next to me. "So the Warden has feelings after all."

I shot her a plain look and wiped at my nose.

"I'm teasing you." She gently knocked her shoulder into mine. "I always knew there was a softy hiding in there."

I sniffled. "I never cry at the end of the year. I don't know what's wrong with me."

She laughed and dabbed the corner of her eyes. "I cry *every* year, so I can't tell you."

I stood, fixing my rumpled blouse and patting away the tears in an attempt to save my makeup.

"A group of us are having drinks and appies to celebrate the last day. Are you in?"

My hand crumpled Whip's note in my pocket. He had wanted to meet at seven, and a few hits of liquid courage might be the ticket. "I'd love to."

"I'll text you the address once we figure it out, but the plan is to only work in our rooms for an hour or so and then head over."

I smiled at her. "Sounds great." As she walked toward the door, I stopped her. "Hey, Rach. Have you ever heard of Trawler's Cove?"

Her eyes sparked with interest. "I have. It's where local kids go to make out." She waggled her eyebrows and smirked. "Why? You going there?"

"What? No." I felt the telltale splotchy heat creep its way up my neck and willed it down. I reached for a plausible excuse. "A couple of kids were talking about it today during small group. I guess my gut was right that they were up to no good."

Rachel smiled. "Trust that gut. It's a good one." She turned back toward her own classroom. "I'll text you in a bit." In the hallway, Rachel shot both arms into the air and shouted, "School's out, baby!"

My laughter rang out, and I hurried to clean my classroom. I needed to run back to my apartment to freshen up if I wanted to meet my colleagues for drinks and still be ready for my secret rendezvous with Whip.

TWENTY-ONE

WHIP

For a thirty-one-year-old man with his shit *mostly* together, I was sweating like a teenager in the awkward throes of puberty. I hadn't been to Trawler's Cove since I was trying to get my first glance at a pair of boobs, but it was secluded and close enough to the marina that Emily and I wouldn't get caught.

The cove was south of the main marina. There was a small beach surrounded by the towering sand dunes, but the cove itself was known for its rocky outcropping.

It was secluded.

Quiet.

I listened to the waves crash against the shore and glanced at my watch. 6:57. My hand tapped a rhythm against my thigh as I waited—*hoped*—for Emily to show.

Low giggling caught my attention as a group of four high school-aged kids lumbered over the rocky edge of the cove's north wall. Two boys helped two girls climb down the edge as they doggedly ogled their dates.

Once they hit the sand, I cleared my throat.

"Oh shit," one kid remarked, his eyes growing wider. "Hey, uh . . ." He looked around at his buddy for help.

I crossed my arms and tipped my head. "Beat it."

One of the girls pulled at his arm and looked at me warily as she whispered, "Come on. We can find somewhere else."

I knew I was being a prick—laying claim to a teenage hangout known for canoodling—but I needed the privacy. I stayed rooted to my spot.

The other boy shook his head. "Yeah, man. Let's go up that way." He pointed to a strip of beach farther up the coastline.

Satisfied, I watched them disappear around the far corner of the cove and exhaled a sigh of relief.

"I didn't realize you were such a curmudgeon." Emily's soft voice floated over my shoulder, and I turned.

My face split into a smile. Emily was dressed in white low-top sneakers with a silver star on the side. Her denim shorts were lightly frayed at the hem and the distressing cut high on her thigh. It was only the beginning of summer, but her skin already held a slight tan. I wanted to run my hands up her thighs and see if they felt as soft as they looked. Her simple V-neck T-shirt was tucked into the front of her jean shorts, and she'd topped it with a soft, oversize cardigan because *of course she did.*

Somehow Emily made casual look effortlessly sexy.

I offered her my hand as she navigated the uneven rocks. "Glad you could make it, Prim."

"You're lucky I did." Emily's feet landed on the sand with a soft thud. "I had to ask around to figure out what Trawler's Cove was, and it sounds awfully murdery if you ask me."

"Why do you always think I'm trying to kill you?" I

teased, remembering a similar comment she made about the dark road that leads to my house on the night we met.

She shrugged, and the carefree movement was a punch to my gut. "A girl can't be too safe, I guess."

I held out my hand. "You're safe with me."

Her hand paused above mine, as if she was still trying to decide how true my statement was. Finally, her delicate hand rested in mine.

"I wanted somewhere quiet where we could hang out without curious eyes." I lifted her hand to my lips.

Her cheeks flooded with the prettiest shade of rose before she smiled and turned to look at our surroundings. Behind us, the cove secluded us from nearby hikers and beachgoers walking atop the dunes, and Lake Michigan stretched out as far as the eye could see in the opposite direction.

"I like it here." She sucked in a deep breath and exhaled. "Feels like you could really breathe in a place like this."

I stepped behind her and wrapped my arms around her. It felt good—too good—to be able to capture her in my embrace without looking over my shoulder. A defiant part of me wanted to demand we go public—fuck anyone who didn't accept that we were together—but it was way too soon to be thinking like that. We had agreed to sleeping together and nothing more.

The canoe I had tied to a rock along the shore bobbed in the water.

"You ready?" I asked.

Her eyes went wide, and she looked at me over her shoulder. "Ready? I thought this was it."

I squeezed her once before releasing her. "Nope. I've

got plans." I held out my hand, and she took it without hesitation this time. "Let's go."

I pulled her toward the canoe. It was sleek and hunter green. The seats were gleaming oak, stained a warm brown and polished until they shone. My supplies were neatly tucked under each seat. I reached in and grabbed a life vest for her. "Put this on."

She eyed the vest. "Where are we going?"

I smiled and slipped on my own vest before buckling it closed. "Just wanted to show you something."

Her eyes narrowed at me. "Hmm. Okay . . ."

I rolled my eyes playfully. "Just get in the damn boat, Prim."

With a laugh, Emily braced the sides of the canoe and carefully got in. I pointed to her seat, and she settled in toward the front. After untying the boat, I moved us deeper into the water before climbing in.

Using the oars, I rowed us around Trawler's Cove. The summer sun hung low in the sky, holding promises of longer days and warmer nights. Splashes of tangerine and golden yellow glittered off the water.

"The water is so clear. It's unbelievable. And the sand dunes are *massive*."

I nodded, loving the affection and awe laced in her voice. There was something about Emily appreciating the place I grew up in that twisted up my insides. "There really is no place else like it."

After touring the cove, I moored the canoe along a desolate stretch of sandy beach beyond where the teenagers had gone, only accessible by boat. Nerves scurried through me like the mitten crabs dancing along the shoreline.

"Hungry?" I asked.

She batted her lashes and my stomach swooped. "Always."

I laughed and hauled up a small blanket and basket from beneath my seat. "That's my girl."

I handed Emily the blanket and basket, then unloaded the compact bundle of firewood and a small foldable shovel from the bottom of the canoe. We walked to a clearing of sand, and I gestured with my chin. "Can you set that up?"

Wordlessly, Emily opened the blanket, arranging it on the soft sand and placing the basket at the center. Using the camping shovel, I dug a circular hole to block the wind. Inside the circle, I stacked a bit of kindling in the center before neatly arranging the logs. I reached into my pocket and pulled out a lighter, igniting the kindling. I leaned forward and blew into the growing fire.

I caught Emily watching me as I turned. "What?"

Her grin widened. "Nothing."

Once settled onto the blanket, I flipped open the top of the picnic basket. Emily sat on her knees at the corner and peered into the basket. I pulled out a half loaf of crusty french bread, two Royal Riviera pears, prosciutto wrapped in parchment, and a hunk of cheese.

She sat back on her heels, her palms resting on the tops of her smooth thighs, and sighed. "You are *full* of surprises."

"How so?" Finally, I pulled out a demi bottle of sparkling wine and two stemless wineglasses.

"I thought you were taking me to Trawler's Cove to make out with me." Her blue-green eyes sparkled in the fading sunlight.

My eyebrow arched, and a devilish grin spread across my face. "Do you *want* me to make out with you?" I moved my eyebrows up and down and stalked toward her on all fours.

Emily snatched the crust of bread and tossed it at me with a playful squeal.

I crowded her space. The fresh, floral scent of her perfume surrounded me. Overwhelmed me. I pressed my lips to hers. She sighed into the kiss, opening for me without hesitation.

I wanted to drown in her.

My cock thickened, and my blood surged with the urge to pin her to the sand and *take*. How is it that I was so attracted to the one woman I couldn't have?

Determined to do this thing right while it lasted, I stopped myself, but not before giving her lush lower lip one last nip of my teeth.

Emily grinned as I went back to organizing our impromptu picnic. She looked around, her gaze landing on the crackling fire, and sighed. "This is . . . really lovely."

Emily's glance lingered as I searched for the right thing to say. "You deserve the world." My words were soft, but I meant every one.

Emily smiled softly and hummed a curious sound.

"What?" I asked.

"You've been hanging out with my dad too much." When I stilled at the mention of her father, Emily continued, but her attention was on her hands. "I had a messy breakup a while ago. It was . . . not ideal. Craig was someone I had uprooted my entire life for. A new job. A new city. For a few years it was all going according to my perfectly thought-out plan." She let out a humorless laugh. "It didn't work out. Then I came to Outtatowner, and I wanted a fresh start, but a lot of it just felt like going through the motions. Dad saw right through me, sat me down, and said, *Melly, you can't go through life like it's a checklist. You'll need to* feel *your way through if you want the life you deserve."*

Her deepened voice and impression of the chief was adorably spot on, and his words were a blow to my chest.

Her soft eyes lifted to mine, and she shrugged. "Sometimes checklists are easier."

I swallowed hard. "Your parents are good people. You're lucky to have them."

"What about yours?" In the firelight, her eyes held a quiet curiosity. "My mom mentioned your mother is out of the picture, but your dad . . ."

My lips pressed together, and I shook my head sharply. "My family isn't like yours. We don't have heart-to-hearts and loving conversations. My mom disappeared when I was seven. Dad said she packed her shit and never looked back."

"Oh my god . . ." Her whisper was drowned out by the waves rolling onto the shoreline.

I didn't want her pity, so I pressed on, opening myself up in a way that was painful but in the quiet firelight felt somehow necessary. "My father is a hard man. His respect is earned. I'm thirty-one and not sure I've quite gotten there yet."

"How do you earn it?" Her question was sincere and lacked any of the judgment I had expected.

"Doing what he asks without question or hesitation." I lifted a shoulder. "Perfect example is your mother."

Her brows scrunched as she sat up. "My mom?"

I nodded. "She's part of the Remington County Historical Association, and they're trying to declare a building that my father wants to purchase as a historical building. He wants me to try to talk her out of it. Dad saw my relationship with the chief as an in. It's his specialty—angling for the win."

For heavy moments Emily watched the flames dance. "You could, though"—she shrugged—"talk to her if you think it's the right thing to do."

I tossed a stick to the side, knowing that had never been an option. "What my father wants is rarely the *right* thing."

Her eyes searched mine, and I stretched my legs in front of me.

"So what are you going to do?" she finally asked.

I looked at the gorgeous woman across from me, her features illuminated by the golden firelight. "I'm going to not worry about it. He's managed the King enterprise without me for this long."

What I left unspoken was the fact that Chief Martin and his wife had shown me more love than either of my parents ever had. They had come to mean more to me than my own blood.

As she sat across from me, the mood slowly lifted as a sense of casual comfort settled over us and we listened to the waves roll in. We laughed over bites of Mimolette and pear, and it was then that one hard truth dawned on me and filled my gut with dread.

Emily Ward was bruising heartache wrapped in a tidy, stubborn little package. There wasn't a world in which I would ever be good enough to deserve her, but for the first time in my life, the prospect of being left behind was unbearable.

TWENTY-TWO

EMILY

"I've got to find it," Whip grumbled as he frantically searched the cab of his truck. His hand raked through his hair, causing it to stick up in places.

I stood back, enjoying the view. Whip's white T-shirt was snug across his chest, and I appreciated the fit of his jeans as I stared at his muscular ass while he tore through the glove box, checked under the seats, and dug into the center console. After our boat ride and picnic, we had erased all evidence of us being on the beach, and Whip had rowed us back toward Trawler's Cove.

Despite my offer to help, Whip insisted on hauling the canoe up the rocky ledge himself before securing the dripping boat on top of his truck. When we got there, a small note was tucked under one windshield wiper.

Good luck finding it.

Clearly a prank from one of the Sullivans, Whip was convinced they'd somehow messed with his truck. After minutes of finding nothing, a realization dawned on me. "How do you know they actually messed with anything?"

He slowly turned to me.

I nodded as the thought fully formed. "What better way to fuck with someone than to make them *think* they did something to your truck, but really did nothing at all. It would eat at you. Drive you mad." I shrugged. "It's what I would do."

Whip stood tall and slammed the door to his truck. "Son of a bitch."

I held up a hand. "I mean—don't get me wrong—I'd still keep an eye or a nose out for something weird, but I'm betting it's a mind game."

A muscle in his jaw worked. "Psychological warfare."

I barked out a laugh. "I mean, maybe less dramatic than that, but sure."

More relaxed, Whip leaned against the door of his truck and peered down the quiet roadway. "Did you park nearby?"

I shook my head. "My apartment is only a few blocks away. I walked."

He hummed and glanced down the street before settling his attention on his feet. "I could drive you home or . . ." His eyes found mine. "We could go back to my place."

Heat bloomed in my core, and I stifled a smile. "I'd like that."

Whip hurried around to the passenger side, opening my door as I climbed into his truck. My hair was tangled from the lake breeze, and anticipation buzzed beneath my skin. I leaned against the window as his truck bumped along the road.

It was getting late, but Outtatowner still hummed with

the flutter of coastal life. Tourist season was in full swing, and the sidewalks were still bustling. I could see King Tattoo was buzzing with life and wondered if that was where Whip had gotten all his tattoos. Mentally, I made plans to trace each line with my tongue. I smiled as we passed the general store, recalling the night Whip and I met.

As the truck rolled to a stoplight, Whip stilled and mumbled, "Fuck."

I straightened, looking around to see what he was looking at.

Just ahead at the crosswalk, my mother's hand was tucked affectionately into the nook of my stepdad's arm.

My eyes went wide as I panicked. "What do we do?"

He lifted an arm, taking the center console with him, opening the bench seat between us. "Get down."

Without hesitation, I swiveled and pressed my torso to the center seat. My face was practically in his lap, and my heart thundered. After what felt like an eternity, the light changed, and Whip's truck rolled forward. As he drove through the intersection, I watched in horror as his arm lifted in a silent salute.

"Did they see you?" I hissed.

"Oh yeah," he gritted through a smile. "Definitely spotted."

"Shit. Do you think they saw *me*?"

Whip's arm casually rested along my back, rubbing a small circle where my shirt separated from my jean shorts.

His warm fingers dipped past the waistband and stroked my skin. "I think we're good, but maybe just stay down to be safe."

"Okay." I stared ahead, directly at his crotch, and waited, my hands tensely gripping his thigh. My face was in his lap as he kept driving. As I crouched down and stayed pinned in place, I realized he'd become hard.

"Are we out of town yet?" I didn't dare peek.

"Oh yeah, have been for a while." His smug words had me rolling my eyes and playfully slapping his thick thigh as I sat up.

"You're the worst." I shifted back to my side of the truck.

Whip laughed. "Can't blame a guy for enjoying that, just a little." He shifted in his seat, adjusting himself in the most obscenely masculine way. A bolt of lust shot through me.

I crossed my arms, still pretending to be annoyed and to hide the fact that my nipples had puckered into hard little points. When we finally turned down Whip's quiet stretch of road, I relaxed. The sun had finally disappeared beyond the trees, and in the twilight, I could just make out the shape of his expansive house.

When he parked near the outbuilding and not in his garage, I looked at him in question.

"I wanted to show you something." Whip got out and rounded the truck to open my door.

I grinned at him as I climbed out. "I could get used to the princess treatment."

A smirk hooked at the corner of his mouth when he swept the hair from my shoulder and leaned in. "I'll give you the princess treatment now because once you're on your knees, begging for my cock, you'll have earned it."

Shivers racked my spine, and my knees went soft. I gripped his shirt. "That's a deal I'll take."

"Good." Whip started toward the garage, and I followed. Once inside, he flipped on the overhead lights. In the center of his workshop was a large boat with what looked like fishing rod holders and ropes attached to the side. It was filthy and seemed to be in rough shape.

On the stern, *Noble King Fishing Tours* had been painted, though it looked like there was something else underneath.

I tilted my head. "A boat? Do you own a fishing company or something?"

Whip's smile was soft as he tucked his hands into his pockets. "No. This boat was supposed to be a big *fuck you* to the Sullivans. Check it out." He stepped forward, using his fingertip to outline the layer of paint hidden beneath the boat's new moniker. It was painted over, but you could still see the outline of a name.

"Juney?" I asked.

"The late Mrs. Sullivan's name was June."

A twinge pinched in my chest.

Whip's lips pressed together, and he nodded grimly. "My father has always had a hard-on for knocking the Sullivans down a few pegs."

"Because of the rivalry," I confirmed.

His head twitched. "It's more than that for him. Sure, we fuck around and prank each other, but that's all petty, harmless shit. This was personal."

I stayed silent, feeling the weight of the room, and waited for him to continue.

"Red Sullivan—their dad—is a farmer but saw fishing tours as a lucrative tourism opportunity. It probably would have been a good one too."

Dread oozed into my stomach. "Would have been?"

Whip nodded, his eyes never leaving the boat. "Red got sick. Early-onset dementia, I think. Dad bought the boat from under him only to slap his name on it and docked it in a prominent slip at the marina, simply because he could."

"That's . . ." I had no idea what to even say to that.

"Shitty?" Disgust tainted his words. "Yeah, it was."

"And why do you have it?" I searched the side of his face, my chest squeezing.

"Giving it back to its rightful owners. A gift from my sister Sylvie to Duke. We're stowing it here and I'm going to do a few repairs on some of the interior woodwork, if I can."

Admiration caused a swell of emotion, but worry pricked at my brain. Whip was nothing like his father. It gnawed at me that Russell King was so heartless he would wield his influence and power over his own children. "How does your dad feel about that?"

He lightly scoffed and put an arm around my shoulders, dragging me against him and dropping a light kiss on the top of my head. "You're pretty smart, Prim. You know that?"

I preened and leaned into his warm embrace. "The plan is to hope he doesn't notice but deal with the fallout when he does. Come on." Whip sighed and guided me back toward the exit before he flipped off the lights and locked the workshop. "I've got plans for you that don't include talking about my fucked-up family."

In a swift movement, he slapped my ass and I yelped, taking off like a shot across the grass to escape him. I ran, but heavy footsteps thundered behind me. A giddy zip followed by a primal squeal tore through the darkness. Despite my best efforts, Whip caught me around the middle and hoisted me up. I giggled and fought his hold.

Though I struggled and kicked, Whip jostled me until I was in a firefighter's carry, upside down over his shoulder. "No fair! You've done this before!"

Whip effortlessly held me in place while he unlocked his door and hauled me toward his bedroom. With two hands, he braced my hips and let me slide down his front.

His eyes bore into mine. "I promise you, Prim. I've never done anything like this in my life."

A deep greediness ripped through me. I wasn't foolish enough to think I was the only woman to ever be with Whip, but I carried an innate feminine knowing that, for the time being, he really was *mine*.

I pulled my lower lip between my teeth, locking my eyes with his. Slowly, I sank to my knees, never breaking eye contact. "Is this how I earn the princess treatment?"

My fingers teased the waistband of his pants, brushing the taut skin of his lower belly. He clenched at my touch.

"It's a pretty good start." His ice-blue eyes were hungry. Every muscle in his body went rigid at my teasing touch. I may have been on my knees, but I held the power as I slowly unzipped his pants and watched him fall apart in front of me.

The sight of his cock, even then, took my breath away. It bulged through the smooth surface of his black boxer briefs. I palmed its length, tracing over each barbell that ran underneath its width.

It wouldn't be the first time I'd been on my knees for him, but instead of tearing at each other's clothes, fighting for the finish line, I wanted to tease.

Torture.

I planned to use my mouth to make him see stars. I wasn't at all worried about Whip coming first—experience told me he would more than make up for it.

"I don't trust that look in your eye." Whip's voice was a rasping husk that sent tingles cascading down my spine.

I shot him a wicked grin as I lowered his pants and underwear, freeing him. "I'm going to ruin you for all other women." I slowly licked a prominent vein on the underside of his cock.

With a deep groan, Whip's head fell back. Then he glowered at me before his hand caressed my cheek. "You already have, Prim."

My nipples pinched painfully in my bra. I wanted him to throw me down and take me, but I was determined to drag this out for him. Adjusting my position, I gripped him with one hand while I teased the head of his dick. Slowly, I started taking him deeper into my mouth, lashing my tongue across the metal barbells.

My eyes watered, and my head bobbed as I took him deeper still. Saliva pooled in my mouth, and I used it to suck and tease. I moaned around him, feeling my pussy grow wetter. Sex with Whip was salacious and freeing. I'd never experienced anything like it, and I wanted *more*.

Releasing my grip, I kept my mouth on him and my eyes glued to his. My free hand dipped between his legs, gently stroking the soft skin of his balls. Carefully sucking in a lungful of breath through my nose, I took him as deeply as I could. Whip shivered and his hips twitched. Teasing the sensitive spot behind his balls, I worked him deeper and deeper until my jaw ached.

With Whip I was wild, free. An idea bloomed in my mind, one that was filthier than I'd ever dared to imagine. I sat back, swirling my tongue across his head as I smiled up at him.

"I have an idea. Can we try something?" A shy blush heated my cheeks as my lashes lowered.

Whip reached down and hauled me to my feet. "Anything."

I quickly unbuttoned my shorts, letting them fall to the ground, and slipped out of my sneakers. My shirt was next, hitting the floor, followed by my bra and panties. I stood, bare and humming with anticipation in front of him as he made quick work of undressing himself.

The cut lines of his abs bunched as his breaths sawed in and out of him. He reached for me, slicking a finger between my legs. "You're fucking soaked, Prim. Tell me you're so wet from taking my cock down that tight little throat."

Before he could push that finger farther, I stepped back toward the bed. "I want more." I clambered onto the bed. His eyebrow popped up when I lay on my back with my feet stretching away from him. Then I shimmied to the edge and hung my head off the bed. "Like this."

His eyes were dark and wild as he stroked his cock with a hard tug and stepped forward. "You want me to fuck your throat?"

I licked my lips and nodded.

"Open your mouth."

I did as I was told, pressing my tongue flat to accommodate him. "Good girl."

My fingers found my clit, and I started working it in slow, torturous circles as he slid his cock into my mouth.

"Fuck."

One syllable, ground out as he thrust to the back of my throat, was a jolt to my system. I wanted so badly to feel his cum slide down my throat because *I* made him fall apart. I hummed my approval and eagerness as he slowly dragged in and out of my mouth. I reached back and gripped his hips. He allowed me to set a comfortable pace as he fucked my mouth.

His rough palms passed over my nipples. He pinched and twisted them. My thighs pressed together as my whole body hummed with pleasure.

He gripped my breasts. "I'm going to come, Prim."

My grip on his hips tightened as I doubled my efforts, encouraging him to let his orgasm go. His fingertips dug harder, and with a moan, I took as many inches as I could as hot, thick cum spurted against the back of my throat. I worked him and swallowed and held him deeper as the final pumps of his orgasm dripped down my throat.

He shook, his knees giving out as he slid from my mouth. I rolled to my stomach, wiping the mess off my chin and grinning at him. There wasn't a challenge I wasn't ready to face head-on, and dick sucking was no exception.

"That was . . ." He laughed. "Holy shit, Em. I'm dizzy."

"A-plus work? Five stars?" I teased with a soft, excited giggle.

Whip grinned at me. "Out of this world. I think I saw God."

Heat scorched my cheeks and I looked away.

He prowled toward me and captured my face in his hands as he looked down at me. "Why are you blushing, Prim?"

I leaned into his hands, hoping to distract him and focus his attention elsewhere, but he held me, waiting.

"It's just . . ." I gathered my courage and looked him in the eyes. "You make me feel different. Confident. I've never been very adventurous in the bedroom. I'm glad you liked it."

His mouth lowered with zero hesitation as he kissed me long and hard and deeply. "You make me feel different too."

A wicked glint shone in his eyes as his body covered mine. "Now it's my turn to show you," he threatened with a playful lift of his brow.

As I sank into the plush stack of pillows piled at the headboard, Whip's hands caressed down my body. I expected fire and fervor, but his lips were soft and warm.

Slowly, he moved down my body, spreading my knees until I was completely bared to him. He dragged out my orgasm with his face buried between my legs as I gripped the pillows and screamed his name.

Later, when he nestled his hips in the cradle of mine, he teased my opening before slipping inside. Eyes locked, he pinned me to the bed with his delicious weight. My legs wrapped around him as my arms wound around his neck. My hands fisted his hair. Whip buried his face into my hair, murmuring my name and easing himself inside.

In the darkness of his bedroom something shifted, altered something inside me.

In his embrace I realized that it was no longer two sort-of friends fucking and having a good time. It was two souls baring themselves to each other and finding that our broken parts somehow clicked together perfectly. His name was a whisper of my breath as he finally filled me completely.

TWENTY-THREE

WHIP

Next to Emily, I slept like the dead.

It was no secret that firefighters often struggled with healthy sleep habits—just a perk of the job, I guessed. But next to Emily? Wrapped around her soft body with the smell of my shampoo after I washed her hair—something I never could have imagined myself doing before her—I could rest for *hours.* Floating somewhere between dreaming and awake, I curled around her.

A good fuck was one thing, but last night had been altogether something new and unexpected. Emily had felt it too. I saw it on her face when our pace morphed into a gentle ebb and flow of reverent exploration. Gentle kisses. Whispers in the dark. Unspoken promises.

I should be exhausted after hours of tracing every line of her body and committing it to memory, but I was keyed up. I could slay a dragon or climb Everest.

It was a total mind fuck being this attracted to the one woman you couldn't have. I pulled her closer and buried my face in her shoulder. "Stay with me."

"Mmm." Emily hummed and pressed her ass into me. "I

can't. I have a planning lunch with the Bluebirds for the carnival." She stretched and groaned before turning in my arms to face me. Her hand cupped over her mouth.

I frowned down at her, suppressing a laugh. "What are you doing?"

"I have kitten breath," she said from behind her hand.

I grinned and pulled her hand from her face before planting a smacking kiss on her lips. "Can I feed you before you go?"

Her cheeks flushed before she glanced at the clock, noting the late morning hour. "I really need to get moving. You're making a bum out of me."

I stretched back in the bed, resting my hands behind my head as she sat up. "If you ask me, you worked overtime last night."

My blood hummed just recalling how intensely satisfying it had been to watch her arch in pleasure as I worshiped her.

Emily stood, naked and unashamed, and flashed me a wicked smile over her shoulder. I stared at her bare ass as she confidently padded across the hardwoods and disappeared into the en suite bathroom. I closed my eyes and soaked in the moment, confident nothing could ruin a more perfect morning.

~

Well, my day was about to get absolutely shit on.

But damn if it wasn't going to be worth it to see the look on my father's face when I told him if he wanted to go toe to toe with the Remington County Historical Association, that was on him. I wouldn't be stepping in to talk with Marilyn Martin or anyone else on his behalf. In fact, if the conversation went the way I was planning it to, I'd be lucky enough to withstand his wrath, and when he saw I was immovable in my stance, he'd cut me out completely.

Only difference was, I was now beyond caring. I didn't need him or his influence to define me any longer.

When he wasn't away on business, my father lived in a luxury condo on the dune-lined shores of Lake Michigan. It wasn't long after my mother left for good that he'd transferred ownership of the King estate to his sister. We grew up in that house and endured the occasional visit from my father while Bug and the paid staff raised us the best they could.

When my father's Porsche wasn't parked outside his building, I headed down the winding roads toward the King estate. It was common for my father to be gone on business for long stretches of time, lining pockets with generous donations to seemingly charitable organizations. Organizations he undoubtedly had a hand in and received plenty of kickbacks in the form of tax breaks or favors he could carry in his pocket.

Wherever he was, Aunt Bug seemed to be able to keep tabs on him, and I had a lifetime of issues to unload on him.

My family estate loomed large on the horizon as I pulled my car onto the long, winding driveway. The grand mansion, a testament to the King family's wealth and pride, seemed to glare down at me with the same haughtiness my father often did. As I parked, I took a deep breath, preparing myself for the confrontation I had postponed for far too long.

The ornate oak front door creaked as it opened, its hinges complaining against the weight of time and echoing through the silence of the house. The air inside was thick with the scent of polished wood and old money. I glanced around and knew the house remembered every argument, every broken plate thrown against the wall in anger, every unfulfilled promise.

Heading toward the study, I braced myself for the clash with my father, where I expected to find him drowning his arrogance in a glass of whiskey. The heavy oak door swung open, revealing a room cloaked in shadows. A figure hunched behind the mahogany desk, cigar smoke stale in the air. The tension in the room heightened as I prepared to speak, but the figure remained silent.

As I stood there, ready to unleash the words I had rehearsed for years, the figure rose, making me stop in surprise. In the dim light, Aunt Bug's face emerged, her usually composed demeanor replaced with an air of anxiety.

Aunt Bug jolted when she saw me. "Whip," she stammered, her voice trembling like autumn leaves in the coastal wind. She laughed and placed a hand over her chest. "You scared me."

I took a step forward, sensing that something was off about her. "What's going on, Bug? Are you all right?"

She flicked a strand of silver hair from her face and laughed again. "Of course I'm all right. You startled me, that's all."

"I was looking for Dad. Have you seen him?"

Her eyes ticked toward the door at my back, as if she were afraid of prying ears in her own home. "Work took him into the city. He should be back in town in a few days."

My lips formed a hard line. I'd wanted to confront my father, but his unsurprising absence took the wind from my sails. I pinched the bridge of my nose and exhaled, letting my shoulders sag.

When I opened my eyes, Bug was wringing her hands. I searched her eyes. "What's going on?"

After a beat, she gestured with her chin. "I found something in the basement, something I think you should see. Follow me."

Descending the staircase at the back of the house, the polished wood groaned beneath our footsteps. The air in the lower levels was damp and musty, filled with the scent of long-forgotten memories. Bug led me to a dim corner, where an old, dusty box sat neglected.

She opened it tentatively, revealing a mix of mementos —faded photographs, a well-worn denim jacket, and a haphazard stack of papers. Among the stack of papers were official documents that turned my curiosity into a knot of anxiety.

"Bug, what is all this?" I asked, my gaze fixed on the official-looking papers.

Bug hesitated, her eyes avoiding mine. "I was looking for old baby pictures to bring to Sylvie when I came across this box. I didn't know what was inside, so I opened it and found all of this."

I reached in and picked up a small plastic rectangle and turned it over. She would have been in her early sixties now, but smiling back at me was my mother frozen in time—light-brown eyes sparkling, her blonde hair styled in loose waves. The resemblance to my sister Sylvie was striking and a sucker punch. She was exactly how I had remembered her before she was gone.

I was seven when my mother left. Old enough to remember that she would hum and tickle my back to help me fall asleep, but young enough to not recall the actual tune. My mother's name—Maryann—became a curse word, and we had each learned early on that the punishments for lamenting her absence were swift and harsh. My father never wanted children, but I assumed we became a way to keep my mother content. Eventually that wasn't enough, and she left us all behind with the man who never wanted us in the first place.

My heart quickened. The room seemed to close in around me as I processed the possible implications of her driver's license being in a box in a basement all this time. Long since expired. "Why would she leave these behind? And why are you just finding them *now*?"

"I don't know, Whip." Bug shook her head, a mix of confusion and fear in her eyes. "I—I just don't know."

I pulled out the denim jacket and clutched it in my fist. "Is this hers?"

Bug only offered a sharp nod.

I flipped the driver's license back into the box and stuffed the jacket on top before closing the cardboard flaps. "It doesn't matter," I said despite the growing sense of dread clawing at me.

I stood, and Bug bent for the box and shoved it into me. "Take it. I don't want this in my house." My aunt cleared her throat and dusted off her shirt. "I have a luncheon to go to—planning a carnival takes work, and I don't want to be late."

With her shoulders set and chin raised, Bug dared me to defy her.

Just like a King to sweep something under the rug.

Leaving the dim basement, unanswered questions hung in the air like shadows, and the weight of my family's secrets pressed down on me, leaving me with an unsettling certainty that things were not entirely as they seemed. Bug knew something, and she was either too afraid or too loyal to my father to say anything. I just wasn't sure which.

I turned to my aunt as we walked toward the front door. "I'll text him and let him know I'm looking to talk."

Bug shook her head and let out a soft sigh. "A child's shoulders were never meant to bear the weight of his father's choices. But you know your father. If it's not on his terms, it won't happen at all."

I bit back the comment that maybe we'd all been bending to his will for too long. I knew it wasn't Bug's fault that she'd gotten caught up in my father's business dealings—leaving would have meant abandoning us in the same way our mother had.

The cardboard box was heavy in my hands. I nodded goodbye to my aunt and tossed it in the cab of my truck. An unsettling ache curdled my stomach as I gave the box one last sidelong glance. Something about knowing my mother's possessions were there, sitting in a forgotten box right next to me, made her more real than she'd ever been.

My thoughts rambled back to Emily, and I closed my eyes and laid my head against the seat of my truck. She had swept into Outtatowner with her perfect smile.

Perfect family.

Perfect life.

All I had was a family name and with it a box of tangled, thorny secrets that refused to stay buried.

TWENTY-FOUR

EMILY

I CAN'T EVEN REMEMBER the last night I slept in my own apartment. Actually, that was a lie. It was weeks ago when Whip finally told me to stop sneaking around town and just leave some clothes at his place.

So much for casual.

Tightness still gripped my chest when I skirted questions from my mother about what I'd been up to, but otherwise Whip and I had been doing a clever job of keeping our relationship under wraps. If anyone noticed the absence of my car at the apartment, no one had said a thing.

Cocooned in his plush comforter, it felt like no one and nothing in the world could touch us. I stretched and reached for him, only to find his space in the bed empty. It was cool to the touch, so I shifted and gathered the blankets around me, hoping to steal their warmth. Lying on my back, I wiped the sleep from my eyes and stared up at the wood beams in the vaulted ceiling.

"Why have such a big house for one person?" It was a rambling, inside thought that tumbled from my lips.

For a moment it was quiet until I heard Whip answer

from the bathroom. "I wanted to be sure my siblings had a place to stay if they ever needed it."

Affection pierced my heart. "Do they ever stay?"

"No." His clipped, one-syllable response was heart-breaking. I rolled to my belly and curled into his side of the bed. "Good morning." Still groggy and feeling well used, I kept my eyes closed and smiled into Whip's pillow.

"Morning." The sleep in his voice made the syllables rough and cracked. I felt the bed dip under his weight before a light kiss brushed the top of my head. When he retreated just as quickly as he'd come, I blinked my eyes open.

Across the room, Whip's back was to me as he was riffling through one of his drawers. He was already dressed for the day in slacks and a button-up shirt.

I sat up, tucking the blankets around me. "Early day?" I asked.

It was moments like these when unease skittered under my skin. Moments when I had to remind myself I had no hold over this man and that our arrangement was supposed to be casual.

Even when they feel anything but *casual.*

He turned, hitting me with the full force of Whip King, impeccably dressed in dark slacks and a shirt and tie. My stomach tightened at the way his chest filled out his shirt and nipped in at his tapered waist.

"My interview for lieutenant is today." His face was unreadable.

"You're a shoo-in." I smiled brightly, though it didn't quite reach my eyes. "Dad loves you."

Whip's reply was only a strange, dismissive grunt as he turned to the mirror for one last check of his appearance.

My brain scrambled. "You deserve the promotion. He'll see that."

Whip offered a flat-lipped smile and nod. Worry pricked at my brain. I had picked up on a few signs that things were slightly *off* between us, but I'd found ways to rationalize each and every one.

Extra hours in his workshop. *He's finishing up his project while I worked with the Bluebirds on details for the carnival.*

The internet search about a private investigator I'd peeked at over his shoulder. *Probably something work related . . . maybe?*

The woman's jean jacket hanging in the back of his closet. *Okay, fine. That one is kind of odd.*

Before he left the bedroom, Whip stopped in the doorway. "Meet me for lunch if you're free? Maybe we can drive a few miles out of town and find a quiet country road."

I pouted. "I have plans to finalize the carnival. It's our last hurrah. Plus, I promised Bug to help at the library. According to her, their Children's Department is a *travesty*, and it's the only way I know how to repay her for all her help with the foundation. Rain check?"

"Sure." I got a curt nod before he checked his watch.

I frowned. "Everything okay?"

"Just nerves, I guess." He crossed the room one last time and planted a kiss on my mouth.

I wanted to arch into him, let his cologne cloak me. Instead, Whip pulled back, leaving my heated skin to chill in the empty bedroom after he left.

Sneaking around was fun and forbidden at first, but lately it had been feeling more and more like a burden. Just last week we'd passed each other downtown, and I had to catch myself before I threw my arms around him. Instead, I smiled politely, waved, and kept walking.

It was pure torture.

There was no denying that my emotions were taking the helm. Logically, I knew Whip and I were spending every spare moment together. His actions matched his words. Whatever was blossoming between us was natural and evolving.

I didn't need to worry about past insecurities or that he could use my feelings against me.

I just had to trust my gut.

Trouble was, my gut was telling me Whip may have more secrets than just the fact he was sneaking around with his boss's daughter.

~

The summer sun filtered through the leaded windows of the Outtatowner Public Library, casting a warm glow on the creaky wooden floor. The familiar scent of well-loved books and the hushed murmur of whispered conversations greeted me as I stepped into the cozy building. The soft, ambient hum of fluorescent lights overhead mingled with the occasional squeak of chairs being pulled out and the rustle of pages turning. Mahogany shelves, lined with stories waiting to be discovered, reached toward the ceiling, their polished spines creating a mosaic of colors. The air held a quiet reverence, broken only by the rhythmic clacking of the librarian's keyboard and the distant hum of the ancient air conditioner.

Sunbeams painted patterns on the worn carpet, guiding my steps through the doorway, where adventure and romance awaited readers on every shelf. The air seemed to shimmer with the promise of hidden tales. I sucked in a lungful of breath and closed my eyes.

Since my childhood, libraries had always been a safe space.

A refuge.

Somewhere I could read tales of romance or adventure or live through the perils of a murder mystery from the safety of its walls.

Despite its charm, the library was surprisingly empty as I wound my way through the stacks toward the heart of the building. A few children picked through books, but I immediately understood why Bug had sought out my help. I worked with kids every day and knew that in its current state, the Outtatowner Public Library, with its muted greens and drab beiges, was extremely *un-fun*.

When Bug saw me, she ended her conversation with the librarian and met me halfway. "Glad you could make it. Thank you for coming."

"It's the least I can do for everything you've put in motion for the foundation. How can I help?"

Bug started walking, and I fell in step beside her. "I have volunteered at this library for a long time. It hasn't changed much in those years, but there are some of us who are starting to feel like that's a problem."

I hummed and considered as she continued.

"Our adult programming is strong, but the programs for kids are underwhelming. We see fewer and fewer children every day. We can't keep up with phones and video games. I was hoping someone with your experience could help generate a few new ideas. Help liven things up around here."

I rubbed my palms together. "First, I am honored you thought of me. I have always loved what libraries can do for their communities." I looked around and thought about what the children of Outtatowner could gain from visiting the library. "I guess my first thought would be whether or not you've developed programs for mid-kids or teens?"

"Mid-kids?"

"Kids around first grade until middle school. They're not babies, but they're also not teenagers yet. A lot of fun learning happens in those years. It's during that critical time, you establish the library as a safe haven of sorts. They'll be more likely to hang around as teens if you've lessened the barrier to entry. Kids love tech. The library should fully embrace that."

A half-formed vision filtered into my imagination. I could see children building, exploring and laughing within those walls. It could be done with the right amount of vision, and resources, of course.

I only hoped Bug could see it too. "A library doesn't need to only be a place where people come to check out books. It can be a place to gather and commune with their neighbors. It has the power to change communities—even make something like the King–Sullivan rivalry obsolete—but you have to start with the kids. Give them a place to gather. Somewhere they can explore, connect, and be inspired."

Bug planted a hand on her hip. "Quite the impassioned speech for someone so new here, but I like your style."

"There's always been something about a library that feels—I don't know . . . hopeful?" I raked my fingers along the spines on the shelf.

Her eyes narrowed at me, but her lips held a faint smile. "You're a bit of an odd bird."

I smiled widely at her. "Thank you."

Bug smirked. "I mean that in the best possible way, of

course. When you live here as long as I have, you realize that many of the people born and raised in a small town often have small-town ways of thinking. We hate to admit it, but sometimes outsiders can bring in fresh perspectives. I will talk with the board to see about some of these changes. Can I get you to write a few ideas down that I might present to them?"

Realizing a compliment from Bug was a rare thing, I simply smiled. "Of course. I'm glad I could help."

I turned to leave, but Bug stopped me when she raised a hand in the air. "One last thing before you leave. This thing between you and Whip. Will it be a secret for much longer?"

I went still, the walls of the room pressing in on me. I froze, unsure of how to react.

When I didn't respond, Bug's eyebrow lifted in challenge. "Do you deny it?"

Wide eyed, I barely shook my head as the blood *whooshed* between my ears.

A satisfied smile crossed her lips. "Just as I thought."

"How did you—" I sputtered.

Bug smiled. "Not much gets past me around here. People ramble, mostly to hear themselves talk, but if you really *listen*, you hear all kinds of interesting things."

Panic seized my chest as I imagined my father finding out what we had been doing. "Do you think my father knows?"

Her lips pursed. "Would that be the worst thing in the world? For you to be involved with a King? You're both consenting adults."

I shook my head. "It's not that. My dad, he—" *Ugh. I don't know how to put this.* "For me, in the end, it would be fine. My dad is protective, sure, but for Whip . . . he *really* deserves that promotion, and I don't ever want to be the reason he doesn't get it."

"We all make choices." The ominous tone in her voice sent shivers down my back. "Chief Martin seems rational enough to promote a man based on his merits and not the company he keeps. Plus, I'm certain my nephew is smart enough to know when to call it quits, and when to fight for what he deserves. Don't ever forget—he's a King."

I wasn't sure if she was talking about the job or something else entirely, but the finality in her statement had me nodding along like an idiot. "Yeah, I'm . . . I'm sure it's fine. We just hadn't really talked about making anything *official*. Things are still kind of new."

"Of course, I understand. But for discretion's sake . . ." Her eyes flicked down my front as her eyebrow crept up her forehead. "You may want to wear something other than my nephew's T-shirt if you're planning to keep gossip to a minimum."

TWENTY-FIVE

WHIP

Interviews were my time to shine.

Typically I could sit back, relax, and confidently convey how I planned to successfully execute the requirements of the job before me. That was significantly more difficult to do when you were sitting across from your boss and remembering exactly how hard his daughter made you come the night before.

Chief Martin studied me from across the table as he and a panel of interviewers reviewed their questions and took note of my final answers. Sweat prickled at my hairline, and I shifted in the hard plastic seat.

I sat at his table, ate his food. Jesus, the things I did to his sweet little girl . . .

Guilt racked me, and I couldn't muster the balls to look Chief Martin in the eye. Instead, I directed my next answer to the battalion chief. I was the first to interview, which was fine by me. Word had spread that only the top three candidates were getting interviews, and I was happy to set the bar by which the others would be judged. Only now I was starting to panic that the bar I set would be pathetically low.

Chief Martin's face was unreadable as he sat back in his seat and made a final note on the pad of paper beside him. "Thank you for your time. We'll be letting all candidates know our final decision in the upcoming days."

I nodded and stood, holding my hand out to him. "Thank you, sir."

I made my way around the room, shaking each interviewer's hand before making a hasty exit. Once the door clicked closed behind me, I tugged at my tie, pulling it from around my neck and stuffing it in my pocket.

"Aww, Bill. Don't tell me you're nervous." Lee Sullivan's smart-ass laugh grated on my nerves. He was dressed in his navy tactical pants and OFD T-shirt. I couldn't wait to get out of my suit.

"I'm not nervous. I'm late for my shift." I brushed him off, pulling my dress shirt from the waistband of my pants and walking down the hall toward the barracks so I could change.

"Relax. I'm just busting your balls," Lee called after me. I turned in time to see him pop an M&M into his mouth. "You've got this in the bag."

I didn't need a vote of confidence from Lee fucking Sullivan of all people.

For a fraction of a second, I wondered what it must have been like—growing up without having to constantly prove your worth to a man who was supposed to love you. To have a mother who didn't pack her shit and leave you behind for something better.

Only, what if she didn't?

I stuffed down the very thought that had been nagging me ever since Bug shoved that box into my arms. It taunted me from the corner of my workshop, where I'd dumped it. I had no fucking clue why I had the urge to hang the denim jacket in the back of my closet, only that it felt too depressing to leave it crumpled in a forgotten cardboard box.

Resting my forearms on the top bunk, I let my head hang. Even having the *thoughts* I was having was a betrayal of the King name.

I just couldn't seem to shrug off the feeling that there was something *more*. Something I was missing.

Despite years of trying to forget, it was easy to remember how drastically our lives changed—how distinctly my childhood could be separated into *before* and *after*.

I had often thought that my younger siblings were the lucky ones, too young to remember her at all. But there had to be something that I was missing. Maybe Abel or Royal remembered something I hadn't noticed or had forgotten in time. Something that made sense of why our mother's belongings would be shoved in a box and buried in a basement.

I knew my father had the answers, but I could never go to him. The person closest to him, my younger brother JP, couldn't be trusted. He was only a few years away from becoming exactly the man my father wanted him to be. He was more and more like our dad with every passing year.

I dug my phone from my pocket and fired off a text to my older brothers and hoped it wasn't the first of many mistakes.

We need to talk. It's big.

ROYAL

If you're trying to come out of the closet, it's no big deal. We already know.

Fuck off.

ABEL

Royal, stop being a dipshit. But seriously, Whip, if that's it, we're cool with it.

I SIGHED and rolled my eyes to the ceiling. I was in the middle of a crisis, and my brothers were taking the opportunity to bust my balls.

It's about Mom.

A SERIES of bubbles popped up, then disappeared, and popped up again. No doubt that the bomb I just dropped rattled them both.

ROYAL

The shop's open. We'll be able to talk in private if you want to meet here.

ABEL

I can find someone to cover the brewery. What time?

I'll come by after my shift.

ROYAL

Parking downtown will be nonexistent because of the carnival. Try the alleyway around back. I'll leave the back door open.

IT WAS PROBABLY paranoid of me to delete the text thread with my brothers, but then again, I was well aware of the power Russell King held. I needed to refocus, and for the rest of the afternoon, I dedicated all my attention to checking and rechecking equipment and performing my duties.

Later a text came through from Emily, and it was the only bright spot in my day.

EMILY

Will I see you at the carnival tonight? How did the interview go? I can't wait to hear all about it!

I SMILED DOWN at my phone as I typed my response.

Interview went well. And are you asking me out on a date?

I SHIFTED my weight as nerves rolled through me. The carnival would be a very public place to have a date.

EMILY

I am! My mom mentioned taking Dad to dinner out of town so I figured you wouldn't have to worry about your mean old boss knowing our business. I can make an honest man out of you. Well . . . sort of.

I NEEDED A NIGHT AWAY. Time to get my head right, and I couldn't think of anyone else I would rather spend time with than her.

I could probably be talked into a corn dog and a Ferris wheel ride.

EMILY

I'll wear a disguise.

THINGS WERE SHIFTING. Emily and I had agreed to be casual, but being seen together at one of the biggest events in our small town would be the opposite of casual.

Her school year was over, and my interview was done. I couldn't help but hope that the shift I was feeling was because things were finally clicking into place.

ROYAL WAS RIGHT, of course. Because of the carnival, parking in Outtatowner was nonexistent. Even at the back of the building, cars were crammed in every available parking space. It took me twenty minutes, but I finally wedged my truck in between Ms. Tiny's Cadillac and a dumpster.

The tinny, rhythmic beat of carnival music echoed in the air as I walked up the street toward King Tattoo. I offered quiet waves and gentle nods to the families and neighbors I passed along the way. Excitement for the carnival, which was held two blocks from the main thoroughfare in town in an empty field owned by the city, hung in the air.

The two-day carnival had been set up with rides, games, and even a stage for live music. Anticipation of seeing Emily hummed in my blood, but I had something I needed to take care of first.

I had no doubt that discussion about our mother was about to go over like a lead balloon, but I needed answers. When I reached King Tattoo, I held open the door for a pair of college-age-looking girls who were showing off and laughing over their matching best-friend tattoos.

I took in the shining black-and-white checkerboard floor of the tattoo shop. The space was brightly lit with my brother's artwork framed along the walls. Over time, he had hired other artists, and their work hung alongside his. The King name may be on the building, but my brother valued the artists who worked alongside him.

The hum of the tattoo machines filled the air, and I caught the eye of Luna, the woman who worked the desk and was also the resident piercer. Studs lined the shells of both her ears, and diamonds for dimples winked in the fluorescent lighting.

I pointed to my right cheek. "That one new?"

Luna smiled and tilted her head to show off her newest piercing. "Had to get the other side to match." She batted her lashes.

"Stunning as always. Is Royal around?"

She tipped her head. "He's in the back. Your other brother is already here." She laughed and shook her head. "Jesus, I forgot how scary that one is."

I smiled. "Abel? Come on. He's a teddy bear." Her barking laugh pulled out one of my own. I dragged my hand across my chin. "Yeah, maybe that's a stretch. I'll see you around, Luna."

"Bye," she singsonged and wiggled her fingers in a gentle wave.

My boots echoed on the linoleum as I made my way toward the back room, which served as Royal's office.

The door was only partially closed, so I knocked twice before pushing it open and walking through. "It's me."

Royal's voice greeted me. "It's open."

When I entered, he was behind his desk, stretched out in the leather office chair, his hands folded behind his head, and his long limbs stretched out, boots resting on the desk.

Abel lurked in the corner, his shoulders hunched and hands stuffed into his pockets. I laughed at Luna's previous assessment of my oldest brother. A teddy bear he was not.

When I shut the door all the way behind me, Royal's eyebrow went up in question. "You've got secrets, little brother."

I crossed my arms. "Yeah, well, I'm not the only one. But I need to know that this conversation doesn't leave this room."

"Did you hurt someone?" Familiar pain seeped into Abel's strained voice.

I clamped a hand on his shoulder. "No man, nothing like that. We're all good."

His hulking shoulders relaxed at my words.

Royal moved his boots off his desk and planted his feet

on the ground. "Why do you wanna talk about Mom? Why now?"

I looked around Royal's office. The likelihood anyone would be listening in was low, but I still felt uneasy. "A few weeks ago, Bug found a box in the basement. She was rattled. It had some things in there that were Mom's."

"I thought Dad burned everything," Abel said.

"Yeah, well, he didn't burn this." I sighed and looked at my brothers.

"Why did Bug give it to you?" Royal questioned.

I shrugged. "I don't know . . . because I was there. Maybe?"

"What was in it?" Abel asked.

Tension wound its claws around my shoulders and settled into my neck. "Some old paperwork, a couple of photographs, a jean jacket. Her driver's license."

Royal's eyes whipped to mine. "Driver's license?"

I paced a few steps in his small office. *I knew I wasn't completely off base for thinking it was fucking weird her license was in there.*

"How does somebody leave and start a new life without their driver's license?" Abel's harsh voice was barely above a whisper.

His words validated the exact questions that had been running through my mind.

"Was it expired? Like an old one, from before she left, maybe?" Royal asked.

I thought for a moment. "I guess it's possible. I didn't look that closely at an expiration date or anything. Do either of you remember when she left? The exact month?"

"September 13." Abel's eyes didn't leave the spot on the linoleum.

"How do you know that?" I questioned.

His dark eyes lifted to mine. "Because it was four days before my twelfth birthday."

"Fuck." Royal scrubbed a hand against the back of his neck. "I'd forgotten about that."

"Look, I don't know what this means, or if it means anything at all, but all I know is that that box has been down there for a long time. And when Bug found it, she was freaking the fuck out. Have you ever seen her lose her cool?" I searched my brothers' expressions, and they both gave me a solemn shake of their heads.

I didn't know what else to do. "Do you think maybe it's time? Maybe we should try to find her?"

My brothers were quiet, until Royal finally asked, "Are you okay with the fact that she may not want to be found?"

My gut twisted, but I answered anyway. "Of course."

Abel straightened. "I know someone who may be able to help. My former PO has a few contacts. I can reach out and see if he wants to take it on. He can start poking around and asking questions."

I nodded. Abel had a former parole officer who'd become a friend of sorts. There was a chance one of his contacts may be able to help, and it was better than a local doing the digging.

I looked between my brothers. "But we agree this stays here between us. I don't think we need to drag the girls into this if it's nothing. And JP . . ." My thoughts trailed off.

"Yeah, we know," Abel finished.

I held out my hand to my oldest brother. "All right. Let me know if your guy is up for it, and we'll go from there."

I turned to shake Royal's hand, and he gripped mine. "Go have fun on your date with the chief's daughter." I froze as he grinned and raised his eyebrows. Royal always was a shit stirrer. "You're not as sly as you think, little brother."

I laughed and shook my head. "Apparently not. Just don't fuck this up for me."

"Nah." Royal laughed and shook his head. "I'll let you do that."

TWENTY-SIX

EMILY

Under the velvety cloak of a starry summer night, the carnival unfolded like a fairy-tale dreamland. The air was saturated with the sweet scent of cotton candy, intertwining with the warm, buttery aroma of freshly popped popcorn and fried corn dogs. The distant laughter of children echoed through the air, punctuated by the joyful melodies of a carousel's calliope.

The warm breeze carried the tang of the nearby lake, infusing the atmosphere with a hint of fresh water and exhilaration. Ahead, colorful lights adorned the simple booths and carnival rides, casting a soft glow on the faces of the townsfolk who reveled in the excitement of the carnival. The Ferris wheel, a majestic sentinel against the twilight sky, provided breathtaking views of the distant shoreline and the sparkling waters of Lake Michigan.

Gravel paths had been laid to guide people from the parking lot to where the games and rides were set up. With every step, the crunch beneath my feet created a rhythm that matched my heartbeat as I grew closer to the fervor of the people. Whip and I had agreed to meet just outside the west entrance. I checked the time, and a giddy thrill zipped through me.

After a few excruciating minutes, I recognized his familiar stride. His long legs ate up the distance between us as he made his way from the parking lot to the entrance. Tamping down a laugh, I pulled the Groucho glasses from my purse and slipped them on.

My stomach bunched. We'd had a few moments that felt *off*, and I had more than a few questions—namely, why was there a woman's jacket hanging in his closet?—but I didn't want to be that kind of girl. We'd agreed to be casual, and, for the most part, that was working for me. I wanted his actions to prove to me the kind of man he was, and I prayed it was enough.

As soon as Whip spotted me, his thick laughter cut through the air. I stifled a laugh when my nose twitched. The attached mustache tickled, but I set my face into a serious expression.

Whip casually sauntered toward me. "Excuse me, sir?"

I grinned beneath the ridiculous nose and mustache.

"Do you think you can help me? I'm looking for Emily Ward. She's about yea tall"—Whip held his hand up to my height—"has blondish hair, eyes like the lake after a storm, and a rockin' pair of tits."

A laugh burst from me. I slowly removed the fake-nose glasses and gave him a cheesy smile.

Whip's eyes bugged. "Holy shit. I had no idea."

My body hummed, called to him. I wanted to melt into him and be swept away in the timeless magic of the carnival's embrace, without having to worry about who might see us.

Instead, I let my laughter fade and slipped the glasses back into my purse. "Fancy meeting you here."

He nodded. "Total coincidence. You hungry?"

I turned toward the entrance. "Starved."

Together we melted with the crowd, funneling through the roped entryway and into the heart of the event. It was a time capsule of childhood nostalgia, where the rides seemed to have grown up right along with you—a little creaky but still chugging along through life.

"It's funny how every carnival is always exactly the same," Whip noted.

I turned to him. "I was just thinking the same thing." My attention wandered to the chipped paint and rusted lettering of the nearby Tilt-A-Whirl. "I'm one thousand percent positive this carnival company is the same one that would do the carnival in the town I grew up in. The foundation had to pay them in *cash*." I shook my head and laughed. "Probably the same workers too."

Whip looked around us. "I wouldn't doubt it." He sucked in a deep breath. "Who would have thought the smell of funnel cake and engine oil would be so appealing."

"Yes, funnel cake!" I grabbed his arm and dragged him toward the first food vendor I saw. My hand dropped from his biceps as soon as we got in line, and I itched to touch him again. Being this close, out in the open, felt forbidden and exciting.

He looked at me. "Looks like you pulled it off."

I glanced around at the smiling faces. The circus calliope music played behind us as we waited to order. "Everyone loves a carnival. I was surprised by how much I really loved all the planning that went into the fundraisers. It makes sense, I guess. I love a good plan."

We stepped forward, and he looked down at me. "What is your plan, Prim? What's next for you?"

When Whip's slate eyes bore into me like that, the

world seemed to fade away. He had a way of making me feel seen. *Chosen.* The sick irony was that I'd been chosen by the one man I couldn't have.

His question held a silent weight, as if my brain was also asking, *What's next for us?* With the way things were, I'd never be more than a secret. I knew it would be safer to not let whatever it was that was building inside me go too far. Things would get only messier if my feelings went uncontained. Instead of letting my tumbling feelings get the best of me, I stuffed them down and focused my attention on having a fun time.

"Well, school's out." I smiled. "Mrs. Kirk officially put in her resignation, so I would like to transition to a full-time teacher at Outtatowner Junior High."

His eyes studied my face, and then he shrugged and looked forward. "You'll get it."

His vote of confidence infused me with pleasure, and I grinned. "I think so too."

After we ordered—funnel cake for me and a corn dog for him—we continued weaving our way through the people. So many had gathered that I recognized only a handful of faces in the smiling crowd. Despite the number of strangers that surrounded us, something about Outtatowner always felt safe, welcoming. The town sign promised it was a place where strangers became friends, and that was exactly how it felt.

I breathed in a lungful of July air and sighed. "I really like it here."

Whip looked around. "It's a great place." His pace slowed and he glanced at me. "I'm surprised you haven't been here more often."

I tossed my used paper boat into a nearby trash can and dusted off my fingers. "I visited my parents once or twice, but by the time Dad got the job as chief, I was already living in Virginia."

Whip's lips formed a line. "Did you like it down there?"

Apprehension coiled in my stomach. "Um." I hated talking about that time in my life and the mistakes I had made. "It was okay at first." We walked side by side, and he gave me space to continue. With my eyes trained in front of me, I searched for the guts to open up to him. "The guy I was dating had gotten a job down there—that's how I ended up in Virginia in the first place. He's a firefighter."

"Ahh . . ." Humor danced in Whip's eyes. "So that's why you hate us."

I laughed. "I don't hate you, I just . . . *know* you."

"Oh yeah? What do you know?" he asked.

"Just the type." I waved my hand inarticulately in the air. "Adrenaline junkies. Always looking for the next exciting thing. Running into fires and saving cats from trees to get a kiss from the stay-at-home mom."

His brows pinched down. "That is oddly specific."

I lifted a shoulder. "Well, in my case, the next exciting thing wasn't the stay-at-home mom, it was my best friend and co-teacher."

He shook his head. "Ouch."

"Yeah, that was very un-fun information to find out. After I caught them—in *my* car no less—I couldn't even look at her, let alone teach in the same room and be everything our students needed." The familiar pinch of failure to see the year through poked my ribs. "So I quit. I left at the end of the semester. Came here and took a pay cut and Mrs. Kirk's maternity leave job just to finish the school year."

"Well, it wasn't because he was a firefighter." The rasp in his voice rolled over me. "It was because he's a fucking idiot."

I preened, knowing that maybe Whip also thought Craig lost something when I left. I bumped my shoulder into his. "You know, I liked you better when you hated me."

"Liar." He laughed. "Besides, I never hated you. But maybe I hated the way you made me feel."

Tingles spread through my chest. Light danced across his features as I stopped to face him. "How did I make you feel?"

His jaw ticced and my heart rate spiked. "Like I'd burn down my entire world just to have you."

My brain fizzled and my blood buzzed. I pointed a finger toward his nose and grinned. "See. Reckless."

With a laugh Whip grabbed my finger and pulled me closer to him. We stood on the outskirts of the carnival, surrounded by neighbors and strangers, as the world moved around us. Tension crackled between us. My attention bounced from his lips to his eyes. His tongue darted out to wet his lips.

A shove from behind sent me crashing into him. I turned to see Robbie Lambert with his hands in the air.

"Oh shit! I mean shoot. Sorry, Miss Ward."

I gathered myself and smiled. "Hey, Robbie. It's okay." My eyes flicked from his new shoes to his face, and my heart sank. I narrowed in on a bruise coloring his high cheekbone with shades of deep purple seeping into a putrid greenish-yellow edge.

I reached my hand out but snatched it back when he retreated a few steps. "What happened to your face? Are you okay?"

His fingertips brushed along the bruise. "Oh yeah. It's nothing. Just messing around. See you later, Miss Ward."

"Bye . . . ," I let out weakly as I watched him jog toward his friends and rejoin his group.

"You okay?" Whip asked.

I shook my head. "Fine, it's just . . . did you believe him? About his bruise?"

Whip looked ahead to where Robbie and his friends had disappeared into the crowd. "Sure, why not?"

Something more sinister scratched at my brain. "I think his dad hits him."

Whip frowned. "Do you have proof? Has he ever told you that?"

My lips pressed together. "No, it's just a feeling. He's had some bruises on his arms before but never on his face. That bruise looked fresh and painful."

"You could always talk with Principal Cartwright."

I shook my head and set my shoulders. "I'm a mandated reporter. As a teacher I am required by law to report *any* suspected abuse."

He paused, his eyes slightly widening. "I just meant to get a second opinion. That's all. A lot of those kids play tackle football on the beach. We used to catch a stray elbow every once in a while. I didn't mean anything by it."

"I know, I'm sorry. I think I'm just worried. There's something about his dad that gives me a bad feeling."

"Pokey Lambert is a hothead and a prick, but I don't think he's a child abuser."

I chewed the inside of my lip as I searched the crowd for one last glance at Robbie. "Yeah, maybe you're right."

He was lost in the crowd, so I set aside the gnawing feeling. My mood lifted, and my eyes lit up when I spotted the fun house entrance ahead. "Come on, I want to show you something."

TWENTY-SEVEN

WHIP

THE DARK CORRIDOR of the fun house closed in on us as the floor shifted beneath my feet. I kept one hand locked on the railing and the other on Emily's hip. Wrapped in the safety of darkness, I was free to touch her. My hand slipped down to grope her ass.

"Watch it." She smirked over her shoulder as she ducked under the wall that led to the next turn.

"Oh, I'm watching it." I palmed her butt again, letting my hand slip between her thighs. "I like what I see."

In the next section of the fun house, Emily stood with her shoulders hunched forward, facing the wall. "What about now?"

I stood behind her, taking in her reflection in the fun house mirror. I laughed at the way the convex mirror distorted her image to a short-legged, very rotund version of her typically lithe self.

"I don't know . . ." I stood next to her, watching my own reflection bend and change as I moved. "I kind of like it."

Emily covered her mouth to hide her laugh. "You know,

if I tilt my head like this, you kind of look like Dickie Johnson."

My face fell, and I anchored my attention on her with a dead stare. "Don't. You. Dare," I teased. I ran my fingers over my lower lip. "I don't even have a flavor savor."

Her squeal of delighted laughter floated above the music, and I grinned before wrapping her in my arms. Our reflection stretched in the mirror, distorting the top of my head to the ceiling. "Would you still like me if my head was this huge?"

Her arms covered mine and squeezed. "Well, it would finally match your overinflated ego."

I nipped at her neck with a growl and grinned. Sparring with Emily was always a highlight.

When a couple of teenagers walked past us and disappeared around the corner, I got an idea. "Come here," I whispered against her soft skin.

Pulling her backward into a dead end, I held her close. Tucked away in the corner, the dull hum of the festivities continued just past the walls of the fun house. Surrounded by mirrors, we were exposed, but my skin was dry tinder, and Emily was the fire that threatened to consume me.

I pressed her back against the mirror, savoring the way her body instantly molded to mine. "I could take you. Right here with the whole world waiting outside, not knowing if someone will come walking up and find us."

She hummed and pressed against me. "That would be unfortunate." Her eyebrow lifted in challenge.

"Do you think I wouldn't try?" I challenged.

"Well . . ." Emily's voice was a breathless whisper as she leaned in close to my ear. "You'll have to catch me first." With a peal of laughter, she ducked under my arm and disappeared around a corner.

"Little shit," I grumbled and took off after her, bumping into a wall and having to feel my way around it.

The labyrinth of mirrors continued, each turn heightening the suspense as I pursued her. Laughter echoed, distorted in the reflective surfaces, and all other sounds became a distant symphony. My heart raced, not just from the chase, but from the undercurrent of something more, something building between us.

I squeezed past an elderly couple with a mumbled apology until I finally cornered Emily in a dead-end alcove. Our breathless laughter mingled, and the charged atmosphere enveloped us. She looked at me with playful defiance, her eyes sparkling with mischief. I closed the distance between us, reveling in the electricity that crackled in the air.

The carnival's ambient noise blurred into the background as I pressed Emily against the mirrored wall. The distorted reflections made the moment surreal, like a dream where reality bent to the whims of my desire. Her breath hitched as our eyes locked, the world outside disappearing.

"I could catch you anytime I want," I whispered, my voice a low rumble that mirrored the distant roars of ancient rides. The tension between us was palpable, a magnetic force drawing us closer.

A daring smile played on her lips, and she challenged me with her eyes. "Then go ahead and catch me."

In pursuit of the game, I lunged forward, but she slipped away, navigating the maze with an agility that left me both frustrated and captivated. The mirrors twisted reality, creating a kaleidoscope of images as we danced through the labyrinth.

Emily finally reached the exit and leaped off the fun house platform. Without missing a beat, she continued her escape across the matted grass and through the crowd. Our chase led us to the outskirts of the carnival, behind a ring-toss game, where the lingering sounds faded into a muted hum. As we darted into a secluded corner between two games, the atmosphere shifted. The coastal air was alive with an unspoken tension, and Emily's laughter softened into a shared secret between us.

Breathing heavily, I caught her arm and spun her around, pushing her back against a quiet, darkened trailer wall. The carnival's pulse lingered in the background, but here, in the shadows, it was just us.

"I knew you—"

Mid-sentence I gave in—my mouth crashed to hers.

The world ceased to exist for that stolen moment. The subtle taste of funnel cake lingered on her lips, and the thrill of chasing her intensified. As I pulled back, our eyes met, and the realization of just how far gone for her I was hit me.

In the silence that followed, Emily's sea-blue eyes locked with mine.

My body screamed: *She is everything.*

Movement caught my eye, and I became aware of a figure standing beyond the shadows in the main walkway of the carnival. My eyes widened as I met the stern gaze of Chief Martin. The echoes of laughter seemed to mock me, turning our night into a high-stakes game with consequences I hadn't fully anticipated. I stilled, suspended in a moment of uncertainty, as the energy surged around us, a jumble of emotions swirling in the air.

Emily's father's gaze bore into me, and my heart pounded. I swallowed hard, searching for words that eluded me.

"What is it?" Emily looked around, still laughing and breathing hard from the intensity of our kiss.

Time seemed to stretch as I stood there, caught in the headlights of a realization that this game, this chase, had consequences beyond the fun house walls. The air thickened with a deafening silence, the carnival sounds now far off whispers.

Emily saw her father, and her eyes widened, mirroring the shock that gripped me. We had wanted to keep our date a secret, away from prying eyes, but now the secret was out, exposed in the dimly lit alley. Our energy had shifted from excitement to a tense uncertainty.

"Whip," said the chief, his voice low and measured, cutting through the quiet like a knife. My name hung in the air, heavy with disapproval and an unspoken threat.

I took a step back, distancing myself from Emily, but the weight of the situation pressed on my shoulders. The carnival, with its flashing lights and spinning rides, seemed to dim around us. I searched for words, any words, to salvage the moment, but they eluded me like ghosts slipping through my fingers.

"Dad." Emily smoothed her palms down her jeans as her father stepped forward, his expression a mix of anger and disappointment. "I thought you were at dinner. I—"

"Your mother wanted to see the carnival."

My pulse throbbed in my ears, a discordant rhythm to the scene unfolding. The silence between us stretched.

"I thought I made myself clear," he said, his voice now a controlled but seething force. I wasn't sure if he was speaking to Emily or to me.

I struggled to find my voice, my mind racing to comprehend the depth of the situation. Emily stood beside me, her eyes pleading for understanding, for a way to defuse the impending storm. But the whirling lights and festive chaos had turned into a silent witness to our unraveling secrets.

"Sir, I . . ." My words faltered, and I felt the weight of Chief Martin's gaze. The laughter in the background mocked me, a reminder of the freedom and joy we had sought in coming here.

The silence hung heavy, a thick fog enveloping us. Emily's father took another step forward, and my instincts screamed at me to escape, to run from the storm. But my feet were rooted to the ground, entangled in a web of secrets and consequences.

And then, just as the tension reached its peak, the lights flickered, casting the alley into momentary darkness. In that fleeting obscurity, I glimpsed a knowing smile on Emily's face. A glimmer of mischief danced in her eyes, and before the lights fully returned, she whispered, "Run."

As if pulled by an invisible force, I broke into a sprint, gripping Emily's hand. The energy surrounding me grew to a frantic pulse, urging me forward. I navigated through the twists and turns of the parked trailers, the darkness my ally in our unexpected escape.

The world around me blurred as I ran, the echoes of Emily's laughter and her father's stern voice fading into the night.

We spilled into the parking lot, vibrant lights welcoming us back into the whirlwind of the fun. My heart pounded, and I cast a quick glance over my shoulder, half expecting to see Emily's father in pursuit. But the alley remained silent and empty.

Emily huffed and bent to catch her breath. "Oh my god. I can't believe we did that!"

I held the sharp pain at my side, then pointed at her as I paced. "You . . . are trouble."

She laughed and swatted a strand of hair from her face.

"I don't know what came over me. I just saw his face and freaked out. He looked *pissed*."

She was laughing. *Why the hell was she laughing?*

"It's because he *was* pissed," I huffed.

And confused.

Betrayed.

The kaleidoscope of colors and dizzying rides had returned to their carefree facade. Yet the encounter in the alley lingered like a shadow, a reminder that secrets had real consequences, even in the midst of a night that was supposed to be fun.

The blinking lights and laughter were a bittersweet backdrop to the tumult of emotions swirling within me. The night had taken an unexpected turn, the highs of the fun house chase now tempered by the sobering reality of our less-than-secret rendezvous.

I planted my hands on my hips. "Why are you laughing?"

Emily sighed, and her face twisted in amusement. "Because it's funny? Whip, we got caught kissing by my dad and we *ran*." She cupped her hands around her mouth and shouted into the night sky, "How's that for checking something off my list, Dad?"

Emily chuckled again. "We ran like a bunch of teenagers." Her deep sigh filled the air. "Oh my god, he was right. This feels so good. I haven't had this much fun in forever."

I couldn't shake the image of Emily's mischievous smile in the darkened alley and how fire sparked in her eyes when she whispered *run*. It was a smile that held promises of future adventures, of challenges yet to be faced.

"A King doesn't run. We take our beatings with heads held high." My jaw ticced.

Emily sauntered past me into the parking lot, playfully brushing her finger over the tip of my nose. "That's fucked up."

I sighed and let my hands drop. "Yeah, I guess it probably is."

"I'll talk with my dad tomorrow." She walked backward, seemingly unfazed by the outing of our secret relationship. Emily crooked her finger. "Now get over here."

TWENTY-EIGHT

EMILY

THE CLINK of a spoon against her teacup was the only sound that filled my mother's kitchen. Her eyes slid to mine as my fingertips drummed a silent beat on the countertop beneath me. Perched in my spot—sitting atop the kitchen counter in the corner—I waited just like I had any other time I knew I was in deep shit.

Mom swirled the spoon in her cup. "William is . . ."

"I know."

Her brows pinched. "And his family . . ."

"I know."

She sighed. "And your dad . . ."

"I know."

I thought for a moment. "So is he '*I'm twenty minutes late for curfew* mad' or '*Poppy Kerr and I got into that fender bender* mad'?"

My mother paused her stirring and lifted her eyebrows. "He's '*you got drunk at prom* mad.'"

Oh fuck.

It wouldn't shock anyone to know that I was a good girl in high school. I made perfect grades and hung out with nice kids and rarely made any trouble. But once, during my junior year, I briefly dated a boy one year older than me. He took me to the seniors' postprom after party and asked, "You drink, right?" while he made a screwdriver that was mostly vodka with only a hint of orange juice.

To which, of course, I lied and stumbled, "Definitely. Yes. Love the—that alcoholic beverage."

Spoiler: I didn't love it.

In fact, even thinking of a screwdriver all these years later made the bile rise in the back of my throat. One drink in, and I was shit-faced. Thankfully, my boyfriend was a decent guy, and after I spilled water all over my lap in a failed attempt at being sexy and rendered my khaki skirt completely see-through, he decided to take me home early.

Unfortunately for him and for me, my stepdad had been waiting up just in case I needed anything. It was the only time I ever saw that look in his eyes—the one that clearly communicated, *I'm not mad, I'm just disappointed.*

I fucking hated that look.

I would have much preferred being punished with extra chores or community service—literally anything but having to deal with the mopey look on his face, or how he would go quiet and simply shake his head and walk away. It didn't matter how old I was, disappointing the man who wasn't required by biology to love me, but did it anyway, was gut-wrenching.

When I let my head hang in defeat, my mother crossed the kitchen and placed her hand on my knee. When she squeezed, I gathered the courage to look her in the eye.

Her denim-blue eyes were soft and understanding. "Just hear him out, honey. I think you'll be surprised by what he has to say."

I picked at a nonexistent piece of lint on the frayed hem of my jean shorts. "And what do you have to say about it?"

Her hand patted my knee. "I think you've really come out of your shell in the last few months. You smile more. Of course I love that you're here in town. That happy little Melly I know is right here . . ." She tapped my chest just under my collarbone. "I've gotten to see more of that little girl in the last few months than I have in years. And if that's William King's doing, then I'm happy for you."

Her weighted words landed with a thud in my belly. *Had I even noticed that I had changed? Was it Whip's doing, or was it being in this town? This place that suddenly felt like home?*

"He's a part of it, I think," I admitted. "But it's also that for the first time I feel like I'm where I'm supposed to be." I sighed and let my hands rest in my lap. "I don't know how to explain it."

My mother gripped her hand in mine. "I know exactly what you mean. There's something magical in these Michigan waters." She gave my hand a squeeze, and when I looked at her, she winked. "The men around here aren't too bad to look at either."

I laughed and leaned in to hug my mother. My whole life, she had been steadfast and strong—a lighthouse to guide me while still allowing me to find my own path.

She couldn't always protect me from my decisions, but she had always been there to weather the storm of any consequences that came after.

"Do you think the Bluebirds know?" I asked.

My mother's soft laugh filled her kitchen. "Darling, you were sucking each other's faces off in a dark corner at a highly anticipated carnival in a small town. I doubt anyone is going to believe he was simply performing CPR. I think it's safe to say everyone knows."

From across the room, my dad cleared his throat, and Mom stepped back from our hug. I hopped off the counter, and Mom gave my arm one last reassuring squeeze.

"Good luck, but don't let him fool you. He is still a big marshmallow," she whispered.

I gave her a quick nod and walked across the kitchen, past Dad, and into his office down the hallway.

His home office was much more personable than the one at the station with *Chief Martin* painted on the door. Here, his computer desk was tidy, but framed pictures covered nearly every available surface. Snapshots from family vacations, Christmases, and old black-and-whites of his granddad, who was also a fire chief, added a cozy ambiance to the office. Despite it being summertime, his oversize sweater still hung on the back of his chair.

I turned to face him, leaning my butt against his desk and crossing my feet at the ankles. In the thirty steps between the kitchen and his office, I'd decided that my newfound Emily-ness was something I needed to embrace.

So I gathered my courage to face my stepdad. I took a deep breath and clasped my hands in my lap to keep from fidgeting. "So . . . I think I owe you an apology. I'm sure it was a shock to see the woman you raised in a slightly compromising position last night. However, Whip and I are both adults, and I don't need your permission regarding who I date, so for that I will not apologize."

"Okay." My dad blinked. "Do you think you need to apologize for running away from me?"

"Perhaps." I bit back a smile. "I panicked."

Dad rounded his desk and sank into the chair with a sigh. "Oh, Melly. What am I going to do with you?"

I turned and sat on the love seat across from him. "I'm not a kid anymore, Dad. You don't really have to *do* anything."

He rubbed his eyes. Over the years the fine lines had aged him, but he was still exactly as I always remembered him. "Do you know I fell for you even before I loved your mother?"

I blinked at the man across from me.

"It's true," he continued. "You were three and your mother and I had been seeing each other for a while. She made me wait six months before I met you. Your hair was up in these little blonde pigtails, and you *loved* party dresses. In the backyard you plunked down in the mud, making a mess and having a ball." His eyes went unfocused, as if he could see that tiny version of me so clearly. "I walked up to say hello, and you just looked at me, stuck out your chubby little hand, and said, 'Well, come on.'" He laughed. "That's all it took. Three little words and I was a goner."

Tears pricked my eyes. I had never known my biological father, but the man in front of me was 1,000 percent always meant to be my dad. "I'm still that girl, Dad. I'm just . . ." I looked down at myself and sighed. "Older."

"Time is a thief. You're going to wake up one day and realize that all these days you wished would pass, *have*—and you'd give anything to slow it down."

Emotion thickened in my throat. I hated thinking about my parents getting older and what that meant. Staying in Outtatowner would mean more time with them, and I clung to that thought.

"Which is why," Dad continued, "you shouldn't waste any of it on the wrong person. You and your mother are the reasons my life is as happy and fulfilled as it is."

I frowned, not liking his implication. "What makes you think Whip's the wrong person?"

He smiled. "I never said he was. He's a good man. His work ethic is unrivaled—"

"But what?" I stood, a tiny spark of indignation building in my chest. "That's not good enough for you?"

Dad chuckled and lifted his hand to give me pause. "No man will ever be good enough for you, peanut. That's just the way it is. But if you say he's the guy then, well . . ." He sighed and let his hands fall to his lap. "Then he'll be the guy. Change your mind, and there will be a hundred more lined up behind him waiting for his shot."

I laughed at the ridiculous image he painted. "I doubt there would be *hundreds* lined up," I joked.

He leaned forward. "You give so much of your attention to the man right in front of you that you can't see anything else—and that's not always a bad thing. But I saw it with that dipshit Craig, and I'm telling you, if you would have taken a peek around him, you would have seen what I saw a lot sooner."

My voice was barely above a whisper. "What's that?"

"You're the prize. Always have been."

My eyes dropped to my lap. "Thanks, Dad."

"Ah, go on." He laughed and cleared the emotion from his throat. "You're a grown woman. Go live your life."

I grinned and stood, then leaned over his desk to wrap him in a hug. "I love you, Dad. I'm sorry if I disappointed you."

He smiled. "Love you too. I just hope you know you don't have to hide things—not from me. Your mom and I are always in your corner."

"Thanks, Dad."

I had started walking toward the door, feeling lighter

than I had all morning, when his voice stopped me. "Hey, Melly? Don't forget . . . if he breaks your heart, I can make him disappear and make it look like an accident."

~

WITH MY HEAD HELD HIGH, I let the July sunshine warm my face as I walked through town. I couldn't wait to fill Whip in on my conversation with my dad. I knew he was worried about the promotion, but he would see that my dad wasn't the kind of man to hold our personal relationship against him. If Whip was the best man for the job, he'd get it.

No more secrets. No more worrying we'd get caught. No more lying about where I had been.

If I was being honest with myself, I was definitely going to miss the charged looks he'd send me from across the bar or the brush of his fingertip down my arm when he walked past, but I'd get over it. We could actually *date*.

The giddiness pumping through me added a pep to my step as I smiled and waved at every single person that I passed. With each day I was getting better at recognizing the townies from the tourists and what made this quirky little town tick.

It felt like an afternoon to celebrate. I stopped and looked up at the storefront sign: *The Sugar Bowl*. The town's bakery was always packed—and for good reason. Their coffee was hot, and the man who owned the bakery, Huck Benton, was a genius in the kitchen. An idea danced through me. Whip said people were always dropping things off at the station for the firefighters. I could get a box of pastries and bring it to the station myself. I could shock the hell out of Whip when I pulled him in for a smacking kiss, right there in front of everyone.

I pulled open the glass door to the Sugar Bowl and stifled an excited squeal as the scene played out in my mind. I held it for two little old ladies to exit while I daydreamed of Whip.

It would be perfect, and I was certain that after the initial shock of it, Whip's stormy eyes would darken and warn me of delicious promises to come.

TWENTY-NINE

WHIP

I CHECKED my phone for the hundredth time and frowned at it when she still hadn't texted. Half a dozen times I'd typed out a pathetic text to check in with her, but I didn't want to interrupt if they were still hashing it out. *Clingy* was not the light in which I wanted to be viewed by her, but the truth was I had been crawling out of my skin. I was spending the last few minutes of my shift in the break room and I was anxious to hear how the conversation with her father had gone.

Word spread quickly about Emily and me, and my phone had been buzzing all morning with nosy texts from friends and my sisters.

MJ

Stop ignoring us. We're your sisters and
Emily's friend. GIVE US THE DETAILS.

If she's your friend, then you can ask her.

SYLVIE

Fun ruiner.

SYLVIE IMMEDIATELY SENT an adorable selfie of her squishing little Gus's drooly face.

SYLVIE

How can you keep secrets from this cute face?

If memory serves, he and his daddy *were* a pretty big secret.

MJ

He's got you there, Syl.

SYLVIE

Fiiiiiine. We'll go bug Emily for answers.

Please don't.

WITH HALF A SMILE, I looked up from my phone and around the station. Chief hadn't been in yet, and dread seeped into my gut, erasing any relief my sisters had given me. I knew before I did it that going after Emily was wrong—her father was my boss and mentor. I was shit at relationships, and when I inevitably fucked it up, it would put us both in the awkward position of having to take sides. But now that I was in it, I couldn't get myself out—and didn't want to. My soul called for her, and I would *always* choose her.

I only hoped that was a choice I wouldn't be forced to make.

The longer uncertainty hung in the air, the more agitated I became. Sitting around and waiting for the hammer to drop was excruciating. I drummed my fingers against the counter as I waited impatiently for the coffee maker to hurry the fuck up.

With the first sip, my coffee tasted like bitterness and anxiety as I mulled over the possible outcomes of Emily's talk with her dad. My eyes kept flicking to the clock, each passing second a painful reminder of the unresolved tension. I couldn't shake the image of Chief storming into the station, his face stern, disappointment etched in the lines of his forehead. My heart pounded, a steady beat of dread accompanying each tick of the clock.

"Yo, Whip!" Connor's voice called on the intercom. "You've got a visitor downstairs."

I walked to the top step and looked down at his grinning face. I sighed. "Don't fuck with me. I can't handle another granny gorilla striptease."

Connor barked a laugh. Last year I had gotten a "visitor," and it turned out to be someone dressed as an elderly gorilla. As soon as I walked to the door, the gorilla started playing music and removing her clothing—*complete with granny panties*. I knew Lee was behind it. Hell, I was fairly certain it was *him* dressed in the costume, and it was fucking hilarious—not that I'd ever admit that to him.

Connor jerked his head to the side. "Come on. I think you're going to want to see this one."

Taking the steps two at a time, I bounded downstairs. My heart thunked against my ribs when I saw Emily standing with a large white bakery box in her arms and a wide, bright smile on her face.

"Aww . . ." Her lower lip jutted out. "I thought maybe you'd ride the pole down."

Connor covered his laugh with his hand, and I shot him a look, telling him to get lost.

I stepped up to Emily. *She's actually here—standing in the apparatus bay surrounded by trucks and the smells of rubber and lemon cleaner.*

She hefted the box higher. "I got something for you."

"Is that so?" I tipped open the lid to find an array of neatly arranged pastries from the Sugar Bowl. "The crew will love them. Thank you."

She beamed up at me, and we smiled at each other like fools.

How was this actually happening?

Emily gently cleared her throat. "I talked to my dad."

I searched her eyes, but they were clear and sure. The tightness in my shoulders relaxed the tiniest amount.

"I think we're going to be just fine, you and me."

You and me.

I liked the sound of that.

Sure, I still wanted to talk with my chief about everything that had happened, but for the moment, Emily assured me things were going to be okay. It almost didn't feel real. Things like this didn't work out for guys like me. Women like Emily Ward didn't fall for unworthy men.

"So we're good then?" I asked.

Her gentle, excited nod was enough to send my mind sailing. She shrugged as I relieved her of the pastry box. "I'm sure there's going to be a level of ball-busting I don't really understand, but from where I'm standing, Dad took the news about as well as he could have."

My tongue was thick and my jaw twitched. *Was it really that easy?* If I trusted in the carefree way she showed up at the fire station and the brightness in her blue-green eyes, then yeah . . . I guessed it was.

"I'm taking you out." I grinned.

Her eyebrows shot up. "Oh, really?"

My molars clamped down to hide my cheesy grin. "Damn right. If this isn't a secret anymore, the whole damn town is going to know you're mine."

Her lips folded in as a shy blush pinked her cheeks. "I think I'd like that."

"Be ready by seven. I'll pick you up at the house." I nodded toward the open bay door. "Now get out of here. You're too distracting to be walking around here looking all cute."

She used two fingers to give me a salute. "You got it."

When she turned, I balanced the pastry box in one hand and used the other to playfully smack her ass. She yelped and giggled before stepping out into the sunny July afternoon.

~

"IT'S KIND OF hard to tell." Emily leaned in and whispered as I slid her fruity drink in front of her. The Grudge was busy, and old country classics crooned from the jukebox as a new band set up on the stage.

I grunted a response and sipped my beer. "It's subtle, but it's there." I leaned in to inconspicuously point toward the west side of the bar. "If you look, those are all Sullivans and their allies. You can tell by the way they all have sunbeams shooting out of their asses."

She gave me a dry side-eye and slyly smiled. "And what about the Kings?"

I chuckled and sat back. "That's easy. Any King carries the weight of the world. You can see it in the shoulders."

Her eyes raked over the east side, taking in members of my extended family and those associated with us. "Always ready to fight, huh?"

I nodded and sipped. "Pretty much."

"It's wild that this feud has gone on so long and anyone who's not from here is none the wiser. Tourists just *exist* alongside it and have no idea."

I stretched my arm over the back of her chair and allowed my fingertips to brush along the soft skin at the base of her neck. "We're no fools. This is a tourist town, and because of that, it keeps us in check. The town may be divided from years of rivalry, but neither side would put the town at risk by alienating the main source of income. We rely on families visiting Outtatowner and coming back every year. How our families feel about each other really doesn't matter. Just the way it goes."

My sister walked in, tucked under the arm of Duke Sullivan, and I watched as they took up space directly in the middle of the bar.

"Maybe not so divided after all." Emily was smiling at my sister and gave her a friendly wave, which Sylvie returned.

Duke and I locked eyes, and he tipped his chin in greeting. I lifted my glass to return it. "You might be right about that."

Things were shifting in Outtatowner—you could feel it in the air. Lines were blurred all over the place, and if I knew anything, my father would be the first person to push back. He'd all but disowned my sister.

I swallowed another gulp of beer and pushed away any

thoughts of Russell King from my mind. Tonight was about Emily and me, and he couldn't take that from me.

As the band started their first set, I drummed my hands on the wood tabletop. Then I held my palm to her. "May I have this dance, Prim?"

Excitement danced in Emily's eyes as she slipped her hand into mine. "I would love to."

Slowly, I led her to the dance floor and felt eyes swivel in our direction. Emily had been in Outtatowner long enough now that everyone knew she was Chief Martin's daughter. Word about us kissing at the carnival, only to be discovered by her father, had also blazed through town like an inferno.

I twirled Emily under my arm as we reached the dance floor. Together we swayed to the music. Emily rested on my chest, and I held her close, dropping a kiss on the top of her head. Memories of the night we met swirled in my mind. I'd known then she was something special, but I hadn't had a clue how much she'd completely upend my life.

How much I *craved* that.

Curious eyes swept over us as we confirmed the speculation that Whip King was, in fact, together with Emily Ward. I basked in the knowledge that this fiery, amazing woman was *mine*.

And the only person who could ruin it was me.

THIRTY

EMILY

Publicly dating Whip King was like riding on a parade float—like the star jock set his sights on *you* and everyone knew it. Only instead of high school glory days and mediocre kissing skills, Whip had a pierced dick and kissed like a god.

July was floating by on a cloud of beachy, sun-soaked days and steamy, limb-tangling nights. I'd all but moved into Whip's house, and it was so freeing to know that I didn't have to carry the weight of our secret any longer.

With Whip working, my day was wide open, and I planned to spend all of it stretched out on the beach, working on my tan. But first, coffee. I pushed open the door to the Sugar Bowl. It still surprised me how many tourists flocked to this tiny coastal town. Standing in line, I hardly recognized anyone as smells of cinnamon and roasted coffee beans mingled with freshly applied suntan lotion.

I quickly scanned the menu board before making my decision. When my phone chimed, I reached into my bag to see if it was Mom, confirming she'd secured a spot on the beach for us. I paused, staring at the phone as *Outtatowner*

Junior High flashed across the screen. Stepping forward in line, I held the phone to my ear while plugging the other with my finger.

"Hello?" I answered.

"Miss Ward? Principal Cartwright. Is this a good time?"

"Oh, uh—yeah. Yes. Sorry, I'm at the bakery, and it's a bit loud." I offered a small, apologetic smile to the couple I was hunched against and slid away as the line moved forward without me.

I tucked myself into a corner of the bustling bakery and infused my voice with the practiced calm of a cheery professional. "Thank you for calling, sir. As I mentioned in my letter of interest, I was hoping to discuss my qualifications for the open teaching position."

"Uh, yes." He cleared his throat. "That's why I'm calling."

Yes! I bit back a happy dance and pressed my lips together so he could continue.

"This is a courtesy call to inform you that the position has been filled."

The slow-motion whoosh between my ears drowned out the titter of voices in the bakery. The room spun as I struggled to comprehend the words he'd spoken.

"I'm sorry?" I had to have heard him wrong.

"Mrs. Kirk's position has been filled. I wanted to be the person to tell you and to thank you for your time at OJH."

"Oh, I . . ." I blinked.

"If you need a reference, feel free to use my contact information, and I would be happy to provide a strong recommendation." His uncomfortable pause made my skin itch. "All in all, your work was more than satisfactory."

"More than satisfactory?" Simply repeating his words still didn't make them sink in.

Principal Cartwright sighed. "I know this isn't what you wanted, Miss Ward."

My jaw set. "Was it something to do with my performance? I'm sorry. I don't understand."

He paused, and the deafening silence spoke volumes. "No. It was . . ." He exhaled an irritated sigh, and my stomach dropped. "We received a phone call that shed some light on the fundraising efforts of the educational foundation that the school board simply couldn't look past."

I stilled, my hackles up. I may have been confused, but I sure as hell wasn't going down without a fight. "The foundation? We raised more money in those three events than the foundation had in *years*. Isn't that a good thing?"

"Everyone appreciates your efforts, we do, but—"

"But it wasn't enough?" My professionalism was slipping—I knew that—but rejection burned inside my gut. Hot tears poked beneath my eyelids as I felt my future slipping between my fingers like sand.

On the line, my former principal sighed. "Did you or did you not go around my direct orders to leave Robbie Lambert and his need for shoes alone?"

My mind whirled. Sure, I had been reprimanded about giving him the shoes, but it was Whip who'd organized the firefighters to provide *all* the students with something so that Robbie wouldn't be singled out.

"I mean . . . I—" Hot anger bubbled inside me. "Why is his father so upset about someone caring for his son?"

"Miss Ward, it was not Mr. Lambert who filed the complaint. In fact, the issue of caring for his son is exactly what got us into this mess. Did you also know that a report of suspected child abuse was filed against the family?"

I stilled. Unable to get the image of Robbie and his bruised face out of my mind, I had made a call after the carnival to report my growing suspicions. I had gotten so wrapped up in my secret with Whip being outed that I hadn't taken the opportunity to inform the school of my report quite yet. "Um . . ."

Fuck.

Nerves rippled down my spine as my mind whirled.

Principal Cartwright huffed on the other end of the line. "Exactly as I suspected. Miss Ward, while I appreciate all teachers caring for their students, accusations of this nature are very serious."

"I completely agree, which is why I—"

"Miss Ward, instead of following protocol—trusting your team—you tried to solve this on your own. Robbie Lambert is enrolled in tae kwon do. Were you aware of that?"

I frowned, confused. "No, I wasn't."

"He also recently participated in a sparring competition in which he, very publicly, was the unfortunate recipient of a pretty nasty black eye. Were you aware of *that*?"

Dread pooled in my stomach. "No."

"He won the competition, by the way, but because of your call to Child Protective Services, instead of celebrating that victory, he and his family are actively being questioned regarding your accusation. I've been tasked with putting together names of Robbie's teachers who can provide their insights as well."

A terrible sinking feeling threatened to drown me. "I thought I was doing the right thing . . ."

Principal Cartwright softened. "I understand that, and I do believe it's our right to protect all children. However, you do also need all the facts first."

"Is Robbie okay?" I couldn't believe what I had done.

"I'm sorry, but there isn't any more information I can provide. The investigation is ongoing."

Defeated, my shoulders slumped. "I understand. Thank you, sir."

"Best of luck in your future, Miss Ward."

I didn't even hear his lackluster goodbye as I hung up the phone. My tongue was dry and thick.

How could this have happened?

A job at the junior high was my opportunity to put down roots and finally stay planted. My vision blurred as I looked around the small bakery, feeling everything slip from my grasp.

We were so close to having it all.

~

THERE WAS NOTHING.

Tucked away in a quiet corner of Bluebird Books, I had scoured every school website and job posting search engine for *anything* that was within reasonable driving distance to Outtatowner. Classroom teachers, content specialists, teacher tech support, curriculum development, *anything* in education that my teaching certificate would qualify me for, and I still came up empty-handed.

Frustrated, I slammed my laptop closed. *I thought there was a teacher shortage, for fuck's sake!*

I hated admitting defeat, but there was no denying that I'd gambled and lost. Outtatowner was supposed to be my big do-over, and instead it was turning out to be yet another flop.

A hand at the center of my back drew my attention and had me sitting straighter. Rachel smiled down at me and set a fresh cup of coffee beside me before sliding onto the chair to my right. "No luck?"

I frowned down at the coffee and shook my head. "Not yet."

She tucked her legs and sipped her frothy latte. "I can't believe that spineless prick Cartwright didn't stand up for you. A principal is supposed to have his teachers' backs. You didn't do anything wrong."

I smiled weakly, appreciating her support. "He had every right to hire someone else. And this CPS case is a total mess. Poor kid doesn't even get to celebrate his tae kwon do victory because I couldn't slow down for one minute—I just barreled ahead. Plus, I went against a direct order to leave Robbie and his need for shoes alone, and he totally called me out on it."

"But *you* didn't do it," she offered.

I shrugged. "No, instead the guy I was secretly sleeping with made an over-the-top big deal about it and proved to my principal I was more than willing to go around my boss to do whatever I wanted."

"I think it's romantic that Whip tried to help." Her eyes went wistful, and she sipped her coffee.

Me too.

"Unfortunately romance doesn't earn the trust of your supervisor. I think he just couldn't look past *two* fuckups." I sighed and let the coffee warm my hands. "Whip's at work. He doesn't know yet that I didn't get the job."

Her brow furrowed. "You didn't want to tell him? He could help you mope."

I offered a wry, half-hearted laugh. "Not yet." I toyed with my lip. "I was hoping I could temper the news with an exciting job prospect but . . ." I gestured vaguely at my computer. "Nothing."

She leaned into me. "Please don't give up. This is only day one, and I can't bear the thought of you moving away. There's still plenty of time left before school starts up in the fall. Something will come up, I know it."

"I hope so," I answered, despite not quite believing with the same confidence she had.

"You want to grab a drink tonight? Brooklyn and I are going to a bar a few towns over to listen to an eighties cover band."

I shook my head. "No thanks. I'm sticking around the bookstore for a while. I want to keep looking. The Bluebirds are also meeting tonight, and I want to thank them for all they did for me."

Rachel's face fell. "You make it sound like a goodbye."

Tears threatened to spill over my lashes, but I crammed the emotions down and faked a smile. "It's not."

I only hoped that was true.

LONG AFTERNOON SHADOWS slanted across the carpeted floor of Bluebird Books. Hours had passed as I sat tucked in a corner at the windowsill. Between searches for work, I watched as life in Outtatowner played out in front of me—couples strolling hand in hand, families trekking toward the beach, friendly smiles and waves.

As the clock ticked, the ambient lighting gradually dimmed, and the once-bustling aisles surrendered to a quieter intimacy. The overhead lights were turned off, leaving the bookstore bathed in the soft glow of table lamps strategically placed around the space. Blankets adorned the cozy reading nooks, inviting patrons to curl up with a good book.

The air shifted as the last customers made their way to the exit, the door chiming softly as it closed behind them. The subtle rustle of pages being turned and the occasional clink of coffee cups echoed in the now-hushed atmosphere. A sense of anticipation hung in the air, as though the bookstore itself was holding its breath, preparing for the arrival of the Bluebirds.

And then, just as the clock struck the evening hour, the familiar faces of the Bluebirds began to trickle in. Laughter and greetings filled the space, punctuating the quiet with a joyful cadence. The women, carrying trays of treats and bottles of wine, moved with an easy familiarity, transforming the bookstore into their meeting place.

I took a deep breath, steeling myself before walking toward the back of the bookstore, where the Bluebirds gathered, with a smile on my face.

"Emily, over here." MJ smiled and waved from her spot on a high-back chair. "I saved you a seat." She patted the settee next to her.

"Thanks." I smiled and sank into the plush seat.

"So," she said, her eyebrows bouncing up and down. "We have some catching up to do."

A hot flush crept across my cheeks. Word about Whip and me being found kissing at the carnival had spread fast in that small town way, and our public outing at the Grudge had cemented everyone's curiosities.

I smiled weakly.

"Give her a break, MJ." Sylvie stepped up and handed MJ a cup, then turned and smiled at me. "Hi, I know we've met before but didn't get the chance to talk much. I'm Whip's sister, Sylvie King—I mean Sullivan!" She barked out a laugh and shook her head. "Sorry, I'm still getting used to saying that." Her smile was soft and genuine. "You looked like you had fun dancing at the Grudge. I'm sorry we didn't stay long enough to chat. Apparently my husband has a two-dance maximum."

I smiled, recalling the love in Whip's eyes when he'd shown me the toy box he was building for his new nephew. I reached my hand out to shake hers. "It's nice to see you again. Congratulations on your adorable baby boy."

She smiled sweetly and settled in the chair on the opposite side of me. "He's over a year old already. I just can't believe it."

"He's the cutest kid," MJ added. "He's got his mama's smile."

Sylvie laughed. "Yeah, but also his daddy's attitude."

The two women shared a laugh as they sipped their drinks, and I couldn't help but feel the warm sense of camaraderie. As an only child, I had never known what it was like to have a sister to share secrets with, or talk about boys, or eventually have someone to raise my children alongside.

As the final women gathered, Tootie Sullivan stood at the front of the group and shook a small bell to gain our attention.

"Good evening, Bluebirds. Before we all get settled in, I just wanted to take a moment. We have a special guest here with us tonight." Her kind eyes found me as she gestured toward where I sat. "Emily, would you like to come up?"

I shifted in my seat and rose to stand, collecting my thoughts as I made my way to the front of the room.

"Emily asked if she might be able to speak to all of us tonight." Tootie gestured in front of her. "They're all ears, dear."

I nodded at her and smiled. "Thank you. Hi." I looked out into the sea of friendly smiling faces. "Thanks, everyone. I feel a little silly standing in front of you all."

A few soft murmurs rippled through the crowd, and a couple of the women hunched together, whispering in secret. I wondered if they were gossiping about me and the news that Whip King and I were officially dating. A firefighter and the chief's daughter were prime gossip fodder.

I cleared my throat and pressed on. "I really just wanted to say thank you. With the help and generosity of the Bluebirds, the Outtatowner Educational Foundation has raised more money in the last few months than they had in years. Thank you."

Soft claps and cheerful whoops rippled through the small gathering of women. Their friendly camaraderie set me at ease.

"Eat that, Scooter Kuder," someone playfully called from the back.

A laugh burst from my chest, and the tension in my shoulders dissolved.

"Next year we can go bigger!" MJ called out from her seat, raising her cup.

My eyes caught my mother's, who gave me a soft reassuring smile. She knew what I did—that if the Bluebirds supported the foundation again next year, it would be someone else at the helm instead of me. Confiding in my mother earlier in the day had nearly broken me. Mom reassured me that everything would work out, but as the day wore on, I lacked the confidence she had.

I smiled and hoped it didn't wobble at the edges. "The children in this town are lucky to have you. Thanks again, ladies."

I stepped away from the front of the room to keep my emotions in check.

Tootie placed her hand on my elbow. "Before you go,

there's one more thing." She looked to her right. "Bug, the floor is yours."

Bug King, always strong and proud, stepped forward. When we locked eyes, her quick nod sent surprise running through me. "At our last meeting the Bluebirds took a vote, and it was unanimous. We would like to extend an invitation to officially join the Bluebird Book Club."

Shock was the only emotion that registered, followed swiftly by overwhelming gratitude. I looked around as the women smiled at me. "I don't know what to say."

"Say you'll bring the rum punch next time!" Lark Sullivan called from the back, and laughter bounced through the book club.

I laughed alongside them, feeling the tears sting the corner of my eyes. "It's an honor. Thank you."

My chin wobbled and I took a reassuring breath.

"Well, now that that's settled, you can sit down." Bug gestured with her chin. "We need to figure out how to get Stumpy Larson a wife so he stops messing up our Matchmaker's Gala."

I bit back a smile and scurried back to my spot next to MJ. I didn't know how long it would last, but for tonight, I was a Bluebird.

THIRTY-ONE

EMILY

After meeting with the Bluebirds, I was drained.

Wallowing alone in my apartment like a miserable troll held a certain appeal, but more than anything I wanted to get lost in the warm comfort of Whip's embrace. I needed to confide in him about my call with Principal Cartwright, so after the meeting I hastily tapped out a quick text to him.

Book club just ended. Interested in some company?

WHIP

Been waiting on you all night.

A girl could get used to a man like Whip waiting on her. Desire, hot and intense, swirled with longing inside me.

On my way!

After a quick stop at my apartment to grab a change of clothes, I eagerly made my way to his house. The drive down his winding road had become a familiar comfort. As soon as my car dipped below the canopy of the trees that lined his long driveway, I was safe.

True to his word, Whip was waiting—sitting in one of the Adirondack chairs on his front porch, in bare feet and jeans. I stepped from my car, and he stood, a bright smile on his face. Tears burned the backs of my eyelids as I took him in. Whip was strong and sexy and *mine.*

"Hungry?" he called out. "I have dinner if you are."

I smiled, but my stomach tightened as I climbed the porch stairs. We came together, like it was the most natural thing in the world, and I melted into his embrace. My fingertips dug at his T-shirt as I gripped him tighter.

Whip looked down at me. "Hey, what is it? This isn't still about your dad?" His fingertip brushed a lock of hair away from my eyes, and insecurities danced over his handsome features. "I plan to talk with him—I just need to find the right time. We're going to figure this out."

I swallowed and shook my head. "No, it's not that. Like I said, he's surprisingly okay with it all. He was texting random capybara memes today, acting like nothing ever happened. He's good."

His eyebrows shot up. "Is that right?"

I buried my face into his chest, hoping to steal his warmth. "I mean, sure, he wasn't *thrilled* about the sneaking-around part, but it seems like he's willing to be an adult about it."

Whip's hug tightened. "I'd still like to talk to him, if that's okay with you."

I looked up and smiled. "Of course."

He dropped a kiss on the top of my head. "Come on. Let me feed you."

I followed Whip into his kitchen. On top of the stove was a rectangular baking dish covered with aluminum foil.

He peeled back the foil, and steam rose above the cheesy top. "Lasagna. I hope that's okay. I'm trying something new for the station. It reheats well and feeds a crowd."

My stomach grumbled loudly, and I pressed my hand to it and laughed. "Yeah, I think it'll do."

He grinned, and I wondered if this was what it could have been like—coming home after a long day and existing together in this space. Worry knotted in my stomach. I knew I had to break the news to Whip that I was essentially jobless and uncertain about what my next steps needed to be.

I'd *always* had a plan, and this level of instability about my future was freaking me the fuck out.

Whip moved toward the refrigerator, pulling out a small salad for two and placing it on the kitchen island. He then dug out a metal spatula from a drawer and began cutting the lasagna into large, square portions.

"Now, you have to tell me if this sucks." He plopped a square onto a plate and slid it aside. "Being a good cook is important for a firefighter."

I laughed. "Not the saving lives part?" I teased.

He shrugged. "Yeah, I mean . . . that, too, but bragging rights for the best dinner that week?" He spread his hands, palms up, and smiled. "Come on."

I took the plates from beside him and set them next to each other on the island. Using a fork, I scooped each of us a bowl of salad and arranged those too. The words *I have no job and no future here* clogged in my throat. Whip was clearly relieved that the conversation with my dad went well, and I hated to ruin the moment.

After devouring his lasagna and salad, I gushed over his cooking instead. "Truly, it was delicious. Ten out of ten."

He grinned, looking younger and more playful than I'd

ever seen him. "Thank you. I like the crunchy overcooked corners, but I was worried I'd left it in the oven a little too long."

I licked my fork with a flourish. "It was perfect. Thanks again."

We cleaned our dishes side by side, but in near silence. With so few dishes he hand-washed our plates and bowls, and I let the lull of running water soothe the tension in my jaw.

When Whip finished wiping his hands dry, he turned to me. "Are you sure you're okay?"

I couldn't meet his eyes, but I managed a jerky nod. "I'm okay. Just tired, I think."

Whip pulled out a beer and held another up in question. I shook my head, and he placed it back into the fridge. "How are the Bluebirds?"

I smiled weakly. "They're amazing, as always. They asked me to officially be part of the group."

He smiled. "All right! You're in the cool kids club."

I nodded. My throat was tight. "I accepted, but I think maybe I shouldn't have."

Whip paused with his beer bottle halfway to his mouth. "What do you mean?"

Tears threatened to spill over my lashes. "I didn't get the job, Whip. Principal Cartwright hired someone else."

Whip's shoulders slumped, and his head tilted to the side before he closed the gap between us. "Aww, Prim. I'm so sorry." His arms wrapped around me, and he pulled me in close, resting his chin on the top of my head. "I know you really wanted it."

I wiped my nose before pulling away. "You don't understand. I didn't just *want* that job—I was counting on it. I've looked, and there's nothing else within a reasonable commute." I took a deep breath and dropped my hands. "I think I have to move."

His jaw flexed and his eyes closed. He sighed. "Move where?"

I shook my head. "I don't know yet. Closer to the city, probably? Trust me when I say I looked and looked. Right now there aren't any teaching jobs I can do within an hour's drive. Small towns don't have nearly the demand for teachers that larger suburbs do."

His body went rigid and his shoulders set. A grumble hummed in his throat. "I don't want you to leave."

Exhilaration zipped through me, followed closely by aching sadness. "I don't want to leave either."

He exhaled deeply, as though he needed me to speak those words aloud. With a firm nod, he looked me in the eyes. "Then don't. Get a job doing something else." He scrubbed a hand on the back of his neck and started to pace. "I can ask around. See who's hiring. I'll call Huck at the bakery or see if there's anything at the brewery. Hell, I can always ask Wyatt Sullivan if he knows of anything at the university." Suddenly his footsteps stopped, and he looked at me. "But wait. Why didn't you get the job? Did the principal tell you?"

The words expanded in my throat as my mouth opened, but nothing came out. I didn't want to lie to him but also didn't know how to tell him that, in part, he had inadvertently caused me to be overlooked for the full-time teaching position. I was also dreading telling him that I should have listened to him in the first place about calling Child Protective Services for Robbie.

"Um . . ." I sighed and resigned myself to the facts. "The principal found out about our little work-around to get Robbie those shoes. He wasn't too happy that I went against his wishes to stay out of it." I exhaled and let the rest tumble out of me. "Then, on top of that, I went ahead and called Child Protective Services about the bruises on Robbie's face, and it turns out he's a really good martial artist and I'm just a paranoid substitute teacher." My hand fell and slapped against my thigh with a smack.

"Oh, shit." Whip sighed. "I'm so sorry, Prim. This is all my fault. I never should have stepped in. I fucked this all up for you." He braced his hands on the counter and then pushed off it sharply. "God, I could kill that prick Pokey Lambert. What an asshole."

"It's not your fault. I really should have talked with my principal before I made that call to CPS—like you had said. I made a complete mess for Robbie and his family. I feel terrible." My hands wrung together. "It also wasn't Mr. Lambert who complained about the shoes. I don't know who did, but Principal Cartwright did confirm that it was someone else." I shrugged. "Guess I made some enemies somehow."

Fury contorted his handsome features as his head whipped up. "I doubt that."

Whip stood in front of me, his hands rubbing down my arms. "You did a good thing—trying to protect your students. I'm glad he's okay, but sorry that it worked out the way it did for you."

I looked at my bare feet. "Me too."

"Think about what I said?" The hope in his voice was a knife to my chest. "You could work somewhere else and just stay here. Do you really have to teach?"

We stayed, locked together in an awkward embrace for what felt like hours. Finally, I took a breath. "I'm a teacher, Whip. I can't fathom not working with kids every day.

Being surrounded by learning and laughter and students? I don't know who I am without that."

His eyes closed and he nodded in defeat. "I know."

"I'll find something." God, I hoped I wasn't lying to us both. I hated this feeling—*any* feeling where my ribs poked and my gut churned. Escape was the only logical answer. It had always worked before. "I think I'd like to take a hot shower. Rinse the day off and settle in. Would that be okay?"

He hesitated like maybe he wanted to say more, but instead he clamped his mouth shut and nodded. "Of course. I'll finish up out here."

"Thanks." I hurried past him and went straight to the primary bedroom before I dissolved into a mess of snot and tears. I couldn't let him see me fall apart.

I couldn't even explain what I was feeling. The pleasure in him wanting me to stay. The hope laced in his deep voice when he offered solutions that kept me close. Craig had never done anything apart from expect me to follow him around and keep quiet about all the ways in which I didn't quite measure up.

But wasn't this the same thing? Leaving my passion for teaching simply to stay close to a man? The fact Whip was the best sex of my life didn't change the fact that whatever intense emotions I was fighting were partly because of my fears. Whip was passionate, reckless. He tended to leap before he ever looked, and for a brief moment, I thought maybe I could do the same.

Instead, I lacked any safety net and had landed flat on my ass.

If I stayed only for him, all that Emily-ness my mother was so happy to see again could be lost forever. If I fully jumped in with Whip, I knew my feelings for him would only deepen. Falling in love with him felt like the most natural thing in the world. If I allowed myself to do that, my emotions would be laid bare—emotions that he could inevitably use to hurt me somehow. How long would it be before he expected me to change? Hadn't he already started by asking if I still had to teach?

THIRTY-TWO

WHIP

I STOOD in my kitchen and stared at the countertop, listening to Emily cry as soon as she made it to the bedroom. The door had barely clicked behind her when a muffled, gut-wrenching sob escaped her.

She was leaving.

The kitchen swirled and narrowed around me—the soft lights blurring at the edges until it was just me and the distance to her. I couldn't stand the helpless, broken feelings coursing through me. I knew Emily had said she was tired and wanted to shower. She probably didn't want me to see her cry but . . .

I slapped the dish towel onto the countertop and strode down the hallway toward the primary bedroom. Behind the closed door, I could hear her muffled sobs despite the running water.

I quietly entered the room. Light peeked out from underneath the bathroom door, illuminating my path. Outside the bathroom door, her shaky breath was even more apparent. I raised my fist to knock.

Doubt swirled in my mind.

You're holding on with both hands, and she's leaving anyway.

It was always too good to be true.

You were never good enough to keep her.

My gut lurched and my jaw flexed. "Fuck it."

Without knocking, I twisted the door handle and entered the bathroom. The shower was running, and through the mirror, I immediately spotted Emily's small figure huddled on the shower floor, shoulders shaking.

I made quick work of stripping off my shirt and discarding my jeans and underwear. Without a word, I opened the shower door and stepped in behind her. Lowering to the floor, I folded myself over her and let my shoulders take the brunt of the hot water as it pounded down from the showerhead. My legs and arms cradled her as sobs racked her frame.

I didn't know the right words to say. I didn't know how to make anything better. All I could show her was that I was there.

I would stay, even if she could not.

Emily had big dreams, and she deserved more than upending her life for *me*. She hadn't asked me to leave with her either. It was a panicked thought that ran through me when I was spouting off options to her, but the sheer ridiculousness of it forced me to hold my tongue. We'd only been dating—in secret, at that—for a few months, and it would be rash of me to assume Emily wanted me to follow her anywhere.

But I'd do it.

If she gave the word, I'd give the chief my notice and start looking for something else.

Only I had been too chickenshit to even offer it.

I was pissed off that Emily was being punished for caring for her students. Even more livid that someone had called the school about the donations the fire station had made with the sole purpose of getting her into trouble.

As we sat in the shower in silence, I held her. I vowed to find out who did this to her . . . and I'd make him pay for it.

~

ONCE EMILY'S sobs shifted to quiet sniffles, she relaxed into me. I washed her hair and body, giving her space in my silence to process all the changes that seemed to be happening far too quickly.

When we finished, I carried her to the bed and helped her dress in one of my T-shirts. In the soft lighting of my bedroom, I spotted the hint of a blush as her lashes lowered. I brushed my thumb across the apple of her cheek.

Tucking her legs into the bed, I wrapped my body around her, praying it wasn't the last time I would be able to hold her. With measured breaths, I stared into the darkness as her back rose and fell against my chest. My fingers brushed along the outside of her arm, memorizing every line and curve.

Emily shifted her hips, gently pressing her ass into me, and I bit back a groan. It was going to be a long night if I had any chance of being a decent man and offering only comfort rather than a quick fuck.

Her quiet whisper broke through the darkness. "Whip," she breathed. "Please touch me."

Following her lead, I stroked my fingertips across her shoulder, down her arm, and over her hip. I gathered the hem of her T-shirt and slipped my hand beneath it to feel the soft skin of her abdomen.

She sighed into me.

I hitched my knees higher, tucking her into me as I caressed her soft skin. My lips peppered gentle kisses along her neck and shoulder. My mouth softened against her skin, and I took my time to soak in its warmth and taste her.

Emily shifted, quietly rolling herself toward me. In the low lighting, I searched her eyes for answers. Her soft gaze roamed over my face before she leaned in to kiss me. It wasn't the hurried, frantic kisses we'd shared before. It was languid and deep. I breathed her in as our mouths met and tongues explored.

Using my weight to gently roll her to her back, I hovered over her. Her lashes swept across her cheek, and I pressed every available inch of my body to hers. "You are so effortlessly beautiful. Do you know that?"

Emily smiled but shyly buried her face into my chest with a disbelieving laugh.

I shifted to softly nudge her. "I'm serious. I ask myself every day how I got lucky enough to be with a woman like you." I didn't always have the right words. I wasn't exactly sure how to articulate the tender ache in my chest, but I had to try. "You're my safe place, Prim."

Emily's arm wrapped around my back and pulled me closer, slanting her mouth over mine. My hands smoothed up her sides, dragging the T-shirt with it. I broke our kiss only to remove the shirt and toss it aside. My cock thickened between us as I reached down to slide my hand between her legs.

Emily moaned into the darkness, widening her legs and allowing me access. I rubbed and teased her, holding back from diving in and taking until she was ready. I kissed her jaw and neck while I caressed her. When her hips bucked forward, I slipped one finger inside her, then two.

Her nails dug into my shoulder, and I reveled in the sharp pinch as her pussy clenched around my fingers.

"You," she breathed. "I want to feel *you*."

"I'm right here, baby." My fingers pumped in and out of her, going slower and deeper each time.

She pressed on my shoulders, demanding I meet her eyes. "Please."

I leaned toward the nightstand, where I kept the condoms, but her grip on my shoulder tightened. "Just you."

A small smile twitched my lip as I lowered to kiss her. I spread her legs and notched myself at her entrance. My whole being ached for release, but I was determined to go slow this time—to show her how she deserved to be worshiped.

Slowly, I pushed the head of my cock inside her. Our moans filled the bedroom as I sank into her, each barbell of my piercing stretching her open.

When I was buried to the hilt, I paused and looked down at her. "You feel like home to me."

Her eyes went wide, and her arms pulled me down as she wrapped herself around me. I moved with her, reading her cues and giving her whatever she needed. It felt like hours as we moved together in the darkness.

When we were both worn out and breathless, I pulled her close to me and buried my nose in her hair. Sated and spent, my gaze wandered to the walk-in closet at the far end of the bedroom. Tucked away in a corner, a denim jacket haunted me like a scratch inside my skull I couldn't reach. Talking about my mother was something I *never* considered, but in the quiet moments with Emily, it almost felt safe.

"Can I tell you something?" I whispered in her ear.

She hummed and looked at me with sleepy eyes.

"There's a woman's jacket hanging in my closet," I started.

Emily looked up at me. "I wondered where that came from."

I raised a playful eyebrow. "Jealous?"

A grin crept onto her face. "Of course not. I'm much too mature for that."

My arms squeezed her tighter. "You never have to worry about that. Actually . . ." Fuck, my gut ached even saying the words. "The jacket was my mother's." Emily's sea-blue eyes held me in place, allowing me the space to continue. "Bug found it in some random box in the basement along with some other things."

"What other things?" she asked.

"The jacket, a few photos, her driver's license . . ." My voice trailed off on the last bit of information—the piece that *still* didn't sit right with me.

Emily frowned. "Kind of hard for someone to leave town without that."

Her simple statement confirmed what I already suspected, but I shoved it down. "I remember Mom wearing that denim jacket. She used to cuff the sleeves." I laughed at the mundane detail that was seared into my brain. "I don't know if I really remember it or just recall it from pictures. I was pretty young when she left."

Emily's fingertips gently traced across my eyebrow and down my face. "I don't understand how a mother could leave like she did. I'm sorry you had to endure that."

Emotion thickened in my throat. I didn't want to think about my mother or why I couldn't seem to forget about her anymore. I didn't want to worry that my moments with Emily were hurtling by too quickly.

Instead, I wanted to savor every second, so I pulled Emily closer and cuddled into her warmth. It was soul crushing to think that this thing we found—this magic—could come to an end over something as simple as a job.

There has to be another way.

THIRTY-THREE

WHIP

The next morning I awoke to find Emily's half of the bed cold. I pulled on a pair of sweatpants and went in search of her. She was sitting at the kitchen island—hair styled, makeup applied, and dressed in jeans and a short-sleeved shirt. Her feet were bare and propped on the rung of her stool.

"Morning." I made my way to the coffee maker.

Her head jerked up, as though I'd ripped her from her thoughts. She cleared her throat. "Hey." She smiled. "Good morning."

I eyed her as I poured my coffee and watched her as I took my first sip. Something was off, but I didn't know what. "Everything okay?"

She frowned as if to say, *No, dumbass, everything is not okay*.

Instead, she blinked and quickly replaced her down-turned mouth with a bright smile. "Of course."

Gone was the raw and very real version of Emily I had experienced last night. In her place was the polished, always-ready-to-face-the-day Prim that she often presented to the world. While I had fallen head over heels with all versions of her, I couldn't help but feel like this fake cheeriness was a step in the *wrong* direction.

"What's on the agenda today?" I asked, propping my elbows on the countertop next to her.

Emily slid from her stool, noticeably avoiding my touch. "Busy day." She smiled, but it didn't reach her soft eyes. "I have plans with my mom and then"—she shrugged—"I'm not sure after that. Keep looking for a job, I guess."

I glowered into my coffee cup. "Today's my day off. Am I going to get to see you?"

She smiled. "Maybe. I can let you know what I'm up to later."

My eyes narrowed in her direction. "Prim . . . am I misreading this here? Are you giving me the brush-off?"

Her laugh was too sharp and quick. "No." She lifted a shoulder and smiled before dropping a kiss against my mouth. "I'll see you when I see you. Promise."

The poised mask she presented to the world had slipped into place, and I really fucking hated it. Last night was intense and profound, yet the woman in front of me seemed completely unfazed by any of it.

"Yeah. I guess I'll see you later." Irritated at my own stubborn pride, I strode past her and out the front door toward my shop. Flaying myself open for her last night to simply wake up and have her stare at me was too much. I needed a distraction. Minutes later, when she didn't seek me out but rather got into her car and drove away, was all the confirmation I needed.

Last night didn't change a damn thing.

I spent the next several hours tinkering in the workshop. Sawdust clung to my sweat, and I regretted not grabbing a shirt and shoes before I had gotten to work. I was angry—at myself for opening my stupid mouth, at her for not having *anything* to say in return, at the whole goddamned situation. Everything was fucked, and I didn't see a way to fix it.

An engine cut in the driveway, and I stupidly hoped it was her. Instead, my father stepped from his Porsche. When he headed toward the front door of my home, I seriously considered hiding in the workshop and ignoring him altogether.

Instead, ever the fool, I called out for him. He took his time making his way across the grass to my shop. No one rushed Russell King.

"What do you want?" I asked, too weary for false niceties.

"Is that any way to greet your father?" His eyes ran across my chest, and he sighed. "Jesus. I will never understand this affinity you have for working with your hands."

I wiped my palms, sending tiny particles of sawdust floating between us. "Yeah, I know that, Dad. Did you need something?"

A slick smile spread across his face. "I came to offer my congratulations."

The throb in my head intensified. "Congratulations?"

"Lieutenant King has a special ring to it." He winked. "Almost as good as Chief, but we'll get there one day."

Lieutenant. Holy fuck, I—I got the job.

He reached out his hand as though he might land it on my shoulder, but thought twice and stuffed it into his pocket. "This benefits the entire family, son. Well done. Once the chief's little daughter moves on and is out of the way, we'll be in great shape."

My brain snagged on his effortless dismissal of Emily. *How the fuck did he know about Emily's probable relocation? Fucking small-town gossips . . .*

When I stayed quiet, he filled the silence. "Trust me. I know women like her. Full of big ideas and a soft heart. That's not the kind of partner a future chief fire officer needs." A pompous smirk tugged the corner of his mouth before his eyes hardened. "Let this be a reminder for the future, that when I ask something of you, I'm not asking."

The gears churned and clinked in my head as if they were rusty and groaning with this information. There was something darker about what he was saying.

Irritated, I stood straighter. "You don't have a clue what I need."

He scoffed, his face hardening. "I know exactly what you need. Taking care of problem women isn't something you need to worry about. I can handle that. You focus on the job and keep working toward the next step up."

A terrible sinking feeling pressed down on my shoulders. Emily had mentioned that Principal Cartwright confirmed it wasn't Pokey Lambert that complained about the shoes. Someone else had called the principal and shined a light on Emily's insubordination.

It wasn't gossips that tipped him off to Emily's employment issues . . . he knew because it was him.

Suddenly it was clear that my father had called the principal as a punishment for me disobeying his request that I talk with Mrs. Martin about the historical society building. Undermining Emily's career was his way of flexing his power . . . and it had fucking worked.

Fury burned through my veins.

My father made no qualms about fighting dirty to get what he wanted, and what he really wanted was for his son to climb the ranks in the fire department so he could use me as leverage. He saw what was blossoming between Emily and me before even I did. He saw it and took care of it in the only way he knew how—to destroy it.

Silence and tension stretched between us.

"Whip," my father began, his eyes cold and calculating, "you're old enough now to understand the importance of family legacy. The town looks up to us, and it's our duty to uphold the King name."

I shifted across from him. The time had come to start confronting the ghosts of our past. My thoughts flicked back to the box of my mother's belongings, shoved in some basement and long forgotten. Emily's confirmation of my suspicions replayed in my mind, infusing me with resolve.

"Legacy, huh?" I said, my voice carrying a hint of bitterness. "What about Mom? What's her place in this legacy you're so keen on preserving?"

Subtle shock danced across his face at my audacity of speaking about my mother.

"Your mother . . ." He hesitated, a rarity for a man accustomed to control. "Your mother made the choices that determined her fate, Whip. We all moved on."

I clenched my jaw, my hands forming fists. The room spun around me. "When she left, you mean."

"What?" The lines on his face deepened.

"You said her choices determined her fate, but what you really meant was when she left us. Right, Dad?"

An unidentifiable emotion flickered across my father's face—was it fear? Regret? Or something far darker?

He recovered quickly as his hand smoothed down his suit jacket, and a practiced smile played on his lips.

The room seemed to tighten around us, the air thick with unsaid words and the acrid scent of mistrust. My father's eyes, once calculating, held a glint of discomfort. The weight of my subtle accusation hung in the air, a shadow creeping over the polished surfaces of his carefully curated life.

"Son, you're overthinking things," he said, his voice attempting to regain its authoritative edge. "Your mother's choices were her own. We couldn't control that."

I stared at him, my gaze unwavering. "What choices, Dad?"

An unsteady pause settled in the airy workshop. The lines on my father's face deepened, and for a moment I caught a glimpse of vulnerability—an unfamiliar crack in the facade of the all-powerful Russell King.

He cleared his throat, his eyes avoiding mine and looking around my shop. "Your mother had her reasons, Whip. You were just a child, too young to understand."

I stepped closer, the distance between us closing like a vise. "Try me, Dad. I'm not a child anymore."

A flicker of hesitation crossed his face, a subtle acknowledgment that perhaps, in this moment, he couldn't control the narrative as he always had.

"Your mother was . . . troubled," he finally admitted, choosing his words carefully. "She felt trapped in this small town, in this life. It was her choice to leave and pursue something more fulfilling."

The words were a hollow echo in the workshop, and my unease deepened. Something about his explanation felt rehearsed, as if he had recited this story many times to himself before.

I thought back to the smiling, happy face on her driver's license.

My eyes narrowed. I was determined to get answers. "Where did she go, Dad?"

His jaw shifted as his hands tucked into his suit pants. "Back home to Detroit, I assume."

"Why? Why would she leave her children behind? What am I missing?" Desperation leaked into my voice.

An impassive stare and deep sigh were the only answers my father was willing to give.

"When someone feels trapped, they find a way to break free," I pressed. "But what if she didn't leave by choice, Dad? What if something happened to her?"

His eyes darted, searching for something before a dismissive laugh huffed from his chest. "Whip, you're letting your imagination run wild. There's nothing more to the story. Focus on the future, on your career. Not women who don't matter."

I took a step back, the suspicion growing within me. I knew he was the last person to give a straight answer, and talking to him was like arguing with a brick wall. I shook my head. "Of course, Dad. I'll stay focused."

But I wouldn't forget about Mom. I was going to find out what really happened.

A sinister edge entered his gaze, a warning that I chose to ignore. "That's what I want to hear. Just remember, some stones are better left unturned, son."

As my father exited the workshop, leaving me alone with the weight of unanswered questions, I couldn't shake the feeling that the legacy he spoke of carried darker secrets than I had ever imagined. My determination to uncover the truth about my mother and protect my relationship with Emily burned brighter, fueled by a growing sense of unease and suspicion toward the man who was supposed to be my father.

THIRTY-FOUR

EMILY

Still no job.

And let me tell you . . . trusting that this is somehow going to *actually* work out is getting really fucking old.

Subject: Not Quite the Right Fit

Miss Ward,
Thanks for applying, but we're after a teacher who can break free from the monotony. Your style doesn't quite cut it.

Principal Jennings

Subject: Thank You for Applying

Dear Miss Ward,
After careful consideration, we regret to inform you that

your application doesn't align with our vision for an innovative educator. We're seeking someone with a more dynamic approach to teaching. Wishing you success in finding a better match.

Sincerely,
Douglas Educational Committee

Subject: A Polite Pass on Your Teaching Talents

Dear Miss Ward,
I trust this email finds you in the midst of wrangling the intriguing minds of your students. Our prestigious private school recently had the pleasure of reviewing your application, and I must say, your qualifications sparkled.

However, after much contemplation, we've decided to embark on a journey with someone whose approach to teaching aligns more with interpretive dance and less with traditional lesson plans. We believe it's time to let our students embrace their inner dance prodigies.

Please don't consider this a rejection, but rather an invitation to explore the world of teaching through the art of movement. Who knows, maybe you'll discover the hidden dancer within!

Wishing you all the best in your future endeavors,
Principal Dandecaff

The bruise from banging my head against the desk was starting to feel permanent.

Sigh.

But finally, after searching school websites, cold emailing principals, and attending countless virtual and in-person interviews, my heart stopped when I read the newest subject line.

Subject: Congratulations! Welcome to the Team!

Dear Ms. Ward,
It is with great excitement that we extend our warmest congratulations! Among many worthy candidates, your interview stood out, and we are thrilled to invite you to join Stella Baines Middle School as our newest educator.

Your passion for teaching and dedication to fostering an engaging learning environment align perfectly with our vision. We believe your unique approach will bring a breath of fresh air to our classrooms.

Welcome aboard, Emily! We look forward to embarking on an educational journey filled with inspiration, laughter, and countless moments of growth for our students.

Best regards,
Principal Sipling

My heart raced as I read, and reread, the email. *I got a freaking job offer!* Sure, I still had to work out details like pay, start date, and the stacks of HR paperwork, but the offer was there, in black and white.

I should have been elated. Instead, all I could think about was the fact that the middle school was clear across the state of Michigan in a suburb of Ann Arbor. Desperation had driven me to even apply, but now? A sick sinking feeling settled into my stomach.

What the hell was I going to do?

THIRTY-FIVE

WHIP

THE NEXT DAY AT WORK, irritation still dogged me. Emily had spent the majority of the day with her mom and looking for local teaching jobs. She had returned, quiet and with sadness lurking around her edges, but we both ignored it.

I hated that I couldn't make things right for her.

At the station, the click of the door drew my attention. My eyes whipped up to see Lee saunter into the break room. Over his shoulder, I watched as Chief entered the station and walked down the hall toward his office with our battalion chief. His expression was unreadable, the duo deep in conversation. My stomach somersaulted as I straightened. I still needed to clear the air with him about everything that had happened. HR had confirmed that the lieutenant position was mine, but the chief still hadn't spoken to me about it.

As they walked, Chief glanced at me, offering only a small nod of acknowledgment, but relief washed over me. At least for the moment, he wasn't throwing me out on my ass and giving me what I undoubtedly deserved.

Lee sidled up beside me, a smirk playing on his lips.

"Dodged a bullet there. Chief didn't look too happy this morning, but he's too busy to chew your ass."

A growing knot of worry tightened in my chest. *What if Chief hadn't been as understanding as Emily had made it seem? Would he want me to stop seeing her now that I would be stepping into the lieutenant's role? What if my recklessness had cost me the one thing that finally felt right in my life?*

I could feel myself spiraling, but Lee's low whistle caught my attention. "Man." He chuckled and shook his head as he grabbed a clean coffee mug from the cabinet. "The boss's daughter . . . you've got brass balls, Bill."

My jaw flexed. "Not today, Sullivan."

I wanted to punch the cocky smirk off his face, but the station was one place we'd drawn the line—it was an unspoken expectation that we left the rivalry outside its walls.

Lee's voice cut through my thoughts, sharp and mocking. "You should know, people are talking."

I glared at him, my patience hanging by a thread. "Talking about what?"

His jaw flexed. "Word is you have a hard-on for the boss's daughter, but that you're only using her."

Instinct took over and I pushed him against the counter. "The fuck did you say to me? Are you running your mouth?"

Lee shoved me hard in the chest, moving me back a few inches, and glared at me. Lee leaned in, his tone low but sincere. "I'm just trying to help you out, asshole. They're saying you're only with her because she's the chief's daughter. Rumor is that you were trying to get some special treatment in your bid for lieutenant. I thought you should know."

The words hit me like a sucker punch. Fury surged through my veins, a red-hot rage that threatened to consume me. I clenched my fists, struggling to keep my composure. "It's not like that. Don't twist it."

He laughed, a grating sound that fueled the fire within me, and raised his hands. "I'm not twisting anything. All I am telling you is that's what people are saying. I was giving you a heads-up. You just better hope Chief doesn't find out."

A flicker of doubt mingled with my anger. "He already knows about us."

What if Emily had heard the rumors? What if she believed them?

The need to set things straight overpowered my instinct to keep a low profile. I couldn't let these lies poison what we had, especially when it already felt like we were on shaky ground.

Anger crept in at the edges of my vision, and Lee was the only person around to catch my wrath. I stepped forward with a finger in his face, fury blazing in my eyes. "You listen to me, Sullivan. My relationship with Emily is none of your damn business. You spread these lies, and I swear, I'll make you regret it."

His hands went up as he rolled his eyes, seemingly unaffected by my outburst. "I told you as a *friend*, dipshit. This town is well meaning, but damn if they don't stick their noses in everyone's business. If I hear the rumors, I'll set it straight, but you might want to watch your back."

With that, he grabbed his coffee and sauntered out of the break room, leaving me seething with frustration and feeling like a total dick. The station's familiar camaraderie now felt like a facade, a thin veil covering the hostility simmering beneath the surface. Lee hadn't deserved my anger but had taken the brunt end of its force.

As Lee walked away, I took a deep breath and tried to regain control of my temper. Chief was too busy at the moment to interrupt with my meaningless excuses and half-hearted apologies. I needed to find Emily and set things right before these rumors spread beyond repair.

~

THE DRIVE HOME felt longer than usual, the weight of Chief's impending conversation and Lee's goading pressing on my shoulders. As I stepped into my house, I half expected to find Emily waiting for me, ready to talk and ease my troubled mind. But the living room was empty, the air heavy with an absence that sent annoyance running down my spine.

"Prim?" I called out, my voice echoing through the quiet house. No response. Anxiety churned in my gut as I checked the kitchen, the bedroom, each room a reminder of her absence.

I reached for my phone, fingers fumbling like a teenager as I dialed her number. The call went straight to voicemail, and frustration simmered beneath my skin. *Where was she? Why hadn't she come home?*

The feeble excuse she gave through a text only added to my unease.

EMILY

> Hey, sorry. Something came up at home. Can't make it tonight. Rain check?

Something about her message felt off, the tone too

vague, too distant. I typed a quick response, my worry bleeding into the words.

> Sure, no problem. Is everything okay? Let me know if you need anything.

Minutes ticked by, each one stretching into an agonizing eternity. The phone remained silent, Emily's reply elusive. I paced the living room, the tension building with each unanswered text.

Just as my frustration reached its peak, my phone buzzed. I eagerly grabbed it, hoping for an explanation. Emily's response, however, only deepened the knot in my stomach.

EMILY

> Thanks, Whip. It's just some family and job search stuff. Nothing at all to worry about. Let's talk tomorrow.

The vague reassurance did little to ease my concerns. Family stuff? Job search? What could be so pressing that she couldn't confide in me? Doubt gnawed at the edges of my thoughts, a growing fear that something heavier lurked beneath the surface.

Just as I debated whether to push for more information, my phone rang, and Abel's name flashed on the screen. I answered, a mix of frustration and curiosity in my voice. "What's up, Abel?"

His voice, usually gruff and impatient, held an unusual stillness. "Hey, we need to talk. It's about Mom."

My breath caught in my throat, the mention of our mother stirring up memories better left buried. "What about her?"

"You might want to sit down," Abel urged, and I sank

into a chair. "I got in touch with a private investigator, courtesy of my parole officer. The guy did some digging, and there's nothing—no record, no trace of Mom after she left all those years ago. None. She's a ghost."

The words hung in the air, a heavy silence settling between us. My mind raced, grappling with the implications of what Abel was saying. Our mother had vanished without a trace. The uncertainty, the mystery surrounding her absence, sent a chill down my spine.

"Are you saying she's . . . dead?" The word caught in my throat, a bitter taste on my tongue.

Abel sighed, the weight of the revelation evident in his voice. "Honestly, we don't know. The odd thing is, the investigator couldn't find a death record either. She's just . . . gone. He's going to look into whether or not she could have changed her name or anything like that. He plans to keep digging, and I don't want to jump to conclusions, but thought you should know."

A heavy silence enveloped the conversation, the implications sinking in. The revelation about our mother, coupled with the unspoken tension with Emily, created a riot of emotions within me. The ground beneath my feet felt unsteady, and the shadows of the past cast long, haunting tendrils into the present.

As I absorbed the shocking news, Abel's stern voice broke through the haze. "We'll figure this out. We can't keep living in the dark. We'll talk more later."

The call ended, leaving me in a state of turmoil. This newfound information about my mother weighed heavily on my shoulders. The air in the room felt charged with an unsettling energy, and I couldn't shake the feeling that the answers I sought were just beyond reach.

I forced myself out of my house and walked toward my

workshop. Maybe a few grueling hours creating something would ease the gnawing dread in my stomach.

I had loved my mother. She had loved us too. Of all the things I had forgotten, *that* I remembered.

I glanced up. Ominous clouds gathered on the horizon as I strode toward the barn and grappled with the shadows of my past that were seeping into my present. I may have been only a child when she disappeared, but in her wake she'd left the most important lesson I'd ever learned: no matter how much I loved someone, I wasn't worth sticking around for.

THIRTY-SIX

EMILY

Stress was eating me alive.

I couldn't help the impending sense of dread that pooled in my stomach. I felt *off* and not at all like myself. Plus, I still hadn't made a decision or told Whip about the job offer. He had been acting weird for *days*, and despite our public outing, the whispers behind our backs only seemed to intensify. It was a startling realization that the pressures of small-town life were no joke. In the span of days I'd gone from feeling on top of the world to floundering in daunting silence.

Whip didn't have work in the morning, so in an effort to find some kind of normalcy, I'd asked him to take me out. By the time we reached the Grudge, nearly every table was full, and the band was deep into a set of country classics. The dance floor was packed, and we skirted the crowd to find somewhere to sit on the King side.

When there wasn't a single seat, I squeezed his arm. "There's a few over there." I bounced my chin toward the opposite side of the bar. "Maybe one night doesn't matter."

His face crinkled. "Of course it matters. We're not sitting over there."

"Okay . . ." Annoyed at his clipped tone, I kept searching. "What about in the middle? Maybe we can be like Sylvie and Duke."

A dismissive grunt was his only response. When minutes ticked by and the crowd got only thicker, Whip grabbed my hand. "You know what? Fuck this. Let's go."

Taken aback by his abruptness, I allowed Whip to lead me toward the exit and out into the warm summer evening. Without stopping, he continued down the main sidewalk toward the beachfront.

"Hey, slow down." I dug my heels in and slowed us to a stop. Annoyance rippled over Whip's features. I hated that I didn't understand why. There was still so much about the man in front of me that I didn't fully understand. When we dove in headfirst, we'd been temporary, at best. Then before I knew it, he'd become the center of my world.

Part of that felt so *right*, all the while I actively ignored the ping of warning bells at the back of my mind. The same ones that reminded me of this familiar pattern. But something shifted the other night when we'd made love. He hadn't told me he loved me, but there was an intensity to him that was unmistakable.

Would he still care about me if I had to leave? Why in the world wouldn't he replace me with something—someone—*easier and closer to home?*

I wanted him to beg me to stay. If he only said the words, I'd do it.

The pleading that seeped into my eyes was uncomfortable. I wanted to scream at him that I loved him. Terrified of being that vulnerable, I held back.

Maybe it's not enough.

I worried that carving out a piece of myself, leaving behind everything I had worked for would only rot us from the inside.

Whip sighed and held my hand, not saying the words I so desperately needed to hear. He shook his head. "Turns out I can make a mess of things just like Dickie Johnson."

My brows pinched together. "What?"

He shook his head in dismissal and headed toward his truck. "Maybe he was the better choice after all."

He winked but instead of feeling the playful zip, my chest hollowed. "Why would you say that?"

He didn't look my way. "I was just kidding."

"Fine." I scoffed, feeling wrung out and annoyed. "Just make a joke to avoid the mess."

When we reached his truck, he wrenched the passenger-side door open. "It's no joke. You just haven't realized it yet."

A rush of emotion washed over me, too tired to beat the feelings back down. Tears swam in my eyes as I stood in front of the open door but didn't get in. Understanding of the man in front of me finally came into focus. "You know what? Fine. I think I do finally believe you."

His hand dropped, but his defenses were visibly rising as he crossed his arms. "And what's that, Prim?"

I bit down to keep from crying. After a steadying breath, I finally looked him in the eyes. "I can't make you want to see the good in yourself. Sure, I might not always be the best at showing my feelings, but I would be the best at caring for the man you hide from the world, and I can only do it if you stop hiding."

His arms spread wide. "I'm not hiding. I'm right here. Maybe you just don't like what you see."

I scoffed as hurt morphed into anger and bubbled inside me. “Somehow it always boils down to me, doesn’t it?”

“I didn’t—” Whip sighed. “Prim, come on.”

I shook my head. “No. As soon as things get hard or ugly, you’re pulling back.”

His eyes reflected dismay and irritation. “*I’m* the distant one?”

His words were a slap in the face—too close to accurate for me to not feel hurt.

And next thing you know, he’ll find someone less closed off.

Gathering my courage, I brushed past him. “I’m going to stay at my apartment tonight.”

“Why?” It was impossible to ignore the annoyance and panic in his voice. “Look, I’m sorry I said that—I’m just having a bad night.”

I sniffed and hated myself for it. “It’s fine. I just need a little space to think. Don’t make this a big deal.”

Whip slammed the passenger door closed. “It *is* a big deal. If you haven’t noticed, you’ve become my *whole* deal, and now you’re acting like I’m some needy boyfriend.”

My control was slipping, and my voice cracked into the night. “Look, I am trying *so hard* here!”

He shook his head as sadness seeped over his handsome face. “That’s the thing, Prim. You don’t have to *try*.”

I angrily swiped under my eyes and let out a frustrated groan. “Do we really have to do this on the sidewalk? We both knew what this was.”

He settled his hands on his hips and frowned at me. “I thought I did. Do you?”

“We’re having fun. Casual, right?” I forced a smile, but it didn’t reach my eyes.

Please, Whip. Tell me I’m wrong.

Tension vibrated between us. Whip raised a hand to point in the direction of his house. "Have you completely forgotten about the past few days? The past few *months*? I had hoped I'd have a little more time before you pulled the rug out from under me, but apparently this is it. You know what? Fine. If you want to run, run." He scoffed in dismissal as I shrank in on myself. "Your exit was overdue anyway."

I shook my head as hurt seeped into my bones. "What are you talking about? I am right *here*!"

I could physically feel him pulling away despite the mere feet that separated us. A knot twisted in my stomach until I felt sick.

"Why are you doing this?" His voice was broken.

"Doing what?" I pleaded. *Why was asking for space to think so wrong?*

His molars ground together. "You know what I'm asking. You're the one pulling away. I can see it happening."

My emotions were stacking—one slamming on top of the other—and I could feel my control slipping.

He gestured between us before I could speak. "Why are you acting like you don't feel this?"

I desperately needed to get this conversation under control before I completely lost my way and threw myself at his feet. A deep part of me needed to prove to myself that I didn't need anyone, that I could stand on my own, but my world was crumbling. I was grasping, desperate to control the unraveling of my life.

"I got a job offer." The words came out flat and unemotional.

"What?" He softened. "That's great. Why didn't you tell me?"

I clenched my jaw. "It's near Ann Arbor. If I take it, I

would definitely have to move—there's no way I could make that commute work."

His gaze was steely as hurt flashed across his face. "Oh. I see."

"I have to figure out what to do." I swallowed hard against the bitter truth that was rattling in my brain. "We talked about this, right?" I paused, willing the words to not sound as hollow as they felt. "We both agreed it was just sex."

I bit back the words, but it was too late. Old Emily had reared her head, and instead of leaning into what I was feeling, I hid behind my walls. Sure, the words were true, but they weren't *true*.

For the briefest moment, his eyes bounced between mine as if he was searching for the lie—confirmation that whatever was between us was far from casual.

"You should have told me about the job offer." His anger bubbled over at my dismissal as he rounded the truck.

I lifted my chin. "I wanted to find the right time. I wasn't planning on doing this *here*." My arms spread wide to make a point that standing in front of the Sugar Bowl and airing our issues was less than ideal.

Whip shook his head and yanked open the driver's-side door. "Trust me, Prim, I wasn't planning on falling in love with you!"

Realization of what he said jolted through me. I was dumbstruck at my own ignorance, but I knew in my bones his words were true. Despite my sharp tongue and shoving down my feelings, Whip was fighting for me anyway.

He was in love with me, and I knew I would do anything I could to keep him.

Shock overtook my face as my eyes went wide and my

mouth dropped into a little O. "Wait, what? Whip. I haven't decided—I . . ."

Frustrated, Whip dragged a hand through his hair. "Look, I get that you're leaving. I hate it, but you were bound to leave eventually. Just don't treat what we had like it was only some summer you fucked a firefighter behind your dad's back."

And without looking back, Whip closed the door and drove away.

THIRTY-SEVEN

EMILY

WHIP KING WAS in love with me.

So in love with me that he yelled it at me and then left me on the side of the road.

I sighed and dropped my head into my hands.

What. The actual. Fuck?

He was in love with me, and I took the coward's way out by tucking tail and running to my lonely apartment rather than finding a way to fix things with him. After turning off my phone, I cried myself to sleep and woke up feeling like total shit.

No part of me wanted that job in Ann Arbor, but what choice did I have?

I lightly banged my head on the tabletop of the window seat at the Sugar Bowl and groaned.

The bakery buzzed with the low hum of conversation and the clinking of coffee mugs. I sat alone at the window, anxiously stirring my latte. The air was thick with the aroma of freshly ground coffee beans, and soft jazz music played in the background.

A soft hand at my back drew my attention, and I sat up.

Sylvie stood beside me with a warm smile. Her eyes held a genuine kindness, and though we weren't friends quite yet, there was a certain understanding between us.

We're Bluebirds.

An aching warmth passed through me.

Sylvie set down a triangular slice of cheesecake in front of me and gestured toward it. "You looked like you could use a pick-me-up. This one's white chocolate with raspberries—personal favorite." Her voice carried the warmth of a friend as she winked. "On the house."

I smiled and slid the plate closer. "I didn't realize you still worked here."

Sylvie leaned a hip on the counter beside me and sighed. "Now you sound like my husband." Her hand wiped across the white countertop. "I enjoy watching life unfold in this town." She leaned down and lowered her voice. "You see a lot when no one thinks you're watching."

A shameful blush heated my cheeks as I wondered how many people had seen our little public meltdown last night. "Did you see us?"

Her laugh was breathy and light. "Of course I did." She gestured toward the large picture window. "There's a lot you can see from this window." She tapped her nose. "But I know all about keeping secrets."

I smiled, remembering the story of how she'd begun a relationship with a Sullivan and hidden it for nearly a year before getting pregnant. A tiny seed of hope burrowed into my chest.

Sometimes impossible things worked out, didn't they?

I sighed and dug my fork into the cheesecake. After the delicate flavors exploded on my tongue, I let out a soft moan. "Oh my god," I mumbled around the delicious bite.

"Told you," she singsonged.

I frowned down at my dessert as I swallowed. "This is hard, Sylvie." I couldn't look up from my plate as I confided in her. "I know he wants me to stay, but I don't know what to do. My whole life has been working hard and being the best teacher I could be."

Sylvie softly nodded, giving me the space to ramble on. "On one hand, I'd do almost anything to stay—not just for him but all of it. My parents, this town, and yeah . . . for him too. But what does that say about me if I give up everything that I've worked so hard for?"

She shrugged. "I don't think it has to say anything. The only person you have to answer to is yourself."

The door chimed open, and in walked Russell King. His commanding presence was like an ice storm brewing on the horizon, zapping any warmth from the bakery. I tensed, feeling a shiver run down my spine. Sylvie noticed my discomfort and squeezed my shoulder as we both tracked the man's movements in the small bakery.

Russell exuded an air of authority that drew people in like a magnet. Townies and curious onlookers alike flocked to him, as if he was the most important person to walk through those doors. The bakery became a sea of excessive adoration, and I couldn't help but feel a sense of discomfort. Whip's father had a way of commanding attention, and it did nothing but make my skin crawl.

As Russell made his way through the smiling crowd, his eyes locked onto mine. I could see a flicker of recognition, but it was quickly overshadowed by his apparent disinterest. From my side, Sylvie shot him a subtle glare of thinly veiled disgust. She knew better than anyone the emotional scars he'd inflicted on his children.

How many tiny cuts had he inflicted on Whip to cause so many scars?

I hated him.

I observed Russell, seemingly oblivious to Sylvie's disdain, as he continued his regal march through the bakery. His eyes scanned the room, and when they finally met those of his daughter, he simply looked away, as if she were invisible.

Sylvie's gaze lingered on her father for a moment, something swirling in her eyes. I couldn't help but feel an ache for her—the daughter yearning for acknowledgement from a father who seemed too wrapped up in his own world to notice. Sadness washed over me when I realized Russell King didn't even acknowledge his own daughter's existence. But when I looked up at her, she didn't look all that sad about it.

Sylvie was content with her choices. *Maybe I could be too.*

Just as Russell was about to leave, coffee in hand, our eyes locked in a tense confrontation. The room seemed to fade away, leaving only the two of us in a silent standoff. It was a battle of wills, a clash between a father's indifference and a loving woman's determination.

I maintained eye contact with Russell, refusing to let him intimidate me. His harsh, cold stare bore into mine, but I held my ground, my gaze unwavering. I could sense the tension building, the unspoken challenge lingering in the charged air.

Seconds stretched into eternity, and I wondered if I had dug my heels in too far. But then, ever so subtly, Russell's stern expression wavered. A crack in his facade appeared, and his eyes dropped first, breaking the intense connection.

I felt a surge of triumph. It wasn't just about me silently defending Whip. It was about standing up to a man who had wielded control as a weapon for far too long. As Russell walked away, a sense of empowerment washed over me. I turned to Sylvie, who met my eyes with a mix of gratitude and admiration.

"Jesus." The words whooshed from Sylvie in an exhale. "I hate when he comes in here."

In quiet whispers and secrets shared only in the dark, I had come to learn the difficulties of being raised by a man like Russell King. I could imagine how profoundly Whip's mother's absence only deepened those wounds. Sadness wrenched in my chest for the little boy who lost his mother and the passionate, giving man he'd become.

The man I am head over heels in love with.

"You know," Sylvie said and bumped her shoulder into mine, "it's just my opinion, but I think you're exactly what this family needs. I hope you figure it out."

I swallowed hard as tears pricked behind my eyelids. "I will." Sylvie turned to leave, but I stopped her. "Can I ask you something?"

She nodded.

"Was it worth it?"

Her brows flicked downward before a smile bloomed on her face. "I can't imagine my life without Duke and Gus. Nothing will ever make me regret my choices."

I stood, wrapping Sylvie in a hug that had her letting out a surprised *Oh!*

"Thank you." I squeezed her harder. "Thank you."

Loving Whip was worth the risk.

Sure, a part of me was terrified that I was repeating the same mistakes with Whip as I had before—giving up pieces of myself to satisfy someone else. But he was *nothing* like Craig. He had never once asked me to change. I had been the one to place that chip on my shoulder and pressure myself into being perfect. I refused to let bad memories of my ex ruin what I could have with Whip.

Somewhere along the line Whip helped me realize that when you allow yourself to truly *feel*, good things happen. He had faith in me, and I had faith in us. We could get through the storm.

Together.

I was done being afraid. Whip felt things deeply, in a way that I had learned was terrifying. But I was done with feeling afraid.

Whip was offering a version of himself reserved solely for *me*.

"I'm sorry, Sylvie, but I have to go!" A sense of urgency propelled me forward, and I left behind the plate and coffee.

"Good luck!" Sylvie called out with a laugh.

I didn't look back but shot an excited goodbye wave into the air. I needed to make a plan, tell Whip *everything*, and finally make this right.

THIRTY-EIGHT

WHIP

I DIDN'T KNOW it was possible to feel so low. I'd checked, and rechecked, my phone for what felt like the millionth time, and there was still no contact from Emily.

How had things gotten so far off track so quickly?

After I drove off, it took only a minute to come to my senses. I'd circled back to beg for forgiveness for losing my temper, only to find her already gone. Worried, I drove past her apartment, and when I saw her safely climbing the stairs and entering, I decided I needed to give both of us a little space.

I spent the night staring up at my ceiling and replaying our argument over and over in my mind.

We both agreed it was just sex.

I knew the moment she said those words that they were a challenge. She needed me to fight for her, and yet I was the stubborn prick whose feelings got hurt because I was scared she would leave. Instead of calmly talking with her and working out a plan, I got defensive and screamed in her face that I loved her.

Real smooth.

The next morning, still irritated and uneasy, I went in search of the only person I knew could set me right.

My knuckles rapped against the door to the Martin home, and I shifted in my boots. The front door pulled open, and Mrs. Martin smiled at me. "William. This is a pleasure."

She widened the door and gestured for me to enter.

I stepped inside, tail tucked and shoulders slumped with shame. "Thank you, ma'am."

Her laughter was gentle and quick. "Marilyn, please."

I nodded and cleared my throat. "Is the chief in?"

A sly smile spread across her face. She tipped her chin toward the long hallway that split the center of the house. "He's in his office."

"Thank you." I had turned to leave when her hand stopped me.

"Thank *you*." My shoulders shifted to face Emily's mother. She was beaming up at me. "Thank you for really seeing her and caring so deeply for her."

Warmth pierced my rib cage, and I dragged a hand across my jaw. "I'm not sure it was much of a choice, if I'm being honest." A soft chuckle rattled through me.

She patted my arm. "Even so. I couldn't be happier."

My throat went thick and tight. The implication that Mrs. Martin wouldn't be upset, but rather *happy* Emily and I were together was overwhelming.

I have to fix this.

With a slight nod, I left Mrs. Martin in the kitchen and found the chief's office at the end of the hallway. My knock was swift and sure.

"It's open."

I pushed through the doorway to find Chief Martin behind his desk, feet propped and reading a book. Despite the warm summer day, a sweater covered his shoulders, and his glasses were perched low on the end of his nose. His steely eyes met mine, and he closed his book.

My lips formed a flat line, and I dipped my chin. "Sir."

A slow smile spread across Chief's face as he tossed his reading glasses to the side. "Have a seat, son."

His choice of words pierced my heart, and I settled into the plush chair across from his. My insides were tight, and my palms were already sweating.

"I was going to wait until I saw you at the station, but I suppose now is as good of a time as any." His hand stretched across his desk. "Congratulations, Lieutenant."

I shook his hand and looked him in the eye. "Thank you, sir. I won't let you down."

"I know you won't." His legs stretched beneath the desk. "I do want to get something clear, however." His eyes were focused and intense. "You *earned* that position. It has nothing to do with any personal relationships you have outside of work nor any of my personal feelings toward you."

A swell of pride tightened in my chest. Chief Martin was an honest man, and it meant a lot for him to have so much faith in me. "Again, thank you." My knee bounced. "Though the job isn't really why I came to speak with you."

His laugh rumbled in his chest. "I didn't think it was." I searched his eyes, but there was nothing in them but kindness. The knot in my gut slowly unfurled.

"Uh . . ." I cleared my throat. "I'm not exactly sure how to start this."

Chief shrugged and clasped his hands together. "From the beginning is usually a good place."

My lips flattened. "Maybe, but in this case it's probably best to start at the end. I'm in love with Emily."

His eyebrows bounced up once. "Is that so?"

My jaw set. "Yes." I had never been more certain of anything in my entire life. "Now, if we're talking about the beginning, when we first met, I didn't know Emily was your daughter—stepdaughter?" I looked to my mentor for help, but he only nodded for me to continue. "When I did find out, I want you to know that I took that information very seriously. I had no intention of continuing a relationship with her at that point."

A chuckle filled the office. "And why the hell not?"

I blinked. "Oh, I—I guess I figured you would have an opinion about that . . ."

Chief Martin smiled. "I do, as any father would, but I also have faith in my daughter's ability to make her own decisions regarding her personal life."

I let out a humorless laugh. "Yeah, but, come on." I gestured at myself. "You know our type."

"And what type is that, William?"

So he wasn't going to make this easy after all.

I sat straighter in the chair. "Adrenaline junkies. Spouses who work long hours and chase the thrill. Cheaters. People not worth sticking around for." Giving voice to my deep-rooted fears was draining. That last one was *definitely* considered more personal than a widely acknowledged trait of our profession.

The chair creaked as Chief sighed and sat backward with a shake of his head. "We do have a reputation." He sighed again and continued: "But I've learned that any reputation can be wrong. Being a firefighter or cop or any position of power, for that matter, doesn't make you a cheater. It only gives you more opportunities to do what you would have done anyway. Are you really going to sit there and tell me Lee Sullivan is going to step out on his woman?

That Amanda Gates isn't the fiercest, most loyal mother you know?" His face twisted. "Give me a break."

I thought over the examples he provided. He was absolutely correct—Lee would never dream of cheating on Annie Crane, and I'd witnessed firsthand what it looked like when Amanda went into full-on mama bear mode.

"Maybe it's me," I finally admitted, unable to look my friend and mentor in the eye. "I love her, but she's going to leave. It's probably for the best, because I know I'm not worthy of a woman like her, but it hurts like hell, sir."

"You're a good man, William." His voice was low and stern, and his words set my chest on fire. "Am I disappointed that you didn't trust me enough to have a conversation with me, instead of sneaking around? Of course."

Shame burned across my neck and down my spine. "I'm sorry, I—I was afraid."

"Don't even mention it." His smile was back, and humor danced in his eyes.

"That's it?" I was used to my own father holding things over our heads for *years* after any perceived slight. It felt wrong for Chief Martin to simply state his peace and move on.

"If you agree that, moving forward, we trust each other enough to have the hard conversations, then yes."

A swell of emotion nearly stole my voice. I didn't deserve the kindness and respect he was offering so freely. I grunted to clear my throat and stood. "Yes, sir."

Chief Martin stood and rounded his desk. When he placed his palm in mine, he tugged me forward. Despite my height on him, his thick arms banded around me and held me in a tight embrace. My jaw flexed as I fought back tears.

He held me at arm's length. "You're a good man, and I

never thought you for a fool, but that's exactly what you are if you give up."

"Thank you." My rocky whisper left me feeling more vulnerable in his presence than I could ever recall. "I won't."

His hand slapped my back as he released me. "No thanks necessary. Just know that I told Emily I would dispose of your body if you ever hurt her. I kind of like you, William. Please don't make me a murderer."

I grinned. "I'll do my best, sir."

His hand slapped my shoulder. "Good enough." He jerked his head toward the door. "Now go on and find her. Marilyn said she's been moping around town all day."

Excitement raced through me as a thought bloomed in my mind. I needed to move—and fast—if I was going to pull it off. I turned toward the door, but before exiting, turned again and said, "Do you think you could keep her occupied for the rest of the day? I have an idea, but I need some time."

A conspirator's smile twitched the corner of his mouth. "I'll see what I can do."

A thrill I'd never known rippled through me. If I could pull it off, I'd prove to Emily just how much she belonged in our small town.

THIRTY-NINE

EMILY

WHIP

I'm sorry for everything. I'd like to prove it in person. Can you meet me tomorrow morning at Bluebird Books around nine?

I STARED at my phone and frowned. *Tomorrow?*

First, the man blurts out that he is in love with me and then ghosts me?

Annoyance buzzed under my skin as my inner critic whispered, *Sucks to be ghosted, doesn't it?*

I nearly growled with irritation as I stomped down the beachfront, kicking up sand like a child and frowning at all the happy, freckled faces of tourists enjoying Outtatowner's immaculate beach. After coming to the realization that I would do just about anything to stay, I went in search of Whip and came up empty-handed.

Defeated, I had chosen the beach as a way to bide my time.

I glanced at the concrete pier that jutted out into the Lake Michigan waters and stopped at the lighthouse at the end. It had always seemed so picturesque and magical. Fishermen dotted the pier, casting long lines into the water. Everything about Outtatowner felt like *home.*

My phone vibrated again, and my heart rate ticked higher. When I glanced down and saw a message from my mom, I sighed.

MOM

Can you come by? I need your help with something.

Her message was annoyingly vague, but ever the dutiful daughter, I quickly typed my reply.

Of course.

With my sandals in hand, I swiveled and headed back up the beach, past the Sand Dollar Snack Shack, and toward the marina. The sun beat down on me, warming my shoulders and lifting my spirits. Laughter swirled around me as children built sand castles and ran through the tumbling waves.

Ahead of me, I spotted Lark, propped in a beach chair alongside Wyatt Sullivan and sunning herself while they both watched little Penny play in the shallow waters with a friend. Wyatt leaned into her, whispering something in her ear, and a shot of laughter rang out. She eased into him, allowing his arm to wrap her in an embrace that held secret promises.

My heart pinched. *That could be mine too.*

Sure, Whip and I had definitely started things off on the wrong foot—no one really expected a one-night stand to turn into what it had. Hell, it had been my assumption that if you had a one-night stand, you never saw each other again . . . I never, *ever* expected for our relationship to morph into what it had become.

Regardless of how things started, Whip and I had always been drawn to each other. I glanced up at the lighthouse and smiled. Much like the tower, he was strong and unwavering. Like one of the ships bobbing in the waters, I found solace in his reassuring glow, his affection and confidence in us guiding me through the murky waters of living my life so guarded. He'd never asked me to change—to be less rigid or less careful. Whip even showed me that a man would stand by you when life wobbled.

Love and affection for him burst through me. There was no way in hell I could wait until tomorrow to see him. My feet kicked through the sand as I took off in a run down the beach. I weaved through sunbathers, ducked past a volleyball game, and came out onto the pavement panting and exhilarated.

When my phone rang, I answered without even looking at the caller. "Hello?" I was panting and out of breath, but eager to find Whip.

"Emily." I placed Bug King's voice in two beats.

"Hey, Bug. How are you?" I swallowed and tried to level my breathing.

"Better than you, it sounds. Is this a bad time?" Bug's voice hinted at the slight irritation that always carried in her voice.

"Uh . . . no. No, it's fine. What can I do for you?" My mind raced, certain that word had spread to her about the argument between her nephew and me.

"I need you to come see me at the library immediately. Are you able to do that? It's important." *Always to the point.*

I smiled as my breath finally evened out and checked my watch. While I was itching to seek out Whip, I certainly didn't want any interruptions when I threw myself at his feet, begged for forgiveness for our argument, and spent the following hours—if not days—completely tangled in him. "I can come by now, if that works?"

A rare smile floated through the phone. "That's perfect. I'll see you soon."

We hung up, and I brushed off sand from my sundress and swiped at the bottoms of my feet. Slipping my sandals on, I walked up the hill toward town. Winning over Bug was no easy feat, so I decided I'd pop back into the Sugar Bowl and get her a coffee or pastry to help my case.

As I passed King Tattoo, I spotted Whip's brother Royal taping large sheets of brown kraft paper over the storefront window.

"Hi, Royal," I called out.

The tattooed beast of a man turned with his ever-present grin. When he saw who had called to him, his eyes went wide. "Oh, hey. Emily, right?"

I stuck out my hand. "Nice to officially meet you."

His grin widened as he wiped his hand across his black pants before extending it to me. "Pleasure."

I eyed the brown paper over his shoulder. "What are you working on?"

His eyes shifted, and he stepped to the side, as if he could block me from whatever it was he was doing. "Just a little town project."

My eyes narrowed. I smelled bullshit but didn't know why. "Okay, well . . . your aunt Bug asked to meet me at the library. I'm hoping to win some extra points. Any suggestions before I head to the Sugar Bowl?"

The mischievous twinkle in Royal's eye gave me hope. "Junkers."

My eyebrows lifted. "What now?"

He smiled. "Junkers. That'll win her over for sure. They're these little bits of homemade biscuit dough discards that are rolled in cinnamon sugar, then baked. Huck sells them till they run out, so you might be shit out of luck but" —he shrugged—"it's worth a shot."

"Got it." I smiled and sent him a salute. "Thanks, Royal!"

Leaving him to his oddly secretive window project, I ducked into the Sugar Bowl. Thankfully, the off-menu item was in stock, and I left with a white paper bag in hand and a major pep in my step.

When I reached the library, I stared up at the aging building. It had so much potential, if only the right person would give it the love it deserved. Once inside, I wove through the stacks until I found Bug standing behind one of the small librarian desks.

Her subtle frown morphed into a small smile when she recognized me. "Glad you could make it."

I smiled and held out the white paper sack. "I stopped for an afternoon pick-me-up."

Her eyebrow tipped up as she took the bag and unrolled the top. When she recognized the pastries inside, she let out a small sigh. "Now that's not playing fair."

I smiled. "Haven't got the slightest idea what you mean. Now what can I help you with, Bug?"

She slipped the treats into a drawer and rounded the desk. "Walk with me."

Together we wound through the stacks, observing the people of Outtatowner. A young man worked with an older patron on how to access his email account. Another couple huddled on the plush seats stacked in a quiet corner. A librarian pushed a cart to restack returned books. The hum and rhythm of the library was a surprising comfort—much like the afternoon I'd spent inside Bluebird Books.

"There's someone I'd like you to meet." Bug motioned toward the row of office doors down a back hallway in the library. With a knock, we were allowed to enter and stood in front of an elderly woman with kind eyes. "Dottie, this is Emily. She's the woman I was telling you about."

Dottie moved around her desk and offered her hand, which I took. "Pleasure to meet you. Bug has been absolutely *raving* about you."

I glanced to my right to see Bug's stern face give a subtle eye roll. I stifled a laugh but allowed the compliment to settle over me. "That's very kind. It's nice to meet you, too, though I'm not sure why I'm here exactly."

Dottie laughed and swatted the air. "Oh, leave it to Bug to be all cloak-and-dagger about it."

Bug softly grunted beside me.

"I'll cut to the chase," Dottie continued. "I would like to offer you a job. Head librarian of the Children's Department, to be exact."

My jaw dropped open. "Oh . . . I'm sorry. What?"

Dottie's smile widened. "I believe you're aware, but we've been attempting to revitalize our children's section for a while now—without much luck, unfortunately. We could use someone with your experience with children, along with your fundraising background. It was quite impressive what you accomplished for the educational foundation, and the ideas Bug shared with the board were a big hit."

I blinked. "Oh, I—I mean . . . it was really the Bluebirds who got the ball rolling with all of the fundraising."

"Nonsense," Bug interrupted. "We brainstormed a few ideas, but it was Emily who planned and executed everything with precision. We'd be fools not to hire her."

I stared wide eyed at Bug King.

Dottie's tittering laugh filled her small office. "I'm not disagreeing with you." She turned her attention to me. "Emily, we think you'd be perfect."

My thoughts tumbled, one on top of another in a jumbled mess. "I mean . . . I'm a teacher. Don't I need a special certification or something?"

Dottie shook her head. "No. In fact, I think it's your experience as a teacher that makes you uniquely qualified. If you happen to be interested in a library science degree, that's always a possibility, but not a requirement. Here at our public library, we're looking for someone passionate about children, learning, and this town. The public library is the community backbone of Outtatowner, and we need someone who can reach the hearts of our youngest learners. I'd love for you to consider it."

"Yes!" My answer shot out of me, louder than I'd anticipated. I laughed. "I'm sorry. Yes. I would love to."

"Wonderful!" Dottie clapped her hands together as Bug nodded beside me. "In your role, you would be in charge of programming as well as head of the youth outreach program. With school starting up soon, we'd love to start your orientation as soon as possible."

"Thank you." Tears threatened to spill over my lashes, but I tamped them down, and my professionalism slid into place. "I'm honored. I won't let you down."

"Of course not," Dottie said. "Come by next week, and we'll get everything we need to get you started."

Dismissed, we exchanged pleasant goodbyes and left Dottie's office. Once in the hallway, I wrapped Bug in a hug. "Thank you," I sniffled.

"You are very welcome." She offered a small but kind

pat on my back. "You earned that position by your own merits."

I swiped under my eyes and looked at her. "I'm in love with Whip."

I was overtaken by the need to tell her as the words fell from my lips.

Her stern face softened. "I was hoping you had finally realized that." She patted my back once more. "I think you two will figure things out in time."

Her eyes flicked to the clock on the wall. "Now I have to get back to work, but I will see you on Monday."

I nodded and couldn't wait to find Whip to tell him everything.

I was staying.

I was in love with him, and everything had finally clicked into place. Undeterred that I hadn't heard from him after his previous text, I left the library and headed toward my car.

FORTY

WHIP

HIDING from Emily Ward was no easy maneuver. That woman was tenacious. For nearly eighteen hours, I dodged calls, slinked through town, and pulled every string I could in order to pull off the greatest feat of my life.

But it was time.

My heart pounded with anticipation, a mix of excitement and nerves. Today was the day Emily would see the town transformed—the day I hoped she realized how much she *belonged*—not just with me but here, in my small town.

I stood in front of the bookstore a full thirty minutes early because if my gut was right, my Prim would be early. Sure as shit, a full eighteen minutes before she was supposed to arrive, I spotted Emily walking down the main sidewalk.

She wore a soft blue dress that fluttered in the breeze and made my heart thunk. Her feet were tucked into casual white sneakers, and I followed the path up her smooth tanned legs. My heart hammered in time with every step she took.

Her eyes met mine, and a smile tugged at the corners of her lips before she took off in a sprint toward me. I stood my ground in front of the bookstore and grinned. When she reached me, she flung herself into my arms. I hauled her up and held her tightly, squeezing her ass and pulling her mouth to mine.

The world around us melted as I allowed myself to be lost in her—in us.

When I finally set her on her feet, she beamed up at me. "Hi."

I swiped a finger across her forehead to tuck a loose strand of hair behind her ear. "Hey, Prim."

"You are a hard man to find," she teased as her hand smoothed down the front of my shirt.

"You're a tough woman to shake." I winked and linked our hands.

"I'm sorry, I—"

I shook my head to stop her. "No. It's me who owes you an apology. I was being a paranoid hothead and let my doubts get the best of me. Take a walk with me? There's something I want to show you. It's my apology."

Still smiling, Emily eyed me carefully as I turned to face the bookstore. Instead of walking, I shifted us toward the window of Bluebird Books. The simmering tension in the air was palpable as Emily's curious gaze lingered on me a second longer. I could practically *feel* the wheels in her pretty little head cranking as she tried to figure out what I had in store.

I squeezed her hand and gestured toward the window. "Check it out."

Hand-painted bluebirds adorned the window, each holding the end of a sign in their beaks that read, "Welcome Home."

Emily gasped, her hand covering her mouth. "What is this? It's beautiful."

I looked over at the woman I loved. "It's just the beginning of what I *hope* is a well-received apology." I scanned the roadway. "Okay, come this way. Let's see this one next."

With giddy excitement, Emily followed.

The Sugar Bowl's window portrayed a couple sharing a cup of coffee, surrounded by steaming mugs with heart-shaped latte art. She squeezed my hand, and I felt her warmth radiate through me. Through the window, my sister Sylvie waved and gave me an excited thumbs-up.

"Come on." I guided Emily down the street as we made our way to the next window.

I stopped in front of King Tattoo. In the window display, Royal had painted an intricate mural. Swirls of violet and electric blue swirled around a portrait of a man who was a dead ringer for me. Prominently displayed, the man had the word *Prim* tattooed on his neck in large, script letters.

Emily's eyes went wide as she sucked in a breath. Reaching over, she pulled down my collar to check my neck and laughed. "Oh, thank god." She leaned into me. "I was worried you went all in for a neck tattoo."

I grinned, pulling her close. "I thought about asking Royal to make it official, but *Prim* in Old English seemed a bit much." I shrugged. "At least on the neck."

She laughed, and electricity crackled inside my skin. "You made the right call."

With each unveiling, the town seemed to come alive, from the hardware store to the library to the Snack Shack. Each window mural echoed our relationship, from the school to the carnival to a couple holding hands on a beach. The storefront owners had been given free rein to help me convince Emily that not only did she belong, but she belonged here—with me.

Next was the fire station. The front window proudly displayed a drawing of a firefighter in action, rescuing a damsel in distress. As we got closer, I frowned at it, and Emily burst into a fit of giggles. Instead of the firefighter rescuing his girl, it was very obvious that the woman was holding the firefighter in *her* arms.

She pointed to the damsel. "Is that supposed to be me or you?"

I bit back a laugh. "Lee was in charge of this one." I shook my head. "What a douche . . ."

Her laughter only doubled as she squeezed my forearm and bent over in a fit of giggles. "It's perfect. I promise, I love it."

I smirked, playing along and pulling her close. "Well, I guess it's fitting since you did save me, after all."

She flirtatiously blinked her lashes at me. "Oh, is that so?"

Seriousness overtook my face as my heart hammered. "You did. You rescued me from a life without meaning. A life of hiding."

Emily filled her lungs. "You saved me too. I was so afraid to let go—afraid that I'd get hurt all over again. But I'm not afraid anymore."

I filled my lungs, hoping that I could manage to tell her everything that needed to be said. "I love you, Prim. Head-over-heels, drowning-without-you love." I planted her hand on my chest and covered it with mine.

"Whip, I—"

I shook my head and closed my eyes. "I need to get through this." My hand squeezed hers. "I'm yours. Whatever the future holds for you, I'm with you. If we need to make long distance work because of your job, I'll do it. If you find something you love, I can go with you if that's what you want. If I need to wait here until things get worked out, I'll do that. I will wait for you."

Emily stayed quiet, and I gathered the courage to open my eyes. She was beaming up at me, and my heart rattled against my ribs in piercing thumps.

She swallowed back tears and shook her head. "No." Dread pooled in my gut as I searched her eyes. A single tear slipped from beneath her lashes. "We're not doing long distance, and you're not quitting your job for me . . ." Her hazy aqua eyes lifted to mine. "Because I'm not going anywhere."

I exhaled a sigh of relief and squeezed her shoulders. Emotion expanded in my throat. *She isn't leaving.*

"I love you, Whip. It was never just sex for me, and I shouldn't have said that. I am so sorry." Emily's shoulders stiffened. My chest cracked open as her words settled over me. "I love you and I love this town. I was never going to take that job. I knew the moment I got the offer that I couldn't stand not living here with you. But . . . in the end it all worked out." Her chin tipped up, and a prideful smile spread across her gorgeous face. "You're looking at the newest head librarian of the Children's Department of the Outtatowner Public Library."

Instinct took over as my arms wrapped around her, and I hoisted her into the air. My mouth took hers, and I poured everything into that kiss.

From the open bay doors, whoops and hollers from my crew rang out. Lee Sullivan's voice shouted over the racket as he yelled, "Gross! Get a room!"

I smiled as I kissed my woman and flipped him off. It didn't matter who saw us.

Just this once, everything in my life clicked into place. Emily was my heart and soul, and though I may never quite deserve her, I would take every opportunity to prove my love to her every single day.

EPILOGUE

Emily

It's funny how you can have a perfect plan for your life, only to have it completely derailed by a cocky firefighter with a charming smile. Funnier still how *not* having a plan created a life far better than I ever could have dreamed.

Autumn had descended on Outtatowner, Michigan, and I had feared I would be saddened by students and teachers heading back to school. Instead, I'd found my passion in turning the Children's Department at the library into a warm and inviting space for our kids. It was only October, but our programs were filling fast, and once it hit three fifteen in the afternoon, kids of all ages could be found finishing homework, huddling together on cozy chairs, or listening to music while getting lost in a good book. My vision to turn the library into a safe haven for our kids was already starting to take shape.

"Excuse me, Miss Ward?" a deep voice cracked behind me.

When I turned, I had to glance up to look Robbie

Lambert in the eye. "Robbie! Good grief, you're a foot taller!"

His sweet, shy smile made my chest pinch. "Mom says I hit a growth spurt."

I laughed. "I can see that. It's so good to see you." I struggled to find the words—to apologize for the strife I had caused his family. My call to his mother had been well received, though Pokey Lambert was still understandably frosty toward me.

"I wanted to see if you might want to come to my belt advancement ceremony next weekend. I'll be earning my black belt."

I swallowed past the lump in my throat. "That's a huge accomplishment. I would be honored to see it."

His cheesy grin made him look young again. "Okay, I will get you the details. Thanks, Miss Ward."

I nodded and smiled through tears. "You bet."

Robbie turned to rejoin his friends, then paused and turned back. "We all think this place is pretty cool." He shrugged. "In case no one told you that."

I nodded a thank-you, too afraid to speak for fear I'd start crying all over him, and that would be *totally uncool.* As he walked away, I noticed his sneakers were the same Nikes I'd worked so hard to get him. They were broken in, but clean and clearly well taken care of.

Thank god they still fit.

I laughed at myself as I busied my hands, rearranging pencils and reining in my emotions. Kids I recognized from class and smiling new faces waved and found their places as they filtered in after school.

"Excuse me, miss?" Whip's familiar rumble had me grinning and turning toward him. My mouth went dry as he stood, feet planted and arms crossed, in his tactical uniform. I ogled him just because I could. "Can you tell me where I might find the head librarian of this department?"

I blinked innocently and placed a gentle hand on my collarbone. "Why, that's me."

His eyebrow tipped up. "Is that so? We're doing routine maintenance on the fire system. Mind if I take a look around?"

Damn he was hot in uniform, and his commanding voice just *did something* to my insides to turn them into absolute mush.

"Right this way." I rounded my desk in the center of the room and led him to the hallway where the control panel was located. The entire way, I could feel his eyes on me, so I was sure to add a little swish in my walk.

In the quiet hallway, Whip crowded behind me and whispered in my ear. "You look damn good, Prim. I told you the night we met I had a thing for librarians."

His warm breath sent shivers racing down my spine. I turned, looping my arms around his neck. "When you get home tonight, I've got a surprise for you under this skirt."

His grin widened. "Naughty librarian? How'd I get so lucky?"

~

After finishing my day at the library, I arrived home to the coziness of Whip's house, now shared by both of us. I walked through the front door and was greeted by the aroma of a home-cooked meal. Despite his long shift, Whip had been busy in the kitchen.

"You're a miracle worker in that uniform, but turns out you're not too shabby in the kitchen either," I teased, wrapping my arms around his waist as he stirred the pot on the stove.

He grinned, planting a quick kiss on my forehead. "Well, a man's got to have some hidden talents, right?"

I leaned into him. Together we settled into the comfort of our routine, cooking together and recounting our respective days. The conversation, filled with laughter and shared anecdotes, flowed effortlessly. As we sat down to dinner, Whip's gaze lingered on me with a warmth that still caught me by surprise.

"You know, your dad came by the library today looking for Bug." I set my glass of wine down.

Whip frowned. "Did he give you any trouble?"

A cracking laugh burst from my chest. "Not a chance. He mostly avoided me. I think he's still pissed he couldn't run me off." I narrowed my eyes and whispered. "He knows I know."

Whip shook his head and chuckled. "I think you might just be the only person Russell King is afraid of."

A sly smile tugged at my mouth. "I don't know if he's afraid of me, but I think he understands that I'm willing to give him a piece of my mind or at least stare him down to make him uncomfortable."

"You really are perfect, Prim." Whip set down his glass and looked at me. "I never expected to feel like this. So effortlessly complete. It's like you've stitched up the holes in my heart I didn't even know were there."

I smiled, my chin resting in my hand. My chest swelled with love. Since officially becoming a couple, Whip was generous with his loving words—we no longer needed to hide from each other or anyone else. "You've brought a kind of happiness into my life that I didn't dare dream of. It's like every day is an adventure with you."

After the meal, we moved to the living room, the flickering flames in the fireplace casting a warm glow. The conversation shifted to the ongoing mystery surrounding Whip's mother. We eagerly awaited updates from the private investigator, hoping for answers that would bring closure to the fractured pieces of Whip's family.

"I can't believe we're doing this together, Prim. It means the world to me," he confessed, his eyes reflecting both gratitude and vulnerability.

I squeezed his hand, reassuring him that we were on this journey together. "We'll find the truth, Whip. No matter what it takes."

A comfortable silence settled between us, the crackling fire providing a soothing soundtrack. In that moment, I leaned into the depth of my emotions, realizing how profoundly my life had changed since Whip walked into it. It wasn't just the love or the laughter, but the shared dreams, whispered confessions, and the solace of knowing someone truly understood you.

He never once asked me to change.

"I never knew life could be this beautiful," I whispered, more to myself than to him.

Whip turned to me with a tender expression. "You've made me a better man, Prim. Before you, I carried fears I tried so hard to bury with jokes and white-knuckling it through life. But with you, those fears have faded. You've given me confidence and a sense of belonging I never thought possible."

His words hung in the air, a testament to the healing power of love. I reached for his hand, pressing it against my heart. "And you make me feel cherished, valued. You've shown me a love that mends and builds, not one that breaks."

Whip's eyes sparkled with a mischievous glint. "Speaking of building, there's something I've been meaning to ask you."

I looked at him, curiosity mingling with anticipation as I sat higher on the couch. Before I could utter a word, Whip slipped off the couch and dropped to one knee and produced a velvet box from his pocket. The room seemed to hold its breath as he opened it, revealing a jaw-dropping ring. It was a brilliant round-cut diamond set in an intricately detailed platinum band. Delicate filigree patterns and small diamonds adorned the band, adding a touch of classic romance.

"Emily Ward," he began, his voice confident and unwavering, "I want nothing more than to call you my wife. Will you marry me?"

Tears welled up in my eyes as I nodded, unable to find words that could match the depth of my emotions. A giggle tumbled from my lips as I finally managed a watery "Yes!"

Whip slid the ring onto my finger, sealing our love with a promise that echoed in the quiet moments of that cozy living room.

Whip laughed and enveloped me in a warm embrace as we tumbled to the floor in a tangle of limbs and frantic kisses.

In his arms, I was safe and warm and *home.*

SNEAK PEEK OF JUST MY LUCK

You might think it's reckless for a single mom to enter into a marriage of convenience with her boss . . .

You would be correct.

To make matters worse, Abel King is a grumpy local brewer with a criminal past. He also happens to be my boss and a total stick in the mud. Every time I come to work with a smile and wave, I'm lucky if I can get a grunt in response.

When I accidentally-on-purpose overhear that he's having trouble securing a business loan due to his criminal record, **I hatch a plan to help the both of us.**

The arrangement is perfect—a business transaction and nothing more. Like having a roommate without having the hassle of other people bugging you for dates.

I will definitely not be falling in love with him no matter how many times he says "my wife" and tingles dance in *all the right places*.

Trouble is as time goes on, things stop feeling like business and start to feel a whole lot like *pleasure* every single day . . . and really, that's *just my luck*. . . .

Pre-order Just My Luck on Amazon!

ACKNOWLEDGMENTS

This book would never have happened without, you, dear reader! From the moment you embraced the Sullivans in One Look, I was receiving messages about the Kings. The more their stories overlapped, the more excited I grew for a series around the mysterious, playful, and hot-as-hell Kings. This series came into existence because you breathed life into the characters and asked for more.

Dare I say I love the Kings?

My dear sweet husband, thank you for putting up with my random Googling of other men's "tackle" and believing me when I say that it's for research. You never ask questions, and I love that for me. Your love and support means the world and I would not have the confidence to live my best life without you by my side.

To every Content Creator who took time to make a TikTok, reel, post, or share - THANK YOU! In a crowded arena, it takes a lot to get noticed and with your support, I do feel seen. I am forever grateful for all the ways you continue to show up for me.

To my Spicy Sprint Sluts (Kandi & Elsie) this book would not exist without your daily cheering and enthusiasm. Your friendship means everything.

To Paula, thank you for experimenting on a new method for developmental editing. It made my writer brain so happy to have you along for the ride!

James, you are an incredible editor and every book we

work on together, I feel like I learn so much from you. Your attention to detail and care for my words is unrivaled.

Anna and Trinity, your beta feedback always makes my heart smile. From tagging swoon-worthy quotes to pushing me to go deeper, y'all are the best!

To Tabitha for your friendship and the laughs—Whip's glitter dick is for you.

HENDRIX HEARTTHROBS

Want to connect? Come hang out with the Hendrix Heartthrobs on Facebook to laugh & chat with Lena! Special sneak peeks, announcements, exclusive content, & general shenanigans all happen there.

Come join us!

ABOUT THE AUTHOR

Lena Hendrix is an Amazon Top 10 bestselling contemporary romance author living in the Midwest. Her love for romance stared with sneaking racy Harlequin paperbacks and now she writes her own hot-as-sin small town romance novels. Lena has a soft spot for strong alphas with marshmallow insides, heroines who clap back, and sizzling tension. Her novels pack in small town heart with a whole lotta heat.

When she's not writing or devouring new novels, you can find her hiking, camping, fishing, and sipping a spicy margarita!

Want to hang out? Find Lena on Tiktok or IG!

ALSO BY LENA HENDRIX

Chikalu Falls

Finding You

Keeping You

Protecting You

Choosing You (origin novella)

Redemption Ranch

The Badge

The Alias

The Rebel

The Target

The Sullivans

One Look

One Touch

One Chance

One Night

One Taste (prequel novella)

The Kings

Just This Once

Just My Luck

Just Between Us

Just Like That

Just Say Yes

Made in the USA
Middletown, DE
30 April 2024

53684307R00250